MURDER IN ASPEN NOTCH

AN ASPEN NOTCH MYSTERY, BOOK 1

KATHLEEN MCKEE

First Edition: September 2019
Revised: June 2021

Cover design by Robin Ludwig Design Inc.
www.gobookcoverdesign.com

ISBN: 9781693186189

Printed in the United States of America

Murder in Aspen Notch is dedicated to the ladies at the Villas of French Creek. Their support and friendship have been immeasurable.

CHAPTER 1

*A*lan and I took a long look at the sparsely furnished living room of the 1950's-style ranch home, staged for a quick sale. From my perspective, the only things it had going for it were the brick fireplace and the striking picture window. The dated ceiling fan and the walls, painted an unpleasant lime green, dismayed me, but as distasteful as they appeared, I considered them a step up from the pumpkin kitchen, with orange everywhere we gazed.

The bubbly real estate agent, arguably knowledgeable, reminded me that a few cosmetic changes could make the home a showcase. In addition, she noted, the large lot with a two-car garage, two additional buildings, and a fenced back yard were unheard of at this price-point in today's market, and they made the place a real gem.

"The street seems rather busy," I noted.

"You're in the borough, on Church Street," she chirped, as if we'd already made our decision to purchase the home. "The town council updated zoning not too long ago, so you could convert the cabin out there to start a business."

"Like what?" I questioned.

"The sky's the limit," she smiled. "I'm telling you, this place will go fast. In fact, I have two more showings today."

"It's definitely a contender," Alan noted, "but my wife and I need to discuss the pros and cons. Can you recommend a place where we can have a cup of coffee and chat?"

Without any hesitation, the agent replied, "You can find Dottie's Café two blocks down on the left. They have good food and reasonable prices, plus you'll like Dottie, as well."

"Great," Alan said, glancing out the kitchen window as he gauged the distance. "Sue and I will talk about it, and get back to you later today."

Though only a short walk to the café, Alan suggested that we take the car and drive around town. Besides the beautiful fall day, he thought we might gain a better perspective of the locale while we made the final decision about moving to Aspen Notch. Recently married, with a second chance at love for both of us, neither Alan nor I felt particularly enchanted with each other's existing homes.

Alan had put his house on the market in early June, just before our wedding day, and by the time we returned from our honeymoon cruise, we were in escrow. We decided that once we found a new home, we'd sell mine, since both of us wanted a slower pace, and we were drawn to the lovely mountain vistas of northeast Pennsylvania.

Alan's oldest son, George, told us about Aspen Notch after he drove through the quaint town last February while he took his family on a ski outing in the Jaworski tradition. George made a convincing suggestion that we consider combining our households there, particularly with Aspen Notch located only about an hour from his home in Middletown, New York.

Alan and I investigated the real estate options using the internet, and decided that the weather forecast made this a good weekend to drive upstate. If anything, we could enjoy the fall foliage in its full and colorful array while we took a closer look at the homes we thought we might like.

The Seat Yourself sign at the entrance of Dottie's Café provided an invitation for us to look around the dining area and choose a booth beyond the counter, away from the hustle and bustle of the early lunch crowd. Actually, we saw only five guests in the corner storefront: an older couple seated at a table near the front window and three elderly men at a booth near the entrance; yet all of them followed us with their eyes.

A slender auburn-haired woman, maybe in her late 40's, arrived with two menus and a friendly, welcoming smile. "I'm Dottie Burkeholder," she stated pleasantly. "Are you visiting or just passing through?"

"A little of both," I replied. "I'm Sue Jaworski, and this is my husband, Alan. Do you own the café?"

"Yes," she nodded proudly. "May I bring you something to drink while you look through the menu?"

Alan ordered two coffees as planned, but then suggested that we might as well also have lunch. I knew he had his eye on the double bacon cheeseburger, though I decided to order the chicken salad on toasted multigrain bread.

Dottie brought over a pot of coffee and filled two mugs, pointed out the bowls of creamers and sweeteners already on the table, then said, "I'll return with your sandwiches in a jiffy."

While we waited, Alan wanted to talk about the three houses we'd viewed, though none of them particularly caught my fancy. The first had no garage, which I considered a deal breaker due to the amount of winter weather I expected in the Poconos. The second had charm and a rural feel, but I didn't like the distance from town. Besides, it boasted two levels with a basement, more space than we needed, and I couldn't see a neighbor in sight. The third had the garishly painted walls on a busy street.

"We don't have to make a quick decision," I noted, "and we can continue looking. Maybe we should check out the real estate in some of the other towns nearby."

Alan nodded his agreement as Dottie arrived with our platters and a bottle of ketchup for Alan's fries. "I couldn't help hearing you mention that you're house-hunting," she said. "Are you thinking about moving to Aspen Notch?"

"Possibly," I smiled. "Alan's a retired New York City cop and I'm foot-loose and fancy-free. We currently live in Chester County, down near Philadelphia, but we both love the mountain vistas around here."

Dottie gazed intently at Alan, checking every nuance of his expression. "Are you applying for the position?" she asked.

"I'm not sure what you mean," Alan said. "We're just here to house-hunt."

"Stan Johnston died two months ago, God rest his soul," Dottie explained. "He was our police chief; our only cop, if you must know, but the poor old guy had a bad ticker. He keeled over when he dressed for work one morning, and kicked the bucket."

"Sorry to hear that," Alan said, "but, no, I'm not applying for a position. We're just looking for a home in the mountains."

"I don't know," Dottie replied. "It seems like a sign to me. We're searching for someone with lots of experience, and you're a retired NYPD cop with time on your hands."

"Thanks for the vote of confidence," Alan chuckled, "but as I said, I'm not interested."

Dottie turned away, still smiling, but deep in thought. I watched her bring a fresh pot of coffee to the table of the older gentlemen, pour them each a refill, then pull over a chair. They spoke in muted tones, while Alan, engrossed with his burger, seemed unaware of the goings-on behind him.

"Maybe Dottie's right," I whispered.

"About what?" he asked nonchalantly.

"A sign," I said. "You have to admit that you often feel bored hanging around the house."

"Not really," Alan shrugged. "I've worked to fix things so we can sell the place."

"I know," I nodded, "but you're like a fish out of water."

Alan shook his head, disagreeing with his eyes. Still, I saw a flicker of interest before he dipped his French fry into a dollop of ketchup. Taking a bite of my sandwich, I reflected on the ways that new opportunities appeared when we least expected them. We could choose to accept them, or let them go.

Alan and I, for example, met at the Alpine Holiday Lodge last winter, and neither of us sought a romantic connection. In fact, Alan had irritated me initially, but as I came to know him, his remarkable qualities won me over. We solved a murder mystery together, fell in love, then decided to embrace the richness of a life together.

"Have we made our final decision to keep looking?" Alan asked as he took his last bite of burger.

I didn't have a chance to reply before Dottie led the three men to our table. Upon closer inspection, they didn't look as elderly as I'd first thought, and two of them actually seemed only a few years older than Alan and me in our early 60's, though the taller, bald man may have been a bit younger.

Dottie introduced each of them, saying, "I'd like you to meet Lou Greene, Bernie Calamito, and Marty Sandler. Lou's the mayor of Aspen Notch."

"Nice to meet you," I replied. "I'm Sue Jaworski, and this is my husband, Alan."

"Dottie told us you're retired NYPD," Lou stated, gazing at Alan with a very engaging smile.

"Yes, sir," Alan said, "fully retired."

"House-hunting, huh?" Lou questioned.

"Yes," Alan replied, "while we take advantage of the fall foliage."

"How about a tour of Aspen Notch?" Lou asked. "We have a nice town here, and my car's right out front."

"We wouldn't want to take up your time," Alan said.

"Nonsense," Lou replied with a convincing smile. "It's the best part of my job. Bernie, Marty, and I serve as the welcoming committee, and we'd like to show you around."

I couldn't help but think that the folks who lived in Aspen Notch seemed quite friendly, and I considered it another sign that Alan and I belonged in such a town.

CHAPTER 2

*I*t didn't take much convincing on their part for us to accept Mayor Greene's offer. The quick drive-around that Alan and I'd made earlier didn't provide more than a cursory glance of Aspen Notch, and we both agreed that we should learn more about the town, other than what we'd seen on the county's website.

Marty reluctantly begged off since his wife waited for his return with a few things from the market, though Bernie joined us. He sat in the back seat of Lou's Subaru Forester with me, while Lou insisted that Alan take the front seat with him, no doubt so the mayor could have Alan's ear.

Bernie Calamito, a talkative fellow of Italian descent, had a New Jersey accent. We hadn't yet turned a corner before he told us about his relocation to Aspen Notch after he retired from a car dealership about 5 years ago. "Once the kids grew up and went off on their own," he added, "my better half and I decided to get out of the city, and we don't have any regrets."

"That's good to know," I said, checking out the shops as we passed by. "Do you live in town?"

"We're a few blocks away," Bernie replied, "in one of the newer developments. Gladys, that's my wife, says we should've downsized more because her knees aren't so good, but I have a nice cave in the basement, so it suits me fine."

Lou interrupted to point out some of the landmarks such as the bank, town hall, and library, though I didn't find them impressive enough to capture my attention. When Lou slowed in front of the police station, an older structure boasting a brick façade and bars on the side windows, he stated, "This is where Stan Johnston hung his hat for 40-some years, God rest his soul. We lost a great friend when he passed."

"That's a long time," Alan remarked. "Was he alone on the beat all of those years?"

"Pretty much," Lou replied, "as long as I can remember. From what Stan told me, he liked it that way because folks knew and respected him. If you ask me, though, he didn't seem the same after his wife died a few years back. I guess he felt lonely."

Alan nodded his understanding since he, too, hit a rough patch after someone murdered his wife on the streets of New York City. Fortunately, his band of brothers on the force gave him the support he needed during that difficult time.

When Lou turned right onto Church Street, he noted the representation of just about every denomination of churches along the main thoroughfare. As he pulled in front of the old Presbyterian Church on the opposite corner of the house that Alan and I had viewed earlier, Lou remarked, "This was the first church in Aspen Notch, built before we barely even had a town. Of course, it's had additions, but you can see the river rock they used for the original structure."

"Do you want to take a look inside?" Bernie asked. "We have a lot of history in there."

"Maybe another time," I said, glancing across the street. "What's the old outbuilding on the property for sale?"

"Now, that's a story in itself," Bernie replied. "Tell them about that log cabin, Lou."

"Abe Whitman would probably turn over in his grave if he saw it now," Lou said, shaking his head. "He built that cabin as his home before the Great Depression, then had the big house constructed back in the early 50's. When Abe's grandson took over the estate, he sold off some of Abe's land, and made some improvements to the cabin, like adding electricity."

"The grandson's selling it now?" I asked.

"No," Lou replied. "He died during the Korean War. His widow, Clara Whitman, lived in the house a good 40 years, give or take, but she never remarried and they had no kids. In her younger years, Clara converted the cabin to a candy shop, and sold her delicious taffies and chocolates, although she closed it when it became too much for her."

"So, why's old Abe turning in his grave?" I asked.

"Well," Lou said, "with no descendants after Clara died, the place went to auction. I should've bought the property, but my wife had no interest in it. Anyway, the couple who got it were nothing but trouble, them and their kids. I can't say I felt sorry to see them go, especially since they wrecked a piece of history."

Lou continued down Church Street for two more blocks, turned right on Chestnut, and right again on Elm. A few stately homes, with their wide verandas and wrap-around porches, caught my attention. Lou verified that Elm Street served as the first developed residential section of town, with many of the homes built by wealthy businessmen from New York City for a summer retreat. The lovely tree-lined park located across the street demonstrated their intention of maintaining a healthy environment for their families.

"How did Aspen Notch get its name?" I asked.

"Abe Whitman called it that," Lou said, "because of all the aspens growing on the ridge just beyond town. Do you want me to take you there?"

Alan glanced at his watch. "Maybe another time," he said. "You probably have plenty of things on your agenda today."

"Quite honestly," Lou replied, "I hoped to convince you to serve as our new police chief."

"You don't even know me," Alan stated.

Bernie interjected, saying, "Lou's a pretty good judge of character, and I have to agree with him. You'd be perfect for the job."

"Why don't you hire a rookie from the police academy?" Alan asked. "Aspen Notch might be a good place to start out."

Lou shook his head, saying, "The younger recruits don't show any interest since they want a town with more excitement. Besides, I'm looking for someone who warrants respect, not some kid wet behind the ears."

Alan glanced over his shoulder to look at me, and I again saw a glimmer of interest. Bernie may have noticed it, as well, because he grabbed the chance to expound on all of the things that he and his wife liked about Aspen Notch while Lou headed back to Dottie's Café.

Pulling up to the curb, Lou turned to Alan. "I know it's a big decision and you need to think it over," he said. "How about if I run a background check while you and the wife talk. If you'd feel better about it, I can make it an interim position with no strings attached."

Alan nodded as he reached into his back pocket for his wallet to retrieve one of his old detective agency business cards since it had all of the information that the mayor would need to evaluate Alan's credentials. The fact that Alan took that initial step surprised me, though I had good vibes about it.

"Can I call you later on this number?" Lou asked.

"Yes," Alan replied. "It's my cell phone."

Lou smiled and shook Alan's hand, saying, "Regardless of your decision about the job, I think you ought to make an offer on the Whitman place. You'd get a good deal, and we'd like to welcome you to Aspen Notch."

CHAPTER 3

*A*lan and I returned to the park on Elm Street to discuss our options since we'd enjoy the charming spot with its colorful array of leaves on a sunny fall afternoon. We found a bench across from an impressive statue of a hunter with a rifle in one hand and a raccoon in the other, which the bronze sign beneath identified as Abe Whitman, the founder of Aspen Notch.

"Before we talk about the house," I began, "you need to decide if you want the job."

"I know," Alan said. "They must feel pretty desperate."

I nodded in agreement before saying, "Right. Who offers a stranger the position of police chief?"

"Technically it's just a title for the only cop in town," Alan replied, "but it makes me wonder."

"Apparently, there's not a lot of crime in Aspen Notch," I said, glancing at my surroundings. I watched as a young woman walked her dog, another pushed a baby carriage, and two older ladies gabbed by the gazebo. They all made the town look pretty safe to me.

"Do you think I ought to take the position?" Alan queried.

I told Alan that I could support his decision regardless of its direction, although I thought the job might provide a good diversion for him without too much stress. Since he liked his independence, I figured he could probably make his own hours and focus on whatever he considered most important.

Alan stared, unseeing, at the statue of Abe, lost in his own thoughts. I hoped the town's founder offered some kind of silent encouragement to back me up because I knew that Alan missed the satisfaction of serving as a police officer to protect citizens from harm.

Alan turned to me, then grinned and grabbed my hand as he said, "OK. I'll do it. It's not every day that something falls into your lap so, if the mayor calls, I'll tell him that I'm available."

"How cool is that?" I exclaimed, giving him a kiss on the cheek. "Everyone will call me the wife of the police chief."

Alan chuckled. "Hold your horses, kemosabe. We'll see if I receive a phone call. In the meantime, we should head back to the house on Church Street. Let's take another look at it before it's snatched up."

THE REAL ESTATE agent walked out of the house with another couple as we pulled into the driveway and parked next to their car. After she waved her farewell to them, she hospitably turned her attention to us, though she didn't seem as chipper as she'd been a few hours earlier.

"Any chance we can do a walk-around?" Alan asked.

"I suppose," she replied, "but I do have a tentative offer, contingent on a loan approval, and I wouldn't want you to waste your time."

Alan glanced at me and I nodded my assent. Strangely, I felt as if I could read his mind, and the house on Church Street with its proximity to town center provided the best alternative for us if the mayor followed through on his request.

"We'd like to make a cash offer, full asking price, with a quick settlement," Alan said. "We'll wait while you draw up the contract."

After her initial surprise, she ushered us into the house and invited us to sit at the dining room table. Once again, the orange kitchen drew my attention, and I inwardly cringed as I pondered the amount of work needed to make the place livable. Still, the house had good bones, and I thought we made the right decision.

"I can't promise that the seller will accept your offer," the agent said when we signed the last of the papers. "I have one more showing scheduled today, but you have a strong chance of getting the property. Go ahead and look around while I contact the owners."

After a quick perusal inside, Alan and I used the kitchen door to take a closer look at the outbuildings. He liked the work-bench in the garage, though the cabin that Abe Whitman built as his home captivated me. Finding the side door locked, I peered into one of the windows, and invited Alan to take a look.

"There's a fireplace," I remarked, "and I think the counter and shelving from the candy shop are still there."

"It's not in the best of shape," Alan noted, "but it probably wouldn't take much to fix it up. Do you plan to start a business?"

Alan's comment tickled my funny bone. "Yeah, right," I giggled, "although I'd like to preserve its history. Can't you just picture Abe sitting in a rocking chair by the hearth and, maybe, cleaning his pelts in this very spot?"

"I wonder where he slept," Alan said as he continued to gaze through the window. "There's no bedroom."

"Abe might have built a loft," I suggested, "or maybe he had a Murphy bed. Wouldn't that be neat?"

"Very," Alan chuckled. "You could make it your woman-cave, or maybe I'll claim it as mine."

"You can have the garage," I quipped. "Let's check out the trees along the back fence. They look as if they're fruit-bearing."

As we crossed the yard, I could imagine planting a small vegetable garden by the side fence since the location had plenty of sun. I usually had success with tomatoes and cucumbers, but I conjured other options when Alan's phone jingled.

He winked at me and nodded, so I knew Alan recognized the mayor's number. The brief call ended with Alan thanking the mayor for his generous offer, and telling him that he'd gladly serve Aspen Notch as the Interim Police Chief.

"When do you start?" I asked when Alan returned the phone to his breast pocket.

Gazing at me with a comical expression, he said, "In two weeks. I must be nuts."

We both began to laugh, and it felt great to release the tension of buying a new home and wondering what the future would bring. Alan pulled me into his embrace, then sealed the deal with an enthusiastic kiss.

"Are you ready for this adventure?" Alan whispered in a voice filled with elation.

"I'm with you, pal," I grinned, "ready, willing, and able."

CHAPTER 4

*W*e had settlement on the Church Street property the second Monday in October. To celebrate, Alan and I took an early lunch at Dottie's Café before he needed to return to his job and I had to meet the movers at the house. Both of us felt tired and hungry by that point, since we departed southeastern Pennsylvania at the crack of dawn.

"I hear congratulations are in order," Dottie said as she pointed to a table near the window. "Go ahead and sit over there. How'd the closing go?"

"It went quite smoothly," Alan grinned, "but we still have the tough part ahead of us."

"I don't envy you," Dottie smiled. "Packing and unpacking are exhausting, that's for sure."

Dottie handed each of us a menu before clearing the table next to us. I thought she certainly knew how to multitask, though I wondered how she managed everything and still remained pleasant. As for me, I tackled one thing at a time, and if it weren't for Trudi, a long-time friend, I'd never have been ready for the move.

"Breakfast or lunch today?" Dottie asked as she filled our mugs with steaming coffee, then welcomed two more couples. With Alan in uniform, both stopped to introduce themselves to him, expressing their delight to have a police presence in Aspen Notch again. Alan replied with a few pleasantries before they selected their tables, then asked Dottie for a stack of pancakes with a side of bacon while I ordered the plain omelet and toast.

The small café, filling up with the lunch crowd as we waited for our food, seemed to attract older couples who probably preferred the friendly diner ambiance, rather than the grab-and-run fast food joints off the highway. Other than a pizza shop, I hadn't noticed any other eateries in the center of town.

I shared my thoughts with Alan, and he agreed, but noted that some of the local business owners took a later lunch. At least that's what he'd surmised during his first weeks on the job while I packed boxes at my home in Chester County.

We both glanced toward the door when another couple entered. I immediately recognized Marty Sandler, one of the three guys we'd met during our house-hunting in September.

Marty strutted toward our table and introduced us to his wife, Evelyn. Alan cordially invited them to join us, though he explained that we didn't plan to stay long since I had to meet the movers shortly.

"Oh, you poor dear," Evelyn said with a charming smile. "We moved into town about 5 years ago and I remember what a hassle it was."

"We had planned to relocate," I chuckled, "just not so fast. Anyway, with Alan starting his job 2 weeks ago and closing on the Church Street house today, we decided to make it work."

"Did you end up with all of the packing yourself?" Evelyn questioned.

"Alan helped on weekends, when he could," I replied, "and one of my friends kept me on schedule. I don't know what I would have done without her."

Dottie arrived with the brunch platters for Alan and me, then took Marty and Evelyn's order. Despite her busy pace, she offered her assistance with unpacking after she closed the café for the day.

"That's so kind of you," I smiled, "but I'll be fine. Besides, you must feel exhausted by the time the last customer departs, so I think you should go home and rest."

Dottie gave a wry grin and said, "Yeah, right. After I make supper for my boy and take him to band practice."

"You have a son?" I asked.

"Rob," Dottie nodded. "He's 15, and a sophomore in high school."

"He's a good kid," Evelyn added, "and an Honor student."

Dottie nodded with pride in her smile. "I've been lucky," she said. "Anyway, we'd be glad to help you. I know you're in a rush, so I'll bring your check when I return with the Sandlers' lunch."

With Alan and Marty into their own conversation, Evelyn chatted with me while I munched. She explained that she and Marty had moved to Aspen Notch after he retired from his tax business on Long Island. They had four children and she stayed home to raise them, though they all now lived on their own and had their own families.

I told Evelyn that I, too, had grown children, a daughter in Colorado and a son in California, and stayed home to raise them, though my first husband had died. Once they went off to college, I worked as a teacher's aide, then an office assistant at a dental practice. When Alan and I found a second chance at love, we decided to marry sooner, rather than later, and thought that Aspen Notch would provide a good spot for our retirement.

Evelyn laughed, then said, "It didn't happen the way you planned, did it?"

"Not exactly," I chuckled, "though we're happy about this new adventure. Do your kids live nearby?"

"No," Evelyn replied. "Our oldest son and his family still live in New York, but the rest have moved all over the country. The youngest works in D.C., and our two girls live out west. Dana's in Texas, while Laurel's in Oregon. They're all married, but we don't often get to see all of the grandkids."

I nodded, thinking that we'd lost the experience of close family ties once the kids went off to forge their own destiny. I didn't neces- sarily consider it a bad thing because it taught them to fend for themselves while expanding their frame of reference, but we missed out on the opportunity to relate with each other on a day-to-day basis.

Though my children and I now spoke on the phone fairly often, Alexa and her family were firmly established in Colorado, and I doubted that they'd ever return to the east coast. On the other hand, Michael, still single by choice, loved to travel. I assumed that his many business trips to Asia prevented his settling down, but I felt certain it would happen eventually.

Dottie brought Marty and Evelyn's sandwich platters and our check as I spread jelly on my last piece of toast. I'd have preferred to stay and chat with Evelyn, but Alan reminded me of the time since we didn't want the movers to have to wait for us, and they still had their return drive to Chester County.

"I really enjoyed meeting you," I told Evelyn. "It sounds as if we have a lot in common, and I sure could use a friend as we settle into Aspen Notch."

"Likewise," Evelyn smiled. "Did you buy the house on the corner of Church Street?"

"Yes," I nodded, "we did."

"It's a great location," she said, "though I heard the inside was awful. I guess you'll have to do some renovations."

Nodding my head in agreement, I asked, "Do you know a reputable painter?"

"Actually, I do," Evelyn replied. "Let's exchange contact information and I can text you his name and number."

As Alan and I departed, I thanked my lucky stars for a new friend, as well as someone who knew the local resources. I certainly needed both.

CHAPTER 5

The movers arrived just after Alan and I opened up the house. We'd already decided to have only the basics brought in, and store the rest in the garage until we had the place painted. Alan wanted to have renovations completed before we moved in, but I thought it made better sense to coordinate the move with our settlement day since Alan already started his job in Aspen Notch and I wanted to be with him. Besides, with November on its way, I worried that the weather would interfere. I'd already had a winter incident on I-81, and preferred not to have another.

The three young men who delivered our furniture didn't lack muscle-power. Two of them lugged the sofa, recliner, and TV to set up the living room, while the other began to carry in the cartons I'd designated as priority items. Wisely, I'd marked each box with the contents and numbered it according to its intended location, so with just a glance, I could direct its placement in the house or garage.

Though we had a cursory walk-through before closing, Alan did a more thorough investigation while I stood by the truck to guide the movers. We already knew from the home inspection report what needed repairs, but we thought we'd have to purchase new appliances eventually, since the existing ones looked dated and dirty.

Once the movers set up our bed and placed the bureau in our room, Alan suggested that I take a look inside to make sure the furniture arrangement suited me. He also added, "I think we should have the movers bring in our dining room table and chairs. Even if we can't use the kitchen, we need a place to eat."

"You're right," I agreed. "Does the oven work?"

"Not really," Alan replied. "Only one burner on the stove-top gets warm, and don't even ask about the refrigerator. I can see why they left it for us to haul away."

I shook my head, wondering how some people could be so inconsiderate. Though we left my older appliances in Chester County, all of them worked fine, and might save the next owner from having to purchase new ones right away. Besides, Trudi and I spent hours cleaning and shining them so they'd look nice.

"I'm fine here if you want to head into work," I said more bravely than I felt. Frankly, I didn't want him to leave everything to me, nor did I know where to begin, yet I simply added, "Maybe we can determine what else we need, and shop for appliances this evening."

"That sounds like a plan," Alan nodded. "Call me if you need anything."

Once the movers had the essential furniture and priority cartons in the house, I let them finish up with the things for the garage, and asked them to take the garden equipment to the shed in the yard. I planned to work inside, particularly gathering the things I'd need to set up the bedroom.

The men made amazing progress in a short time, and by late afternoon, I could sign-off on their work. I gave them each a tip, handed the driver a cashier's check for the final charge, and thanked them for their excellent service.

Finally alone, I thought I'd feel relief that we completed the first stage of our relocation, but I didn't. I wandered through the house, questioning what possessed me to agree to this move since the ugly place didn't feel like home. I wanted to cry, but instead, I texted Alan to tell him the movers had left. The bounce back message I received that he was in a meeting didn't help my sagging spirit.

Hoping to bolster my spirits, I made up the bed with the new set of sheets that I'd purchased for just the occasion. A matching comforter and pillow shams completed the look I wanted, though I made a mental note to add new blinds to our shopping list. The ones on the windows looked dingy and hung at an odd angle.

I thought about trying to find my canister of tea bags, but one step into the kitchen left me cringing, which I could also say about the laundry room. Instead, I lugged a carton to the living room sofa to unpack our dishware and cutlery, then tediously removed the newspaper wrapping from each plate and saucer until the chime of our front doorbell brought relief.

Thrilled to see Evelyn Sandler on the stoop, I invited her in, warning that the house was a mess. She handed me a box of doughnuts while she balanced a carry-out tray with two cups of coffee, then she gazed at the lime-green walls, shaking her head.

"You *do* need a painter," she chuckled, "but don't worry. I brought my box of business cards."

"Have a seat," I said, moving the carton of dishes to the floor. "You've just saved me from a major meltdown."

Evelyn offered me a coffee, which I gratefully accepted. I even indulged in a scrumptious Bavarian cream doughnut after Evelyn reminded me that the move made a perfect occasion for the ultimate comfort food. She obviously remembered her own experience of relocating to an unfamiliar area.

"I'm surprised that your husband couldn't take the rest of the day off, with the move and all," Evelyn noted. "It's not as if he can't make his own schedule."

"He would have," I said, "but the mayor called a meeting. Actually, Lou Greene already scheduled it, but he certainly could have picked a better day."

Evelyn nodded, then said, "If you ask me, Lou could have shown a little more consideration. Anyway, give me a quick tour, then we'll start calling for painting estimates."

~

I FELT SLIGHTLY MORE upbeat by the time Evelyn departed. The painter she recommended promised to stop by in the morning to provide an estimate, and even suggested that we purchase the paint as soon as possible since he could start immediately if we approved his fee.

Because the kitchen required a total renovation, Evelyn picked out the names of two local construction companies from her box of business cards, and I set up an appointment for both the next day. Finally, she had me call the cable company that had the most reliable service in our area, and they scheduled the set-up for the next day, late afternoon.

Nearly dusk when Alan arrived home, he found me in the dining room arranging the stacks of dishes, pots, and utensils on the table, although I left room for the two of us to eat a meal. Of course, I wondered how we'd manage if we needed to gut the kitchen, but I tried not to worry about it. Brushing a wayward strand of hair out of my eyes, I gave Alan a brave smile.

"How was your meeting?" I questioned.

Alan rolled his eyes before saying, "Did I ever tell you how much I hate wasting time? There are some big windbags in this little town."

"It seems to me I recall hearing such a thing," I chuckled. "Take off your uniform and get comfy. I haven't found the carton of hangers yet, but I put your suitcase on the dresser."

While Alan changed, I searched through the boxes under the table for the one I'd labeled with hangers. We'd need that one sooner than later, though I reminded myself not to hang the clothes until we had the closets painted. It frustrated me that one thing hinged on the other, but at least I wanted to be ready.

From the bedroom, Alan declared that he liked the new décor, but the lightbulb in the overhead fixture had died. We'd probably need to pick up some bulbs at the store, so I added them to my list, which grew by the minute.

"Are you ready for supper?" Alan asked when he strolled into the living room, as his gaze checked out the day's progress. "I guess we have a lot to do tonight."

"That's an understatement," I moaned, recognizing that my upbeat performance didn't last very long.

Alan placed his arm around my shoulder, then pulled me into his embrace. "I'm sorry, honey," he said in a gentle tone. "I should've stayed with you. The place looks good, so thank you."

"It looks like crap," I groaned.

"But it looks better than it did this morning." His lopsided grin made me smile, for some odd reason.

"I'm ready," I sighed. "Get me out of here."

CHAPTER 6

$\mathcal{A}$lthough Alan wanted us to have a celebratory dinner at an upscale restaurant, I suggested we reserve that for an evening of relaxation, rather than a night when we had so much to accomplish. Instead, we decided on a quick meal at a fried chicken eatery near the home-goods store.

While we ate, I told Alan about Evelyn's visit and her help lining up appointments for the next day. I also mentioned that I had measured the spaces for the appliances we'd need, though we might have to wait on an oven and refrigerator until after I met with the construction people.

Alan nodded before saying, "I honestly can't believe how much you accomplished today. You even found the yardstick?"

"No," I said, "I remembered to put my measuring tape in my purse before we left."

"You're a smart gal," Alan smiled, "and resourceful, too. Of course, I knew that."

We both laughed, which broke the tension I felt with my brain in overdrive. Changing the subject, I asked Alan to tell me about his earlier meeting, and he shook his head in frustration until he said, "I'm not sure I like some of the politics in our little town."

"Argumentative?" I questioned.

"That's the problem," Alan sighed, "if you can call it one. No one crosses Lou, so it's his way, and that's it."

"Do you disagree with his policies?" I asked.

"I'm still learning the ropes, so I didn't voice an opinion," Alan replied, "but I couldn't help thinking that we have a town council composed of a bunch of zombies."

"Hand-picked by the mayor?" I pressed.

"Like me?" Alan said. "I don't know, but I'll figure it out. Are you ready to do some shopping?"

ALL IN ALL, we had a successful shopping trip. We purchased a new washer and dryer, and set up delivery for three days later, which I hoped gave us enough time to have the laundry room painted.

As far as the oven and refrigerator, Alan and I disagreed on the models, but called a truce, knowing that the construction design would direct our final decision. On the other hand, we didn't find the selection of paint too challenging since we both preferred a neutral palette.

When we returned home, Alan hung the new blinds for the side window facing the street, and replaced the old light bulb in the ceiling fixture, while I moved the rest of our buys to the laundry room. He intended to tackle the back windows in the morning, since he thought no one would traipse through our fenced yard at this hour.

With both of us exhausted by the time we went to bed and turned out the light, I think I fell asleep before my head hit the pillow, but I awoke, startled, in the middle of the night.

I had such a realistic dream that I heard myself call out, "What do you want?" Yet Alan didn't stir. Had I actually uttered those words aloud or were they a part of my dream, as well?

I listened carefully, but didn't detect any strange sounds. As my eyes adjusted to the darkness, I saw nothing out of place. In fact, my dream quickly faded and I remembered nothing but the imagined presence of a stranger.

The next morning, Alan stood in our bedroom doorway with two take-out containers of coffee in his hands. "Rise and shine, sleepyhead."

Groggily, I stretched, then gratefully accepted my coffee as I said, "You went out already?"

"Yes, ma'am," Alan quipped, "and breakfast awaits your presence at the dining room table."

"You're wonderful," I said. "Let me get a quick shower."

Alan had already made a dent in his container of sausage and eggs when I arrived, and I had to admit that they smelled good. Fast food had its place, I thought, recognizing that it made a welcome meal when we had no food in the house other than Evelyn's box of doughnuts, which Alan soon discovered.

"You look particularly handsome in that uniform," I said, taking a bite of my biscuit. "What's on your agenda today?"

"I thought I'd meet the painter with you before starting my rounds," Alan replied as he selected a glazed doughnut. "Lou likes me to cruise the neighborhoods first thing in the morning."

"I'd appreciate your presence," I nodded, "since I need a little moral support today."

Alan raised his right eyebrow, asking, "Do you feel all right? You're not having regrets about the move, are you?"

"I'm OK," I replied. "I guess I just feel sad about leaving the home where I raised my kids, but I'll get over it."

"I know," Alan agreed. "I felt the same way when we sold my house."

"Really?" I queried. "You didn't tell me."

Alan gave a wry chuckle as he said, "Cops know how to hide their feelings."

"You don't have to do that around me," I reminded him. "We can give each other strength."

Alan reached to take my hand in his, and the loving gesture reinforced our unity in this new venture. I recognized the difficulty of change for everyone, but having an ally made it so much easier.

"We're going to upgrade this place to make it our dream home," Alan smiled. "What do you think about knocking out the wall between the kitchen and dining room?"

"I love it," I agreed. "How about a totally open concept? We could possibly have an island to separate the kitchen and living room."

Alan and I hashed out our wish-list for the renovations, though we focused on the more public areas of the house since we thought the bedrooms and bathroom only needed a cosmetic update for now. By the time the painter arrived, we felt pretty confident about our joint decisions.

John Calhoon introduced himself, then gazed around the living room with a surprised expression. I had expected a much younger man, given his voice on the phone. Instead, we met a wiry middle-aged guy, clean-shaven, with salt-and-pepper hair.

"I suppose you can see that the house needs painting," I said after shaking his hand, "but let me show you the kitchen."

The three of us stood laughing in the kitchen doorway before John exclaimed, "Geez! I've never seen anything so putrid in all my life. What were the previous owners thinking?"

Alan and I agreed wholeheartedly before presenting the rest of the house. In the end, we accepted his bid, showed him the paint we'd purchased, and suggested that he start with the laundry room, then the master bedroom sliding-door closet.

"Good thing you bought plenty of primer," John noted. "I can start this afternoon or tomorrow morning, whenever you can pay me the first installment."

Alan offered to pick up a cashier's check during his lunch break if John could begin right away. Although we knew we'd find the necessary upgrades chaotic for a while, we wanted to settle in as soon as possible.

CHAPTER 7

By late afternoon, I felt frazzled, though John didn't cause any of the hassles. He arrived shortly after lunch with a ladder in tow and immediately began to disconnect the washer and drier, then moved them to the center of the room. I watched him lay out the drop cloths and prepare his rollers until the doorbell signaled the first appointment with a construction representative.

Quite honestly, I didn't like the arrogant young guy, who adamantly explained his vision for the place. Our wish list went out the window, while he blabbed on about the strengths of his team and what they could accomplish with the right budget. After his ridiculously high verbal estimate, I told him not to bother sending a write-up.

I didn't consider the next appointment much better. Though a tad more collaborative and engaging, the man's fees included the marked-up cost of an architect and engineer, but we could forego those if we used the company's boiler-plate design. The sketch he presented didn't captivate me since it basically offered the same kitchen with updated counter-tops and new fixtures. I did, however, ask him to send me an estimate for his plan, as well as the cost of incorporating our ideas.

I checked on John's progress while I waited for the cable company. As the ceiling of the laundry room dried, he worked on the spackling of the walls, and impressed me when he said he could finish painting the closet in our bedroom before he departed for the day.

"I couldn't help but overhear your conversation with the construction people," John remarked as he patched a large nail hole. "I suppose you plan to remodel the kitchen."

I shook my head in utter frustration before saying, "I don't know what we should do at this point. The cost seems exorbitant, especially if we try to integrate the design we'd like to have."

"It's the right time to fix it up," John said, "what with just moving in. A paint job and new appliances or cabinets are fine, but you might as well make it into something that you and your husband could both enjoy."

"That's what we thought," I nodded. "Frankly, we both want the open concept, and I'd like to be part of a conversation in the living room even if I'm working in the kitchen."

John moved to another area needing spackle, then said, "It makes sense to me, though you don't know if those are load-bearing walls that you want to tear down. You really will need someone who has knowledge about that sort of stuff."

John's comment made sense to me, and Alan and I had discussed the topic, but we figured it would be part of the deal if we went with a legitimate construction firm. Being new to the area posed a disadvantage, I realized, despite Evelyn's handy business card box. At least she steered us in the right direction with John Calhoon.

When I asked John if he knew anyone I could contact for a more reasonable estimate, he shook his head, saying, "I've done some work for a few builders around here, but they're not interested in renovation jobs. Let me think awhile."

I let John mull while I met with the cable serviceman who had just arrived. Once he hooked up the TV and internet service, I could conduct an on-line search for a reputable construction company, so I decided to put my worries aside.

Close to 5 p.m. by the time the representative installed all of the components for cable and checked the connections, I could finally breathe a sigh of relief. Although I had a hectic day, we'd accomplished a lot, and I looked forward to Alan's return so he and I could discuss what I'd learned.

As John Calhoon washed his paint rollers, he called from the laundry room that he'd thought about someone who might consider helping us. Curious, I stood in the doorway, hoping that he had a good lead.

"I know a retired guy," John said, turning to face me. "He and my father used to hunt together before Pop passed, and I recalled that Deke Hopewell worked as a construction manager for those big factories they built back in the day."

"How old is he?" I asked.

John's eyes twinkled as he said, "I think close to 75, at least. Anyway, while you met with the cable guy, I called Deke to see if he knew of anyone who might have an interest in doing renovations here."

"What'd he say?" I questioned.

"You won't believe this," John smiled, "but he told me that he'd like to take a look. He used to know the lady who had the candy shop in the Whitman cabin, and if you ask me, he might have had a thing for her at one time."

"Really?" I asked. "Could he take on a project like this one at his age?"

"Deke would just manage it," John replied. "Anyway, he knows people in the business, so I'd hear what he has to say."

"It's a good option," I agreed. "When can he come?"

"I told Deke that I'd bring him over tomorrow morning," John explained. "He'll meet with you and Alan to determine the feasibility of the project, then he'll sandpaper the spackle for me. I'll drive him home around lunchtime, after we get a bite to eat."

It sounded like a great plan to me.

≈

DUSK ALREADY DESCENDED and John departed before Alan arrived home. I had just finished checking our bedroom closet that John completed, and I found good workmanship, with everything left in perfect order, which made him a wonderful asset.

Alan changed out of his uniform, then suggested that we eat supper at an Italian restaurant just off the next exit of the highway which Lou recommended for its good food and popular early-bird specials. It didn't take long for me to wash my face, put on a dressier sweater, and dab some lipstick.

After we placed our order, I checked out the décor of La Traviata. It had a cozy ambiance, even with a blazing fire in the hearth by the bar. Alan and I agreed that it reminded us of the dining room at the lodge where we had met, and I considered it a sign that we'd have a pleasant meal.

When the waiter returned with a basket of warm, crusty rolls, Alan requested a bottle of the house wine for our table. Our server returned almost immediately, then poured two glasses, while I realized how much I looked forward to just relaxing. As I took my first sip, I asked Alan about his day.

"Not bad," Alan replied. "Other than a couple of traffic violations and an incident at the pizza shop, I organized files."

"What happened at the pizzeria?" I asked.

Alan swirled his wine, then said, "Sal D'Angelo reported money missing from the cash register. I don't know if he told the truth, but I wrote up the report."

"Why would he lie?" I pressed.

"Lou said that he makes trouble sometimes," Alan stated. "Nothing serious, but Sal likes a little attention."

"What's with this 'Lou said,' all the time?" I queried.

"He knows Aspen Notch," Alan shrugged. "I figure it can't hurt to listen to what he says, at least until I learn enough about town to form my own opinions."

I nodded while the waiter placed our plates in front of us, then added a bowl of fresh salad to the center of the table. I had the lasagna, while Alan selected the penne pasta dish with spicy sausage, and I found the aromas delectable.

While we ate, I told Alan about the successes and failures of my day. He agreed that we should meet with Deke Hopewell, since his past experience in the business might serve us well. If it didn't pan out, we could continue our search for the company that would fit our budget and design.

"Can you stay with me to meet him?" I questioned.

"Sure," Alan agreed. "I have nothing pressing tomorrow morning."

"I wouldn't want to get Lou all riled up," I teased.

Alan raised his right eyebrow, then laughed. "I get your point, so give it a rest. If I'm the police chief, interim or not, I'll determine my own schedule."

"That's the Alan I know and love," I said with a wink.

CHAPTER 8

*J*ohn Calhoon arrived with Deke Hopewell shortly after Alan and I finished our fast-food take-out breakfast. Deke offered a friendly handshake with a wide grin on his well-lined, clean-shaven face. He had thick white hair and bushy eyebrows, and I thought he might have been a tall man at one time, but age left him stooped, walking with a cane.

Alan and I welcomed Deke and John, then invited them to take a seat in the living room. Deke gazed around the room with a look of nostalgia in his eyes, and he didn't seem to notice the glaring lime green walls.

"This place brings back a lot of memories," he said softly. "I hope it gives both of you great happiness."

"John mentioned that you might have known the original owner," I commented as I moved a chair to sit across from them. Alan remained standing, leaning on the back of the recliner.

"Yes," Deke nodded. "I knew Clara Whitman quite well. We first met when I'd stop by to purchase her taffy. She was a wonderful woman, generous and kind to all she met."

"Was she your sweetheart?" I asked, with a side glance to see John's reaction.

Deke laughed, shaking his head. "I wasn't more than a kid back then, with Clara probably a good 10 years older. Once I became a smart-aleck teen, she offered me a job after school and on weekends, mostly just doing yard work or helping her stock the jars of candy. Eventually, I became her handyman for small repairs, which got me interested in construction work."

"So, you know this house, as well?" Alan asked.

"Yes," Deke agreed. "Of course, I wanted to check it out. Clara would turn in her grave if she saw it now."

Alan nodded before saying, "We'd like to restore and modernize the place, but the price seems excessive, so we need some guidance."

Deke's eyes wandered from the ceiling to the walls, then to Alan and me. Whether Clara's spirit guided his decision, or the challenge of a restoration, or my pleading expression, Deke told us that he'd serve as construction manager. He'd contact some of his old cronies, and come up with a plan.

"You're wonderful!" I exclaimed. "When can you start?"

Deke chuckled. "You forgot to ask what I charge."

After he told us the amount for his service, Alan and I agreed in one voice. We considered the cost reasonable, given Deke's experience and knowledge, and he knew people to call in order to complete the job.

Deke told us that he'd spend the afternoon generating a list of what we needed to begin the project. Sure that the wall between the kitchen and living room was load-bearing, he'd contact someone to measure and order the steel beam, then call in a few favors from an electrician and plumber.

John added that he'd finish the laundry room so we'd have it ready for the new washer and dryer, then begin painting the bedroom ceilings. Before he had to leave for work, Alan gave John and Deke a hearty handshake, and thanked them for their assistance.

I felt as if they'd lifted a weight from my shoulders.

∾

JOHN AND DEKE left for lunch around noontime, after John told me that he'd return by 2 p.m. On a whim, I called Evelyn Sandler with an invitation to join me at Dottie's Café, which she readily accepted since Marty went hunting with his friends for the day.

As the first to arrive, I took the last available table. Dottie smiled her welcome when she brought lunch platters to the two patrons across from me, and by the time Dottie had a chance to wait on me, Evelyn scurried in to take her seat.

"Sorry I'm late," she panted. "I had to take a pie out of the oven."

"No problem," I smiled. "Do you want Dottie to give us a minute?"

Evelyn shook her head, saying, "I'm ready if you are."

We both ordered chicken salad sandwiches and iced tea. While we waited, I told Evelyn that Alan and I thought highly of John Calhoon and appreciated her recommendation of him.

"I heard that he's good," Evelyn nodded. "How about the contractors?"

I shook my head. "Neither of them was exactly what we had in mind, but John suggested an older guy, Deke Hopewell. He worked as a construction manager before his retirement, and has agreed to oversee the project."

"I don't know him," Evelyn stated, "though I'm glad John came through for you."

I told Evelyn that Alan and I had met Deke earlier, and he intended to begin work right away. Since he'd line up the people for each phase of the renovation, we felt confident that he'd make sure they properly completed their jobs.

"You can't do better than that," Evelyn smiled. "How's everything otherwise?"

"I'm trying to stay calm," I said. "We're still living out of a suitcase, but I began to hang clothing in our closet this morning, now that the paint has dried. John finished the laundry room, too, and the new washer and dryer will arrive tomorrow."

Dottie heard my comment as she arrived with our plates and beverages, and remarked, "You know, Rob can help. His band director requires community service, so he and a few of his buddies could carry cartons or move furniture."

About to decline the offer, I had second thoughts. After all, with Alan busy at work, and my inability to carry heavy items by myself from our garage to the rooms, I considered it a better idea to make use of the teens.

"I'd really appreciate that," I nodded. "Of course, I'll pay the boys."

"Nonsense," Dottie smiled. "We help our neighbors, so I'll talk to Rob about it tonight."

"That'd be great," I sighed. "Could they possibly come on Saturday?"

"I think so," Dottie replied, "but I'll check, then let you know. You can give me your phone number before you leave."

Evelyn nodded her approval as Dottie left to wait on the next customer. Between bites of her sandwich, she told me about Dottie's situation. Her son, Rob, was barely a toddler when the boy's father died in a freak plowing accident. Dottie managed to scrape together a down payment, purchased the storefront café, and worked hard to make a decent life for the two of them.

"She never remarried?" I asked.

"Her life revolves around this place and her son," Evelyn said. "I think she might have dated someone a few years back, but I suppose it didn't work out."

"That's sad," I said as I took a sip of my iced tea. It made me reflect about the years I lived alone after my first husband's death and our children moved away. You start to believe that another chance at love will never happen.

"Be that as it may," Evelyn said, "Dottie's a good woman. "You can trust her to give you a straight answer, if you know what I mean."

I wasn't exactly sure what she meant, but I left it at that. John would soon return to continue his work, and I didn't want him to wait on me. Munching on my few remaining chips, I told Evelyn that she could stop by for a visit later if she got bored.

Evelyn chuckled before saying that she planned to run a few errands until she had to prepare supper. She didn't know what time

Marty would return home, but he liked a good meal after a day of hunting.

We signaled to Dottie that she could bring our checks, and I wrote my contact information on a napkin. As we gathered our things, Evelyn turned to gaze intently at me. I thought I must have forgotten something until she gave me parting advice.

"Be careful," she whispered. "Keep your eyes and ears open, because you can't trust everyone around here."

CHAPTER 9

$\mathcal{A}$lan informed me after breakfast the next morning that he had meetings all day and didn't know what time he'd return home, but he'd touch base with me by mid-afternoon. My expression may have betrayed my frustration, though I tried to shrug it off because I realized that a new job often entailed extended hours, and I couldn't blame Alan.

Alan pulled me into his embrace, then said, "I'm sorry, honey. I know this move hasn't been easy, and you probably feel as if you're doing it all alone."

"Sort of," I muttered. "I suppose I thought we'd handle this move together, but we barely have a chance to talk during the day, and we're both exhausted by the evening."

"It won't be like this all the time," Alan assured me. "Lou wants to make sure that I've caught up with everything."

"Like what?" I asked.

"You know," Alan remarked, "like who to keep an eye on, if they've had any prior felonies, that kind of stuff."

"It seems to me you could read reports instead of having lengthy meetings," I said.

"True," Alan agreed, "though reports don't tell the entire story. Lou gives me background information that I can use as intelligence, so to speak."

I nodded as if I understood, but I didn't, nor did I want an argument. The vibes I had about Lou's over-involvement didn't sit well with me, and made me wonder if it connected with Evelyn's comment about people not to trust. Did she refer to Lou Greene? I tucked the thought to the back of my mind, intending to ask her when I had a chance.

John arrived with Deke shortly after Alan departed. John went to work on the guest bedroom right away, while Deke sat with me at the dining room table to review his list of tasks. First on the agenda, he noted, would include demolition. He lined up a crew to tear out existing cabinets and remove the wallboard where we planned to open walls, although the studs would stay until we had the beam in place to support the ceiling.

"When will they start?" I asked.

"As soon as you agree to the cost," Deke said. "I assumed you wanted to have the work done quickly."

I nodded my agreement while I reviewed the estimate. As the first phase of the project, we needed demolition before we could move forward, although I had no idea what it should cost. I'd have liked Alan's input, but that couldn't happen with him in meetings all day, so I approved.

"Good," Deke said. "The dumpster will arrive today, and two guys will come first thing in the morning."

"Can we salvage anything?" I asked. "Alan might want to use some of the cabinets for his workshop in the garage, and I haven't yet decided about the old cabin, but maybe a couple of them would fit out there, as well."

"I don't see why not," Deke agreed, "and I always try to use anything not broken. Have you sketched out your design?"

I shook my head, saying, "No, I didn't know where to begin, but I want lots of natural light, an island, and more counter space."

Deke grinned. "I figured you'd say something like that, so I played around with two designs last night. They're not perfect since I didn't take any measurements yesterday, but they could give us something to build upon."

Deke amazed me with both rough sketches because he incorporated modern aspects with very different approaches. He reviewed each element with me and helped me decide what would provide better work-flow and organization. In the end, we had a compilation of Deke's two drafts, keeping the back door and the laundry room in their current location, enlarging the counter space, and moving the position of the appliances.

"Well done," Deke said. "I'll get John to help me with the measurements before lunch, then we'll get out of your hair. You and Alan can select your new cabinets, counters, appliances, and sink fixtures, but don't buy anything until I give my approval."

"Wow," I exclaimed. "This is exciting!"

"It won't be, come tomorrow," Deke laughed. "You might want to find a place to stay for a few weeks."

"We'll be fine here," I stated. "I can take care of errands if the noise level and dust get to me."

"Suit yourself," Deke said. "Anyone I send is trustworthy, so you don't have to worry about that, and I'll check on their progress several times each week, if not every business day."

I really liked Deke Hopewell because he reminded me of my father who had a solid work ethic, but always made time to give support and advice to my sister and me. Dad reassured us constantly that he'd help us handle any problems, though his heart gave out way too soon, which left mom to carry the burden until her death. Still, I missed both of them.

When I asked Deke about his family, his eyes took on a sorrowful cast as he told me that his wife died of cancer 3 years ago. She held a special place in his heart, throughout their 52 years of marriage, and Deke still struggled to accept her death. They had only one child, a daughter he called "sweet Caroline," but she developed leukemia at 10 years of age, and died before her 12th birthday.

"I'm so sorry," I said softly.

Deke cleared his throat. "I'll never forget Clara's kindness to us.

My wife always remarked that we couldn't have made it through such a difficult time if it hadn't been for Clara."

"Clara must have been a remarkable woman," I stated.

"She was," Deke nodded. "It's why I want to help fix up her place-- your place. We'll make her proud."

"Definitely," I agreed with a firm nod.

It made me think that Clara's spirit watched over us, and that comforted me.

CHAPTER 10

The next morning, I finished three loads of wash in my new washer and dryer and, for the first time, I began to feel at home when I hung clean clothing in our closet. With my spirits lifted, I felt better able to handle the chaos that surrounded me.

Before he departed for work, Alan promised to call it an early day so we could explore our options for the new kitchen at the local home-goods store. Meanwhile, John started painting the third bedroom and Deke handled the demolition project with the two husky guys he hired.

Despite the noisy whacking of hammers and the grating sound of cabinets being pulled from their moorings, Deke had control of the situation. For the most part, he perched himself on a dining room chair, acting as if he were the director of the next blockbuster movie. Occasionally, he'd use his cane to totter over and inspect whatever caused a halt in progress, offer his suggestion, then the racket would begin again.

At one such point, Deke called out to me. "Hey, Sue. Come and see what we just found."

I hurried from the bedroom and asked, "What's up?"

I saw Deke flipping through a spiral notepad while the two men gazed over his shoulder. With a chortle, Deke turned a page, then held it up to me, saying, "This belonged to Clara. It must have slipped through the back of the cabinet drawer, never to be seen again, but I'll bet she searched for it."

"How do you know it belonged to Clara?" I questioned.

"I'd recognize her handwriting anywhere," Deke smiled nostalgically. "Besides, these are some of her riddles."

I glued my questioning gaze to the small memo pad in Deke's hand, and recalled having similar notebooks as a high school student since we used them for recording our homework each day or passing notes in class. I still kept one in my purse for jotting appointments or contact information, though most people I knew used a phone app for such things. Nonetheless, I still preferred paper and pen.

Deke wanted me to read Clara's riddles, remarking that she often assigned him jobs using her little ditties. She got great joy from trying to stump him, and he won a taffy if he figured out what she wanted him to accomplish that day.

I took Deke's discovery to the living room, flipping pages while Deke gave additional instructions to his crew. Because some of the yellowed paper had grease stains, I figured Clara wrote while she worked in the kitchen, and probably stored her pad in the drawer. Maybe she searched feverishly when it went missing, and wondered where she could have lost it.

I understood completely because I, too, have misplaced items in cabinet drawers, especially plastic lids to my favorite storage containers. I'd never thought to actually remove the drawers to search within the dark space under them.

I started to return the memo pad to Deke when he joined me on the sofa, but he insisted that I read the riddles to him. He remembered that Clara wrote in elegant cursive, and he didn't think his eyesight could handle the fancy script.

Deke gazed across the room as I began to read one of the riddles, and his smile indicated that Clara's rhymes brought him fond memories.

Red and blue, flickering flame,
Eats the wood, knows no shame.
Winter is coming, time to chop,
Fill the bin to the very top.

"That was an easy one," Deke said with a hearty chuckle. "In fact, Clara used it so often that she wrote the riddle on a piece of cardboard, then taped it to the cabin window whenever she needed firewood."

"How old were you?" I asked.

"I don't know," Deke replied, "but I suppose about 14 or so. I just remember groaning every time Clara put out the sign because I hated the hard work of splitting logs."

"I can only imagine," I giggled. "How big was the bin?"

"It seemed huge to me," Deke smiled, "though, in reality, no bigger than a baby's bassinet."

"That's so funny," I chuckled. "Do you want me to read another?"

"Just one more for now," Deke nodded, "since I have to get back to work."

I flipped toward the middle, randomly choosing the next riddle. I noticed many stains on the page, as if Clara often read it while she made her candies. I scanned it, then hesitated before I continued.

"What's the matter?" Deke asked.

"You be the judge," I said.

Time stood still for one so young,
Dark and bitter, melodies never sung.
Ashes to dust, deep in the ground,
Happiness again never to be found.

Deke sat very still after I finished reading, and I watched as his eyes darkened and his brow furrowed, which made me wonder if Clara wrote the riddle as a eulogy for Deke's daughter. When I questioned Deke, he didn't know, though he mentioned that Clara attended Caroline's funeral, and provided her loving support for him and his wife.

With a tightening of his mouth, Deke told me that Clara took their hands in hers, then remarked that she knew exactly how devastated they felt. She recognized their overwhelming guilt for the inability to save their daughter, and the tremendous sadness that took hold of their spirits, but she assured them that the pain would become more manageable in time.

"Did Clara lose a child?" I asked.

"No," Deke replied without making eye contact with me. "Clara never had any children, although her husband died in the Korean War."

"That's what I'd heard," I nodded. "She must have written the poem to express her sadness for your loss. Maybe she even transposed her own emotions as she recalled how she felt when she learned that her husband wouldn't return from war."

Deke took a deep breath, then slowly rose. "Maybe. It just makes me wonder."

I watched Deke lean on his cane and make his way back to the kitchen. His sadness took shape in his stooped back, as if he carried a heavy burden.

It made me curious as well, I thought, as I placed the pad on the dining room table. I wanted to learn more about Clara Whitman and her riddles, because she definitely used them to send encrypted messages.

I just had to figure out their meaning.

CHAPTER 11

I felt drained after our shopping expedition, and Alan's stamina declined, as well, though he suggested that we grab a bite to eat with a couple of beers at the Black Horse Pub. He and Lou went there a few times for lunch, and Alan enjoyed the bar food and laid-back atmosphere. Honestly, any hole in the wall would have worked for me, as long as I didn't have to smell paint fumes.

The Black Horse Pub, located at the north end of town, didn't look like much from the outside, but the full parking lot seemed a good sign to me. Of course, I knew that Aspen Notch had few recreational options for the locals on a Friday night, so I wanted to check out the place.

Alan pulled open the heavy oak door for me, then led me to a table away from the bar. As luck would have it, a couple had just departed and the waitress finished wiping it clean.

"Perfect timing," she grinned. "Can I get you something from the bar?"

Alan ordered without even glancing at the menu. "We'll have a large pepperoni pizza, an order of spicy wings, and two of the pub's light beers."

"You've got it," she said. "Bottles or tap?"

"Tap, please," Alan replied. We both watched her scurry to submit our order, then check on folks at her other tables.

Though not overly expansive, the tavern could seat a number of guests and offered another section off the main room, which Alan explained held a couple of pool tables. If I felt up to it after we ate, he suggested that we might play a game of 8-ball.

"No dart boards?" I questioned.

Alan laughed, then said, "Yes, they have two of them, but I can't beat you at darts."

"What makes you think I won't win a round of pool?" I teased.

Alan's comical expression made me chuckle because he considered darts my specialty, especially after I'd gloated about my previous champion status. However, we'd never challenged each other to a game of pool, so he didn't know that I could also handle a cue stick, and I wanted to see if I'd lost my touch.

The waitress brought us each a pint of beer and placed a basket of wings in the center of our table. "I'll return with your pizza in a minute," she said as she handed each of us a pile of napkins. "Are you new in town? I haven't seen you here before."

I nodded, then explained that Alan accepted the position of police chief, and we recently purchased our home. Alan added that he'd eaten lunch at the tavern with the mayor, but they sat at the bar.

"Welcome to Aspen Notch," she smiled. "I'm Sally, and I work nights, so I guess that's why I never saw you."

"Happy to meet you," Alan and I both chimed at the same time. "Do you live in town?" I asked.

"Born and raised," Sally nodded. "I thought about moving to Scranton at one point, but then my dad got sick. It's just mom and me now, and she's pretty settled in her ways."

Since Sally looked as young as my daughter, I figured her mother might be my age and had put down roots, which often discouraged relocation. The thought made me realize why I found this move so difficult.

Sally left to get our pizza, while Alan and I tackled our hot wings. As we ate, I recounted the progress on our renovation since John finished painting the guest room and Deke oversaw the removal of our kitchen equipment. "Deke's crew salvaged all but one of the cabinets," I remarked, "then even lugged them to the garage for us."

"That was a good idea," Alan noted, grabbing a napkin for his sticky fingers. "What's next on their agenda?"

"John will begin to paint our bedroom on Monday," I said. "Deke will have his men pull up the old floor and tear out the wallboard. I'll show him the samples we got today, and once he approves, we can place our order."

"Sounds good," Alan nodded. "Do you want me to move the extra bed we stored in the garage? I can set it up in the guest room tomorrow, since we should probably sleep there for a few days until the paint dries in our room and the fumes disperse."

I agreed as Sally arrived with our pizza, which I thought smelled delicious. We thanked her before we each took a slice, then continued our conversation.

"That's a good idea," I said, "but you'll have help. Dottie's son will bring a couple of friends tomorrow afternoon, and they can do the heavy lifting. I also plan to ask them to help me set up the other bedroom as a den."

Alan paused midway between bites, saying, "Did I ever tell you how much you amaze me?"

Although Alan often said that, and I laughed every time, I didn't feel remarkable. In fact, nothing in my life came easy, and each new hurdle made me wonder how I'd manage it, but my darn stubbornness must have made me resilient.

"Thanks," I replied after my usual giggle. "Do you have to work tomorrow?"

"I'll just cruise around a few times," Alan stated. "I want folks to know they have a police presence in town."

"Good," I said, "because I need you."

"Why?" Alan questioned as he raised an eyebrow.

"You're my moral support," I smiled, "and I like spending time with you."

Alan chuckled as he handed me a second slice of pizza, then he said, "Right back at you, pal. I'll work with the teens while you direct the operations."

"That sounds like a plan," I grinned. "By the way, I forgot to tell you what Deke's crew found today."

Alan seemed interested in hearing about Clara's book of riddles, and thought she used a clever way to entice Deke to help her around the place during his teen years since solving puzzles would keep him motivated.

I agreed, but explained that Clara didn't direct all of the riddles to Deke, at least according to what I saw when I flipped through the spiral pad. I almost considered Clara a voice from the past, and wondered if she had something to tell us.

I'm not sure why that idea popped into my head, though I felt that Clara had some unfinished business. Alan again raised an eyebrow, a trick he used when he focused on something I'd mentioned. It made me happy that he offered to take a look at the notebook when we returned home.

"Are you ready for a game of pool?" Alan asked after his third slice of pizza. "I intend to whoop your butt."

I laughed, totally relaxed, then said, "Don't count on it, pal. I'm up for the challenge."

CHAPTER 12

*A*lan gloated the entire way home. Though we played only one game of pool, he beat me fair and square. Had I not sunk the 8-ball on the sixth round, I might have had a chance of winning. Nonetheless, I assured Alan, I considered him the champion, at least until I gained more practice.

After lugging in our purchases, Alan did a walk-through of the house, examining the renovation progress. I kicked off my shoes, plopped on the sofa, and settled comfortably though my brain continued to crank out tasks that I wanted to accomplish the next day. The list grew by the minute.

"Now that I see the space opened up," Alan said when he returned to the living room, "I think you made the right choice with the cabinets."

"I hope Deke approves our selection of those, as well as the appliances," I nodded. "Let me tell you, I can't wait to have a working kitchen."

Alan agreed, then said, "Speaking of Deke, where did you put the notepad he found?"

"On the dining room table," I pointed, happy to see Alan's interest in my activities.

Alan opened to the first page, and read the riddle aloud.

Red and blue, flickering flame,
Eats the wood, knows no shame.
Winter is coming, time to chop,
Fill the bin to the very top.

"This one's pretty obvious," Alan said with a grin. "I guess young Deke had to chop the firewood."

I laughed, then explained that Deke cringed whenever Clara displayed her sign with the riddle. Frankly, I could never imagine my son, Michael, doing anything so strenuous, not that I'd have trusted his ability to use an axe.

Alan turned the page and read the next riddle.

Blade upon blade, pewter and green,
One will meet its match, as we have seen.
It won't last long, this ongoing fight.
The stronger will fail, the weaker has might.

"This one's not so easy," Alan chuckled. "Did Deke have to sharpen knives?"

"I'm not sure," I said. "We skipped ahead in the notebook, so I'll have to ask him about that one. Anyway, what kind of knife blade is green?"

Alan and I tossed out our ideas, challenging each other to solve the riddle. Finally, I answered my own question.

"I have it!" I exclaimed. "A blade of grass is green, and the blade on one of those old lawn mowers could have been pewter, at least in color. So, the mower would seem to be the stronger, but the grass wins in the end because it keeps growing."

"Smarty pants," Alan teased. "I think you're right. We had one of those old push-mowers during my youth, but the blades on our mower weren't pewter. They were orange from rust."

"Probably because you left it out in the rain," I quipped.

"No doubt," Alan agreed, and we both laughed.

"My brain has about had it for today," I said with a loud yawn, "so I intend to hit the sack."

"Now that we have a working TV," Alan stated, "I'd like to watch the news, but I'll join you shortly."

I gave Alan a good-night kiss after he reached for the remote, then said, "Sweet dreams, honey. I love you."

He kissed me back, saying, "I love you, too."

AFTER I FELL into a sound sleep, a strange noise brought me to full attention. It wasn't the drone from the TV in the living room, nor did I detect Alan's movement. In fact, I figured that he had likely fallen asleep in the recliner, a typical occurrence.

The sound I'd heard seemed to come from the back yard. Listening intently, I noticed only the occasional distant purr of a car on the road out front. I padded to the window and peeked between the slats on the blind to see that the full moon cast eerie shadows, but nothing looked out of place.

Wide awake now, I flipped on the light switch, intent on discovering the source of the noise I'd heard. Donning my robe and slippers, I checked the lock on the front door before heading to the back until Alan stirred as I passed by.

"What's the matter?" he asked with one eye open.

"Nothing," I said. "Go back to sleep."

"If you're looking for the rest of the pizza we brought home," Alan remarked, "I ate it."

"No," I replied, "I wanted to make sure that we locked the doors."

"Why?" Alan questioned.

"I heard a noise out back," I stated, "and it woke me up."

Alan knew that I tried never to make a mountain out of a molehill. He also thought I had good powers of observation and a sharp intuition, at least he told me that often enough. Perhaps that's why he grabbed his jacket and headed to the kitchen.

"Stay here," he said in a firm cop's voice.

I paid no heed and followed him out the back door. His loud sigh indicated that he knew I wouldn't listen. He checked the latch on the fence gate, as well as the locks on Abe's cabin and the garden shed, and found everything secure. As I had seen from the window, nothing looked out of place.

"Everything's fine," Alan noted when we completed our search. He locked the back door and turned the dead bolt.

"I know," I replied, still stymied, "though the same thing happened the other night."

"You heard something?" Alan questioned.

"Initially, I thought I dreamt it," I nodded. "In fact, I forgot all about it until just now."

Alan put his arm around my shoulder and pulled me into his embrace, saying, "I'm sure you just had a dream. Besides, we still have to get used to the place, and we'll hear lots of strange sounds, so don't worry about it."

We walked to the bedroom arm in arm, turning off the TV and lights on the way. I gladly accepted Alan's reassurance, but I still wondered about what I'd heard.

CHAPTER 13

*R*ob Burkeholder, Dottie's son, arrived shortly after lunch with two of his high school buddies whom he introduced as Cole and Dylan. None of the boys looked very hefty, but they made up for the lack of muscle-power with their lively spirits, and I quickly pegged Cole as the class clown.

No sooner had they straggled in when Cole pretended to gag as he gazed around the living room. Laughing, I told him that I couldn't agree more, but we'd lose the lime green walls in just a few days.

"It's a good thing you're fixing it up, Mrs. J.," Cole noted. "This place was a dump."

"Were you here before?" I asked.

"Yeah," he nodded. "The kid who used to live here invited me over. I considered him creepy, just like his old man."

All of the boys, including Rob, added their two cents, and I got an earful, with none of it good. The chatter abruptly ended when Alan opened the front door and greeted the boys. He still wore his uniform, since he just returned from his dutiful cruise around town.

Rob, the first to address him, said, "Hi, Officer J. Do you remember me? I met you at my mom's café."

"Good to see you again, Rob," Alan smiled. "Thanks for bringing two of your friends to give us some help."

"No problem, sir," Rob replied. "Besides, we get service points."

After another round of introductions, Alan explained the plan. He and the boys would carry items from the garage to the house, I'd direct their placement, then the boys would help him set up the bed in the guest room. Alan remarked that they could finish in an hour if they worked together as a team.

Within short order, the boys had placed the desk, futon, floor lamp, and spare TV in the den, careful not to mar the paint. After carrying in the cartons I'd labeled for the den, they began the more difficult task of lugging the queen-sized mattress and box springs for the guest room. Luckily, John hadn't yet painted the hallway because it would have needed plenty of touch-ups.

While they carried in the dresser and bed frame, I found Alan's tool box, since I knew he'd need it to put together the frame, then I began to unpack the boxes in the den. The boys not only assisted; they also offered to get rid of the empty cartons.

I kicked myself for not having any soda or water on hand to offer the boys, though it hadn't even crossed my mind, more because the refrigerator didn't work than thoughtlessness on my part. They didn't seem to mind, especially when Alan handed them each $20 for their time.

Rob looked hesitant to accept any money, and said, "We didn't do this for pay, sir."

"Understood," Alan nodded. "Just think of it as a tip. You can accept tips, right?"

"Yes, sir," Rob replied, "I suppose so. Will you sign our service vouchers?"

"Of course," Alan agreed, pulling a pen from his pocket.

"Do you like being a cop?" Dylan asked, handing Alan his paper for a signature.

"Definitely," Alan smiled. "Are you thinking about police service as a career?"

"Yes, sir," Dylan nodded, "but my mom doesn't like the idea."

"Because of the danger?" Alan questioned.

"Probably," Dylan agreed. "I mean, she watches the news, and says there are a lot of kooks running around."

Alan nodded, then said, "Every job has its risks. You can remind your mom that a police officer gets plenty of training. Anyway, you still have a couple of years to decide."

Dylan seemed satisfied with Alan's response, although Cole teased him about being a momma's boy, which he shrugged off. When Alan finished signing each boy's voucher, Rob offered to return whenever we had to move more items. They all readily agreed, perhaps because Alan tipped so well.

"We'll keep that in mind," I smiled. "We have plenty to do around this place to get it in shape."

"Are you going to fix up the old cabin?" Cole asked.

"Sure," I nodded, "after we finish work on the house."

"Cool," Cole said. "I'd like to see the inside of it because we think the loonies cooked drugs or something in there."

Rob nudged Cole, and said, "You don't know that for sure. Anyway, my mom thinks you should have a candy shop, the way it used to be."

The boys unanimously agreed. Dylan remarked that his dad always told stories of how he and his friends would stop there on their way home from school. According to his father, they lost the best place in town when old Mrs. Whitman closed the store.

"So I've heard," I chuckled, "but I wouldn't know how to begin making candy."

"Just buy the candy, then sell it," Cole stated. "That'd be easy."

Alan and I laughed about the boys' insistence that Aspen Notch *needed* a candy shop, and they continued to badger until I promised to consider their pleas. When they finally departed, and I closed the front door, Alan gazed at me with twinkling eyes. "It's not a bad idea, you know," Alan chuckled. "Just think. You could be as famous as Russell Stover."

I could only shake my head with the absurdity of it all.

I LOCATED the sheets and blanket for the guest room and made up the bed while Alan did his next cruise around town. The boys' help and chatter had lifted my spirits, and I had renewed energy to tackle the den set-up. After connecting the cable for the TV, I organized the desk, then stepped back to determine what décor I still needed. I thought I should buy new blinds and a pretty valence, though the bookcase, still in the garage, would also make a nice addition.

The chimes from the front doorbell startled me because I hadn't expected company, but thought that one of the boys might have forgotten something. To my surprise, I found Evelyn Sandler on our front stoop.

"Come on in," I welcomed her. "You won't believe what we've accomplished so far."

Evelyn smiled as she handed me a heavy insulated bag. "I made an extra chicken casserole today. It's in a covered dish, still very hot, so it'll stay warm until you and Alan are ready to eat. I know you told me that your oven doesn't work."

"That's so kind of you," I said as I placed the bag on the dining room table. "In fact, I think we'd both like a quiet night at home this evening since we've had quite a busy week."

Evelyn glanced at the torn-apart kitchen which looked like an empty shell without the cabinets and counters. Despite that, she had an empathetic, yet supportive, expression.

"Wow," she exclaimed. "You don't waste any time."

"It's all Deke's doing," I nodded. "He's a master."

"Will they finish by Thanksgiving?" Evelyn asked. "If not, you and Alan are welcome to join Marty and me."

"Won't your family celebrate with you?" I queried.

"Probably," Evelyn agreed, "but it's not a problem to add two more places at the table."

I laughed, before saying that I hoped Alan's kids would visit. If not, we'd probably drive to his son's home in New York. In any case, I'd keep the Sandler Thanksgiving option open.

"Come see the den," I said. "Rob and his friends were a tremendous help today."

Evelyn admired everything from our choice of wall color to the attractive arrangement of furniture. When I told her that I planned to buy new window accessories and, maybe, a couple of decorative pillows, Evelyn offered to show me the location of a discount store not too far from town.

We decided to do some shopping together on Monday if Deke didn't mind my abandoning him. Actually, I thought he'd be rather happy not to have me in the way of his crew, so I told Evelyn that I'd enjoy the excursion.

I offered Evelyn a cup of tea, but she declined. "Marty will wonder what's taking me so long," she said as we walked to the door. "By the way, we go to St. John's across the street for church on Sunday, then to Dottie's for brunch. Would you and Alan like to join us?"

"What time?" I questioned.

"The service starts at 10:00 a.m.," Evelyn replied. "We can meet you out front."

"I'm not sure about Alan," I chuckled. "He's not much of a churchgoer. I'm not tied to any particular denomination, but I wouldn't mind checking it out."

"Great," Evelyn smiled. "I'll see you there."

I giggled as I closed the door because Alan wouldn't be very happy when I broke the news to him.

CHAPTER 14

*D*eke and John arrived early on Monday morning while Alan and I ate breakfast, then the demolition crew followed shortly after. Despite my recognition that the noise level and debris would soon increase, I gladly welcomed the crew because the faster they started, the sooner I'd have a working kitchen. My mother often identified the kitchen as the heart of the home, and now I realized what she meant.

John started painting our master bedroom immediately, while Deke sat at the dining room table with Alan and me. He told us that the plumber would begin today, working around the men pulling up the old linoleum.

Alan nodded, saying, "The home inspector didn't find any major issues, but I wouldn't mind paying the plumber to double check the whole house. Winter's coming, and we don't want any frozen pipes."

"He'll do that," Deke said, "but he'll focus on the kitchen, unless you also want a new bathroom or something."

"Now that you mention it," I said, with a sideward glance to Alan, "an *en-suite* bathroom in our bedroom would be nice."

Although he didn't immediately respond, Alan raised an eyebrow. Deke, on the other hand, didn't look surprised, and I considered it rather comforting that he seemed able to read my mind.

"I'll talk to the plumber about it," Deke said. "This would be the time to add a bathroom, if that's what you decide."

"Where would it fit?" Alan asked.

Deke told us he'd take some measurements and work up a design. In the meantime, he'd keep the kitchen as the priority, and we now needed to order the fixtures. Excitedly, I showed Deke the brochures and samples for the equipment that Alan and I had selected. He took a close look at each of them before approving.

"I'll order the built-ins," Deke said, "and get the plumber to install a water-line for the refrigerator since you want an ice-maker. You can arrange to have the appliances delivered next week."

That seemed like an amazingly short span of time with all that still needed completion, and I didn't quite believe it. Alan had a skeptical expression, and he questioned, "Are you sure?"

"Yep," Deke nodded, "barring any unforeseen delays. The electrician will arrive tomorrow, then we'll install the load-bearing beam by the end of the week. After that, we just put it all together."

"Wow," I exclaimed. "I'll have my new kitchen in time for Thanksgiving."

"That's the plan," Deke smiled.

BEFORE HE LEFT to cruise the neighborhoods, Alan remarked that he planned to take an hour or two from work after lunch since he wanted to tackle the leaves in the yard before the predicted rain. He thought the timing might provide relief for me so I could enjoy my shopping expedition with Evelyn, and he'd keep an eye on the work crews' progress. Of course, I expressed my delight with a farewell kiss, then made the bed and hung more clothes in the closet.

By the time Evelyn arrived to pick me up, I felt more than ready to leave the chaos behind. Although she ate a sandwich with Marty before leaving her house, she offered to pull into a fast-food eatery for me to order a hamburger and soda to-go. I updated her on the renovation progress between bites, and told her again how much I appreciated Deke Hopewell.

"He really was a fabulous find," Evelyn chuckled. "You must have a lucky streak."

"I'm not sure about that," I smiled. "Did you know that Deke wanted to help us because he knew the original owner?"

"The lady with the candy store?" Evelyn asked.

"Yes," I nodded, "Clara Whitman. Do you know anything about her?"

"Not much," Evelyn replied. "I guess most people think of her as a legend because when they talk about the good old days in Aspen Notch, they always mention her corner shop."

"I want to learn more about her," I said. "When the crew pulled out the old cabinets in the kitchen, they found a notepad with riddles she used to write."

"That's cool," Evelyn remarked. "What kind of riddles?"

"Clara wrote some of them for Deke," I replied. "She hired him during his teen years to do odd jobs around the place, and she used the riddles to direct him."

"He had to figure out the meaning of the riddle to know what she wanted him to do for her?" Evelyn queried.

"Exactly," I agreed, "but some of the riddles have a dark tone, and I'm not sure what she meant by them."

Evelyn nodded as she pulled into a parking spot in front of the outlet store, then informed me that she'd found a few sinister elements in Aspen Notch. When I pressed her for more information, she shrugged it off and opened her car door.

Despite my curiosity, I figured she'd tell me more when we became better acquainted. On the other hand, I wondered if Alan's role as the interim police chief caused her reluctance. Sometimes that posed a barrier to open communication, though Evelyn didn't seem the type to harbor such feelings.

The outlet had an excellent selection of home goods with bargain prices, so I bought everything on my list, and then some. Evelyn, too, picked out a few things that she couldn't resist. All in all, we had a successful outing and I expressed my gratitude to know how to locate the place for future reference.

On the drive home, Evelyn did most of the talking. She told me about her kids and each one of the grandkids, and we laughed about their most recent escapades. I actually enjoyed the diversion, and the time passed quickly.

As we approached Aspen Notch, Evelyn commented that she wanted to stop for a couple of Italian hoagies at Sal's Pizza Shop since she'd forgotten to defrost anything from the freezer for supper, and Marty might enjoy a kick-back evening. I hadn't had a good hoagie in a long time, so just the mention of it made me want one, as well.

"Sal makes the best hoagies," Evelyn said as we pulled in front of his shop. "Honestly, his pizzas and Stromboli are also just as great. Have you tried them yet?"

"No," I replied, "but we just had pizza the other night, so I'll get a couple of the sandwiches."

Evelyn held the door to Sal's shop open while I entered to, surprisingly, find the place empty. "That's strange," Evelyn muttered before calling, "Yoo hoo, Sal. You have customers."

With no response, I remarked, "Maybe he had to run to the bank or something. We could wait a few minutes."

Evelyn glanced at her watch, then said, "The bank closed at 4 p.m."

"How about the back room?" I asked, noticing the closed door behind the meat case.

Evelyn marched behind the counter and gave a firm rap. I don't know why, but I followed her. With no response, Evelyn pushed open the door, then she screamed.

There, lying on the floor, we found Sal D'Angelo in a pool of blood. His wide-eyed visionless stare indicated that he had died, most likely from the knife protruding from his chest.

I reached into my purse, grabbed my phone, and pressed Alan's number, feeling relief when he picked up the call after only two rings.

"Hey, Alan, it's me. I'm at the pizza shop in town, and you'd better get over here right away. Sal's dead."

CHAPTER 15

$\mathcal{E}$velyn, weeping softly, paced the floor as we waited for Alan's arrival. When I reminded her not to touch anything, she nodded, then suggested that we step outside for some fresh air. I agreed, despite the chill as dusk descended, and tried to keep Evelyn calm until Alan pulled up to the curb.

When he met us at the entrance, I stammered, "Sal's in the back room."

Alan greeted me with a serious expression as he entered the pizza shop, and I followed behind to explain that Evelyn and I intended to bring home hoagies for supper. When we didn't see Sal, or anyone else for that matter, we knocked on the door of the back room, then went in.

"So, your fingerprints are on the doorknob?" Alan asked as he donned a pair of nitrile gloves.

"Evelyn opened the door," I said, "but I may have touched the doorknob, too."

Alan glanced around Sal's preparation and storage area, apparently taking stock of the crime scene, then leaned over the corpse as he said, "Please don't touch anything else."

"I know," I agreed.

After Alan checked Sal for a pulse, he asked that I stand at the entrance to prevent anyone from entering unless wearing a police uniform or having official clearance. Since he'd already notified county police, he expected their arrival soon. Alan's request seemed easy enough, at least until I saw the crowd that had formed along Main Street.

Within minutes, Lou Greene, the mayor of Aspen Notch, followed by a county police officer, pushed past me standing in the doorway. Lou insisted that I remain outside with the other on-lookers and, although I didn't think he qualified as having clearance in a police investigation, I decided not to argue.

Evelyn rushed towards me as soon as I stepped onto the sidewalk. Dottie Burkeholder, right behind her, pulled me aside.

"Is Sal really dead?" Dottie asked, grabbing my hand. She looked as pale as a ghost.

I nodded, feeling weak-kneed as reality crept in. Others gathered around, asking for details. Most, I assumed, were shop-owners or passers-by who saw the police vehicles on the street, though Marty Sandler and Bernie Calamito had joined them.

"I really don't know anything," I said, "except that Sal had a knife in his chest. When Evelyn and I arrived, we found him already dead."

"There was nobody else in the pizza shop?" Dottie asked. "That's really strange for this time of day."

Evelyn agreed, saying, "I thought the same thing, but it's possible that customers didn't see Sal, so they left."

"Where'd you find his body?" Bernie asked.

"In the back room," Evelyn replied. "I don't know what possessed me to open the door to search for him."

Evelyn shuddered with the memory, even though Marty placed his arm around her shoulder. We watched as the county coroner's van arrived, and I nudged Evelyn that he should have our parking spot.

We motioned to the driver that we'd move our vehicle, and Marty told Evelyn that he'd follow her home. I admired his concern about her well-being after such a horrid discovery, and wished I didn't have to go home alone. I felt troubled, not afraid, but understood that Alan needed to finish his police business.

As she dropped me off in front of my driveway, Evelyn invited me to her house, but I declined. I honestly thought she needed Marty's presence more than mine, and I didn't want to hash out everything again and again.

"I have so much to do," I said, retrieving my purchases from the trunk of her car, "but thanks. Will you be OK?"

"I'll probably cry on Marty's shoulder, but I'll be fine."

"Call me if you want to talk," I added.

"Same for you," Evelyn nodded.

AFTER FLIPPING ON THE LIGHTS, I wandered through the house to view the day's renovation progress. It felt strange to see through to the kitchen now that the men removed all of the wallboard and left only the studs. In a way, the place looked like a war-zone, although the work crew had swept the debris.

Even arranging the new decorative pillows in the den did nothing to raise my spirits. My thoughts kept returning to poor Sal, and I wondered if he knew his assailant. I assumed he did, because we found Sal lying face-up, which meant the person attacked from the front.

I'd never met Sal, but recalled Alan saying that he filed a police report regarding money missing from his cash register. I thought his death could have resulted from a foiled robbery, but something didn't resonate with me. In my mind, if someone demanded cash, a gun would make a better choice of weapon, not a butcher knife.

My morose reflections disturbed me, and the stillness of the house magnified their intensity. Now fully dark, I yearned for Alan's presence, though I tried to calm myself by turning on the TV. When that brought only controversial news and a flash report of the murder in Aspen Notch, I decided to leave.

Grabbing my jacket, purse, and keys, I fled to the scene of the crime. The crowd had dispersed, and another patrol car replaced the coroner's van. Reporters waited like birds of prey for the next tidbit they could stream to the media, and I knew Alan wouldn't return home anytime soon.

Somehow, I found my way to the shopping center with a grocery store. Rather than searching the outer aisles for healthy food that needed refrigeration, I foraged the bakery, snack, and candy sections. Seeing the Halloween displays, I tossed several additional bags of my favorite mini-bars into the cart. If we had no trick-or-treaters, Alan and I could eat all of them.

Before heading to the check-out lanes, I grabbed two pre-made Italian hoagies, a 2-liter bottle of cold soda, and a giant bag of potato chips. I needed comfort food and realized that I had a binge in store for the evening.

I knew I'd regret it in the morning.

CHAPTER 16

*E*xcept for the muted gleam of the street lamps, the entire block of storefronts, as well as Sal's Pizza Shop, were in darkness as I passed by on my return. A few apartments above the shops had lights on, making the scene appear to be an ordinary evening in Aspen Notch. Residents returned from work, then settled in for a relaxing evening in front of the TV. No one would suspect that a gruesome murder had occurred just hours before.

Relieved to see Alan's car in our driveway, I unloaded my grocery purchases and went to meet him. He greeted me at the front door, and took three of the bags I lugged, though he didn't look pleased with me.

"Why didn't you answer my call and text?" he grumbled. "You had me worried."

Placing the bags on the floor, I reached into my purse to search for my phone, then held up the black screen. "I guess I forgot to put it on the charger. It's dead. Sorry about that."

Turning on his heels, Alan carried the bags to the dining room table and began to rummage. When he came across the hoagies, his expression softened.

"You must have read my mind," Alan smiled as I handed him a plate.

"You had a long night and we needed something to eat, so I went out to find a grocery store," I explained.

I poured two glasses with Coke before joining Alan at the table. Already munching on a few potato chips, he removed the wrapper from his hoagie, then said, "I'm sorry I acted like a grump. Given all the candy you bought, I guess you felt upset."

"That's an understatement," I agreed. "How about you?"

"Tired," Alan said, "and frustrated."

I nodded, knowing that Alan wanted to relax during his retirement, not get embroiled in a murder case. Neither of us expected this level of crime in Aspen Notch.

"If it's any consolation to you," I teased, "I'll share my goodies."

Alan laughed, then reached for the bag of Snickers which he opened and held out for me. Taking one, I asked if Sal had any next of kin.

"Yes," Alan replied, "his wife. Lou came with me to break the bad news to her."

"That must have been awful," I sighed.

"It never gets easier," Alan nodded. "She seemed pretty distraught."

In response to my questioning, Alan told me that Irma D'Angelo lived just a block from us. She used to help Sal at the pizza shop, but she'd had a knee replacement in July and didn't get around very well. Still, she'd worried about Sal, especially with someone stealing money from the store.

"Do you think Sal's murder was a robbery gone bad?" I questioned.

"I don't know what to think," Alan replied, reaching for another Snickers. "Someone looking for cash from the register wouldn't have gone into the back room with a butcher knife, and I didn't see any sign of a struggle."

I told Alan my theory that Sal knew his attacker because Evelyn and I found him lying face-up with the knife in his chest. Alan didn't disagree, but reminded me that he couldn't confirm anything, especially since the crime scene investigator from the county and the coroner still needed to complete their reports.

I could see that Alan didn't want to talk further about the case, and I found the discussion unsettling, as well. Instead, we decided to bring our snacks to the living room and try to relax by watching something on TV. Neither of us wanted a crime show, so we picked a romantic comedy, but Alan fell asleep before the first commercial.

My attention kept wandering and I couldn't get into the show, even with the bag of chips on my lap. I thought about poor Irma D'Angelo, dealing with her husband's death all alone. I hoped she had friends and neighbors with her because I would want a shoulder to cry on.

Too late to call Evelyn to ask if we should reach out to Irma, I put the thought aside since I didn't know if she and Irma belonged to the same social circle. Frankly, I didn't know enough people in town to determine if Aspen Notch had cliques or elite groups, not that I condoned such behavior.

Actually, the more I thought about Evelyn's reaction to Sal's death, the more I wondered why she didn't mention Irma's name or shed tears for Sal's wife. If Irma occasionally worked at the pizza shop, wouldn't everyone know her? Surely Evelyn, or even Dottie, would have shown some concern for her.

The canned laughter on the TV began to irritate me to the point that I turned it off, then decided to get ready for bed. I closed the bag of chips, ate the crumbs nestled in my lap, then put all of the goodies out of sight on one of the chairs in the dining room. When I noticed Clara's notebook of riddles on the table, I flipped to one I hadn't yet read.

With bright moonlight they appear,
Looming dark, causing fear.
Always silent, calm as a lamb.
Unless some movement makes them scram.
The wind is the culprit, I so often say,
Though I'm happy they're gone with the light of the day.

Clara definitely had morbid musings, I thought, feeling goose-bumps on the back of my arms. From the kitchen window, I peered into the darkness of the yard. Looking for the moon, I scanned the sky to find, finally, one almost full. What had Clara seen with a full moon?

I didn't believe in ghosts, nor did I see anyone traipsing through our yard or walking along the street. I noticed only the shadows from the trees until a sudden movement gripped me with fear. Did someone move from behind the large oak tree near the fence?

Pulling open the back door, I yelled. "Who's there?"

The shadow lengthened, then retreated. My pulse raced, and my heart pounded, but I hesitated between going outside and closing the door.

When Alan suddenly appeared at my side, his concerned voice startled me. "What's the matter?" he asked.

"Someone's in the yard," I said.

Once again, Alan did a complete search while I stood in the doorway watching him. Returning, he assured me that he found no one out there.

I pointed to the area where I saw movement. Alan stared, then chuckled, saying, "It's only a shadow, and the breeze makes it look as if it's moving. Come on, honey. Let's go to bed."

I took another peek while Alan put the bolt on the back door. Like Clara, I thought, I'd be happy for the light of the day.

CHAPTER 17

a t breakfast, Alan told me that he intended to bring Irma to the pizza shop to retrieve Sal's personal belongings. With the site still categorized as a crime scene, she couldn't enter unless a police officer stayed with her.

"I'd like to accompany Irma," I said, slicing into the coffee cake I'd purchased the night before. "She shouldn't go in alone."

Alan raised an eyebrow, then stated, "I'll be there."

"I know," I nodded, "but you have official business to tend to, and besides, I can show her empathy."

"You don't even know Irma," Alan remarked.

"It's a woman thing," I shrugged. "Humor me."

"I guess I don't see a problem if Irma agrees," Alan stated. "You can keep an eye on her while I give my instructions to the locksmith."

Though I didn't know if the police typically had the locks changed at a crime scene, I thought Alan made a good decision. By securing Sal's Pizza Shop, Alan had assurance that no one could disrupt the ongoing investigation. I nodded my agreement and asked what time we'd meet Irma.

Since Alan coordinated his schedule with the locksmith, who planned to arrive at the pizza shop by 10:00 a.m., he told me that he'd first do his cruise around town, pick up Irma, then stop back for me.

"That'll work," I said. "Deke and John can handle things here, and I'll have time to straighten up the bedroom."

Alan took another slice of coffee cake, then said, "Did you sleep OK last night? I'm getting worried about your unfounded fears regarding the back yard."

"They're not unfounded," I sighed. "Most times I heard a noise, as if someone's out there, but last night was different."

"How so?" Alan questioned.

I reached for Clara's book of riddles and found the one that triggered my anxiety. After I read it aloud for Alan, he smiled and said, "I know the answer to that one. Clara wrote about shadows from the trees. When the wind blows the branches, the shadows will move."

"Obviously," I replied, "but I saw something or someone move from behind the tree by the fence."

"I found nothing when I investigated," Alan remarked. "Maybe you'd feel safer if we got a dog."

I stared at Alan, before saying, "Are you kidding? Look at this place. It's a disaster."

"Not for much longer," Alan said as the doorbell signaled John and Deke's arrival. While he went to greet them, I pondered his words, but still wondered what I saw. Nonetheless, I totally dismissed his suggestion of a dog, since I could never manage its care with our house ripped to shreds.

DEKE TOLD us that the electrician would arrive shortly, and he'd oversee any necessary electrical work, while John intended to paint the ceilings in the hall, living room, and dining room. Both assured me that I needn't stay home as they worked.

"I sketched out an *en-suite* bathroom," Deke said, holding up a piece of graph paper. "If we use some of the space from the master bedroom, and retain the wall adjacent to the laundry room, we can save a lot on plumbing costs by connecting to the washer's pipes and drain."

"Will the bedroom be too small?" I asked.

"No," Deke replied. "You have plenty of room there, and we can even include a walk-in closet next to the bathroom."

I loved the concept of adding a walk-in closet since our old-fashioned sliding door type already cramped our clothes, and I hadn't even finished unpacking. I gazed at Alan, hoping he would read my mind.

"How much will it cost?" Alan asked.

"I don't know yet," Deke replied, "but a lot less than the kitchen, and worth every penny."

Alan looked closely at the design, and I thought he took more time to mull over something I considered a perfect option. I couldn't help but wonder why.

"I like it," I said with an encouraging smile. "Deke even fit a shower and double sink vanity without taking away too much space from the bedroom, and we'll have a walk-in closet, too."

With a slight shrug of his shoulders, Alan finally gave in, saying, "If it'll make you happy, let's do it."

"You won't be sorry," Deke replied, watching my excited reaction. "You'll have convenience during the night, and privacy when you have guests, so it can't get better than that."

In total agreement with Deke, I assured Alan that we'd have plenty of money for our renovation budget when my home sold. With a skeptical expression, Alan reminded me that we still hadn't received an offer, despite our selling agent's texts about the interest people had shown.

"She's having another open house next weekend," I said.

"Good," Alan nodded. "Keep her nose to the grindstone. Maybe I should make up a riddle for you to send to her."

"Very funny," I quipped.

Reference to Clara's riddles caught Deke's attention, and he asked if I'd read any interesting ones. To my chagrin, Alan told him about my fright last night with Clara's shadow riddle. Deke nodded as if he knew which one Alan spoke about.

"Clara had her fears," Deke said. "She was fine while she had customers in her shop or when I helped her after school but, eventually, she seemed to fear something."

"Like what?" I asked.

Deke shook his head. "She never told me. Read another riddle to me, and see if I remember it."

> *Made of tin, wearing a hat,*
> *We fill it up with this and that.*
> *Full to the brim or begging for more,*
> *It must be gone from the store.*
> *Don't worry, I tell it, you'll be back soon.*
> *But it must wait until the next afternoon.*

Deke chuckled as he explained that Clara had memorized that ditty, even adding a tune which she'd croon to Deke every Monday when he arrived after school. With trash pick-up on Tuesday mornings, Deke had to take the can to the curb, then bring it back the next afternoon.

"I remember those tin trash cans," Alan said. "My brother and I used to play soldiers with the lids, as if they were shields."

"The good old days," Deke nodded as nostalgia colored his expression. Alan agreed wholeheartedly.

CHAPTER 18

*A*lan honked the horn of the police cruiser when he pulled into our driveway with Irma D'Angelo in the passenger seat. I called my farewell to John and Deke, grabbed my jacket and purse, then hurried to the vehicle so as not to keep them waiting.

Irma stared straight ahead while I hopped into the back seat. Not even my cheery introduction resulted in more than a cursory hello from her. Irma's lack of conversation didn't bother me because I recognized that the police escort to a crime scene involving a deceased husband would put a damper on anyone's spirit. Besides, we had only a two-block drive to Sal's Pizza Shop.

Alan pulled to the curb behind the locksmith's van, then turned to remind Irma that he needed to change the locks for her protection during the investigation. He assured her that he'd provide the new set of keys after the police finished their work, and Irma nodded her understanding.

Even with Alan's help, Irma struggled to exit the vehicle. As a large woman, actually quite obese, she could barely bring herself to a standing position, so Alan and I each grabbed an arm, and told her to lean on us until she found her balance. Alan handed her the cane she had brought, and the two of us led her to the front door.

"I've changed my mind," Irma said in barely a whisper. "I don't want to go in there."

Tears welled in her eyes, and one gained momentum along her rotund cheek. She quickly brushed it aside, as if she didn't want us to see her emotions, then took a deep breath. I reached into my purse for a tissue.

"It's OK," I said. "I'll wait with you in the car while Alan's with the locksmith."

"I need the cash in the register," Irma murmured. "I don't have any money."

"Do you want me to get it for you?" I asked.

"No," she replied. "Sal told me he keeps most of it in the safe. Ever since..."

Irma's voice trailed off as she watched the locksmith take his equipment from the back of the van. She appeared nervous, and her hand shook as she pushed strands of salt-and-pepper hair to the back of her ear.

Though Alan tried to show patience, he needed to get on with the job, so I gently said, "Let's go in, and you can have a seat while you think about what you need, then I can help."

Irma reached into her coat pocket and handed Alan a key to the front door. He unlocked it, held it open for the two of us to slowly make our way inside, then Irma plopped herself on two of the wooden chairs arranged near the storefront window for patrons awaiting their orders.

She looked around the room before her eyes focused on a wall of family pictures, and she again became emotional. After I followed her gaze, I asked her to tell me about the people in the photos. Alan mouthed a silent thank-you to me as he went out to meet the locksmith.

"The big portrait in the center," Irma faltered, "shows me and Sal on the day we opened the pizza shop, 18 years ago."

I walked over to take a closer look at a younger, slimmer version of Irma who smiled broadly, with Sal's arm around her waist. They stood in front of the store, under the gold lettering that highlighted their achievement, and both of them appeared proudly happy.

"What a wonderful picture," I exclaimed. "It must have been such an exciting day."

Irma sighed before saying, "We considered it the best day of our lives, but that's not how it played out. I hated this place."

"Owning a small business must be grueling work," I said, giving her my empathy.

Irma's mouth tightened, and she said, "We expected to put a lot of time into the business, but that wasn't the problem. Sal changed so much that I could hardly stand being around him, and we fought all the time."

"I'm sorry," I said, moving on to the next picture. I really had no idea what to say after Irma's admission, so I thought I'd better change the subject.

"That's Sal and his father," Irma said. "His parents owned a deli in Brooklyn, and they provided the down payment on the pizza shop."

"Are they still living?" I asked, thinking that Irma should contact them about Sal's death.

"No," Irma replied. "Sal's mother died of cancer shortly after we married, then his father passed a couple of years ago. My parents have also died."

"Mine, too," I said softly. "Life is so fragile."

Moving on to the third picture, I asked Irma if the young boy sitting cross-legged in front of a meat counter was also Sal. Irma's expression softened, though her eyes glistened when she identified the boy as their son, Francesco. She and Sal gave him her father's name, but called him Frankie.

I didn't want to ask the dreaded question, nor did I need to, since Irma's use of past tense and her body language told me what I feared. Irma explained that Frankie contracted measles when he was in second grade. She didn't worry about a normal childhood disease, and even thought that her son's lying in one position in bed caused his complaint about a stiff neck. Sadly, the symptom indicated meningitis.

"The doctors tried to save him," Irma said softly, "but it didn't help. Sal never forgave me for Frankie's death."

Rushing over to Irma, I sat next to her and took her hands in mine. I could only imagine my devastation if I'd lost Alexa or Michael, as would any mother who faced such an experience.

"My heart breaks for you," I said, feeling my own eyes fill with tears. "You have to know it wasn't your fault."

"It doesn't matter," Irma said. "I'll always blame myself for not calling the doctor any sooner than I did."

Squeezing her hand, I knew I'd feel the same regret since I often second-guessed myself. I supposed we all had misgivings about things we'd done or didn't do, but I'd learned over time that we had to let things go and move on.

Alan glanced our way as he led the locksmith to the back door of the pizza shop, though he probably wondered why we hadn't yet gathered Sal's belongings. When he passed by, he reminded us to put on the nitrile gloves, so I knew I should try to get Irma moving.

"Do you want to take any of the pictures home with you?" I asked.

Irma shook her head. "No, they belong here, at least until I decide what to do about the place. I'll get the money out of the cash register and check the safe."

We found $153.17 in the register, not enough, I thought, to last very long. I wondered if they had any money in savings, but didn't think it my business to ask.

Irma stopped at the doorway of the back room, hesitant to enter, then she said, "Is this where they found him?"

"Yes," I nodded, "near the blood stain. Do you think he'd gone back here to work?"

"As you can see, we used this as our prep and storeroom," Irma noted. "Unless he returned for something, or needed more dough, he'd have waited on the customers out front."

I noticed an industrial-sized refrigerator against the side wall, while metal shelving, filled with containers organized by size and empty pizza boxes ready for use, lined the opposite wall. A large stand mixer with several bins next to it, as well as a double-sided deep sink were at the rear. In front of those was the stainless-steel work table, still dusted with flour.

"Where's the safe?" I asked.

"Behind the picture next to the fridge," Irma replied.

The cartoonish 24"x36" portrait of a rotund guy tossing pizza dough in the air grabbed my attention. Irma slowly made her way across the room and I followed. She tugged on the left side of the picture and it opened outward, like a door. Behind it, I saw a safe, almost as large as the picture.

Irma painstakingly turned the combination lock to the left, then to the right and back again. When it clicked, she pulled the handle down and opened it.

"Bastard!" she gasped.

ooking over Irma's shoulder, I saw that the safe had piles of currency, bundled and stacked entirely to the top, and any packs that protruded looked to contain $100 denominations. We both stared at the enormous stash until I called to Alan, and told Irma we'd better not touch anything until he gave the go-ahead.

"You should check this out," I said in a voice as calm as I could muster when Alan joined us. Irma leaned heavily on her cane, shaking her head in disbelief.

Alan gave a low whistle as he pulled his cell phone out of his jacket pocket. He took several photos, then began unloading the safe, making new piles on the flour-dusted table. I probably would have wiped off the table first, but Alan didn't seem to think it mattered.

Irma seated herself on the sturdy chair located near the stand mixer, watching the money add up with an expression of awe and anger. She had known that Sal kept cash in the safe but, obviously, had no idea about the amount.

"There's close to a quarter-million dollars here," Alan noted, taking more pictures. "Didn't your husband believe in using the bank?"

"I don't know where he got all this money," Irma sighed. "We have a business account, as well as our personal checking and savings, though they're pretty slim."

Alan gave her a skeptical look, then stated, "You had the combination to the safe, so you must have known about the cash."

"I expected a couple of hundred," Irma said, "and maybe more if Sal didn't have time to make a bank deposit, but not all of this."

"You can't use any of the money until we determine how Sal obtained it," Alan replied. "I'll put it in an escrow account."

"I don't want dirty money," Irma huffed.

Alan reassured her that he'd have a full inquiry into Sal's business practices. In the meantime, he'd keep the cash in the locked safe until he filed all of the necessary paperwork, then return for the money with a county police officer after lunch. I assumed that Alan wanted no possible allegation of theft, and thought it a good idea to have additional police presence when he set up an account at the bank.

Irma pulled a notepad and pen from her purse to write the combination, while Alan and I returned the stash to the safe. By the time we closed it and put the pizza-guy picture back in place, we had flour everywhere.

Dusting off my pants, I whispered my concern that the locksmith may have seen us count the money, and I knew Alan wouldn't want that tidbit discussed around town. Alan assured me that the locksmith had left before Irma opened the safe, and he suggested that we take Irma home.

Irma seemed lost in her own world when I turned to ask if she needed to retrieve anything else. I felt great sadness for her because she'd not only lost her husband, but also learned that he had secrets. Something similar happened to me after my first husband died, and I wouldn't want to experience anything like it again.

"I guess there's nothing else," Irma said, looking forlorn.

I pulled open the refrigerator door, then asked, "What about the deli meats? Do you want to take the opened ones?"

"Maybe I should," Irma nodded. "There's probably also some sliced meat and cheese in the case out front, and I'd like the rolls, too."

"I'll get bags and check the meat case," I said. "I saw some large sacks near the cash register."

After I grabbed a number of the plastic bags and filled them with rolls and anything sliced, I noticed an order pad on the counter, with several orders scrawled in a shorthand that I couldn't read. Sal clearly recorded the pick-up times, though, and they looked close to when Evelyn and I arrived. I also found a number of order sheets crumpled and tossed in the trash, so I emptied the waste basket into one of the sacks, then put the pad in my pocket with the intention of giving everything to Alan for his investigation.

I helped Irma fill the bags with any of the opened bulk meat and cheese from the refrigerator in the back room, then Alan carried them out to the police cruiser. I wondered if she had a meat slicer at home, because Sal apparently only sliced what he needed for the day, but Alan urged us to hurry.

Irma stood in the doorway, then gazed around the pizza shop. Eyes misty, she shook her head as if she couldn't believe the turn of events. Finally, she turned toward Alan, and said, "I'm ready. You can lock it up."

ALAN and I walked Irma to her front door, then he and I carried all of the bags to her porch. Shoulders stooped, Irma retrieved her house key and thanked us, though she didn't invite us in.

Back in the cruiser, Alan told me that the mayor wanted to meet him for lunch to talk about the murder case. I, on the other hand, didn't want to go home, given the paint fumes and the electrician working. I told Alan that I'd eat out and, maybe, wander the home-goods store, so he could drop me off to pick up my car.

"Why don't we go to the Black Horse Pub tonight?" Alan asked as he pulled into our driveway. "I challenge you to another game of pool."

"Sure," I agreed, "but I thought you'd have to work late."

"Except for digging into Sal's background, and returning with another cop to retrieve the money in his safe," Alan noted, "I can't do anything until I receive the forensics reports."

Unbuckling my seatbelt, I had another thought. "Do you intend to tell Lou about Sal's stash of money?"

"Probably," Alan nodded. "Why?"

"I don't think he needs to know about it yet," I said. "From what you've indicated, Lou Greene didn't like Sal D'Angelo, and he might influence your findings. I understand that you report to him, but I'd let the police conduct their business first."

"I'll think about it," Alan nodded. "Have fun shopping. If anything interferes with our plans, I'll give you a call."

CHAPTER 20

*A*s I sat in my car parked in the driveway, my thoughts tumbled in overdrive. I really didn't feel hungry, nor did I want to wander the aisles of the store. Rather, my heart compelled me to comfort Irma, although I didn't wish to intrude on her privacy.

Part of me suggested that I just drive over, knock on her door, and invite myself in, but another part said to mind my own business. So typical of me, my indecision occurred often, though I should have learned by now to just follow my instincts.

Finally, I made up my mind to visit the bereaving Irma, as the kindly thing to do, even if she considered me a busy-body. For some reason, the thought of Irma having no one to comfort her at a time like this bothered me.

I pulled to the curb in front of her house and turned off the engine as I observed the uniqueness of each home on Church Street. Most of them, probably built in the 1950's, looked dated or seemed as if they had plenty of deferred maintenance. I could say the same about the D'Angelo residence, at least from the outside.

I noticed Irma hadn't brought in the bags that Alan and I left on her porch, though I recognized she would have trouble managing them with her cane. They provided a good excuse for my return, I thought as I rang the doorbell.

The high-pitched bark of a dog signaled that the doorbell worked, although Irma didn't immediately answer it. I knocked and called her name, even as I wondered if the neighbors gazed from their windows to watch me.

Eventually, Irma opened the inside door a crack while she told the young hyperactive black Labrador to go lie down. Thank goodness, the storm door seemed sturdy enough to keep the pup at bay.

"I planned to do some shopping until I noticed the bags still on your porch," I said with a friendly smile. "May I help you bring them in?"

Irma looked as if she intended to refuse, but changed her mind, saying, "I'd be grateful, but I have to hold the puppy. Can you take them to the kitchen?"

On my way there, I stepped around the dog toys strewn along my way, then noticed the upturned water bowl, which left a large puddle on the floor, and the empty food bowl. After I placed the bags on the counter, I retrieved a towel from the oven door, and wiped up the floor before adding fresh water to the bowl.

"Do you have any kibble for the dog dish?" I called.

"She ate the last of it this morning," Irma replied.

"Do you want me to put the meat and cheese in the refrigerator?" I questioned.

"I guess so," she said.

It didn't surprise me that the fridge had plenty of room. I found a couple of 2-liter bottles of soda on the top shelf, and a pizza box with two dried and unappetizing leftover slices on the next shelf. I placed the deli items in the two bottom drawers usually reserved for produce and the rolls in the freezer.

The last bag contained the contents of Sal's trash basket which I'd completely forgotten. I meant to tell Alan about it, as well as the order pad that I'd put in my pocket, but he had been in such a rush to lock up and meet Lou for lunch that they'd slipped my mind.

Taking them to the living room, I suggested that Irma and I look through the papers to see if anything looked important. The forensics unit must have focused only on Sal's back room as the scene of the crime though, despite my lack of police training, that seemed rather short-sighted to me.

Irma released the pup, who bounded toward me with a playful leap. "Down, Sophie," she hollered, to no avail.

I held the sack of papers in the air with one hand, while I put out my other hand to let Sophie smell me. The enthusiastic pup must not have considered the sniffing part too important because she preferred to play "get-the-bag" with me.

"You'd better take this," I laughed, giving the bag to Irma before returning my attention to Sophie.

Irma stuffed the sack under her expansive hip while I sat on the sofa and gave belly rubs to Sophie. She eventually settled down, and decided to trust me as her new friend.

"That dog will be the death of me," Irma frowned.

"How old is she?" I asked.

"I guess about 8 months," Irma sighed, "but I don't really know. Sal got her from the shelter a couple of weeks ago because he thought she'd be good company for me, but she's a pain in the butt."

"She's still a puppy," I said.

"Sal tried to train her," Irma noted, "but she doesn't listen to me. She just eats and makes a mess, and I didn't want you to see the place like this."

Laughing, I said, "You should see my house. We're having renovations done and it looks like a war zone."

"Why didn't you do all of that before you moved in?" she questioned.

"When the mayor offered Alan the job as interim police chief," I explained, "we decided to make the move right away. In hindsight, we probably should have waited, but I didn't realize the difficulty of managing without a working kitchen."

"How do you cook?" Irma asked.

"We don't," I replied. "In fact, I went to the pizza shop to pick up sandwiches for our supper."

Irma nodded, and I wished I hadn't made that comment because her abrupt silence indicated that I again triggered her emotions. Rather than a focus on the negative, and with Sophie sleeping at my feet, it seemed a good opportunity to take a look at the papers from Sal's waste basket and his order pad.

I pulled the pad from my pocket and handed it to Irma as I said, "I couldn't decipher Sal's handwriting, but it looked as if people needed to pick up their orders around the same time he was…"

"You can say the word," Irma sighed. "He was murdered."

"Right," I nodded. "So, what did they order?"

Irma flipped through the pages, then explained that Sal hadn't completed the orders still attached to the pad since he used it to keep track of what he still needed to make. When customers picked up their orders, he tossed the paper in the trash unless the person wanted a receipt.

Reading Sal's scribble aloud, Irma said that Mary Z. had ordered two pepperoni pizzas, Lou G. wanted a large Stromboli, Ed S. requested an Italian hoagie, as did Jake F. All of them asked to pick-up their orders at or near 6:00 p.m.

"Do you know any of these people?" I asked. "Sal didn't include last names."

"The pizzas were probably for Mary Zimmerman," Irma said. "She orders pizza whenever she babysits the grandkids. I imagine the mayor, Lou Greene, ordered the Stromboli, but I'm not sure, and I don't know the others."

I nodded, saying, "That sets the time of death before 6 p.m. since Sal hadn't yet made any of those orders. Of course, we knew that because Evelyn and I arrived at around 5 o'clock, and we found Sal, already…"

"Dead," Irma said.

"Right," I agreed.

"You don't have to struggle to find the right words," Irma remarked. "What's done is done. Sal's dead, murdered in cold blood, and nothing we do can bring him back."

Irma's words sounded bitter and, for a brief moment, I saw darkness in her eyes, though she masked her expression. I wondered if she directed the flash of anger to Sal, his killer, or both of them. I had no doubt that the stash of money in Sal's safe added to the equation.

"I understand," I said, trying to show empathy.

"No, you don't," Irma retorted. "Nobody does."

"Do you want to talk about it?" I asked.

Irma vehemently shook her head, then reached for the bag of tossed papers. "You can take this stuff with you," she said. "I have no interest in Sal's trash."

Clearly, Irma wanted me to leave, and I understood, even as the memory I had of the days following my first husband's funeral flashed before me. Once I'd learned that he'd frittered all of our savings at casinos and lived a double life, my spirit had withered. I wanted everyone to leave me alone while I grieved for the love we'd once shared.

Sophie stirred when I stood to take the sack from Irma and pick up my pocketbook. Her tail thumped on the carpet for a moment before she closed her eyes again. No doubt, I passed muster, and she found the need for a snooze more important than my departure.

"I can pick up a bag of dog food for Sophie," I remarked as I walked to the door. "I need to go to the store anyway."

"I'd rather you take the stupid dog," Irma muttered. "I don't want her."

CHAPTER 21

y jaw dropped with disbelief, though I knew that Irma still felt yesterday's shock after learning someone killed her husband. I assumed she associated Sophie with Sal, which compounded the situation, but I thought she shouldn't make such a life-changing decision during her time of grief.

"Are you serious?" I asked, glancing at Sophie first, then looking at Irma's resolute expression.

"If you don't take her," Irma stated, "I'll put her out and hope she gets run over by a car or truck."

I gasped, wondering how anyone could act so callous and cold-hearted toward an innocent puppy, although I now understood why Irma had no friends. What happened to the sweet-looking, smiling young woman I saw in the picture at the pizza shop?

"Irma," I sighed, "the renovation has left my house a total mess. Besides the dust and nails on the floor, the paint fumes smell horrible, and we shouldn't put Sophie through all of that."

"Fine," Irma shrugged. "Let her out, then close the door behind you."

I knew I couldn't do that, nor could I leave such a sweet pup without food and basic care in Irma's home, given what she might do in her frame of mind. I knew Alan wouldn't care if I took Sophie, yet I struggled with the reality of our renovation situation.

With clenched lips and unwavering eyes, Irma showed no change of heart, so my gut reaction overcame my indecision. I wanted only to save the puppy.

"Does she have a harness and leash?" I asked, observing that Sophie wore a secure collar.

"They're on the kitchen table," Irma replied. "You can also have her bowl and toys because I don't want anything that reminds me of Sal. May he burn in hell."

With a heavy heart, I gathered Sophie's balls and squeaky playthings, and placed them in the bag with the contents of Sal's waste basket, then I retrieved her leash and bowl in the kitchen. Sophie had awakened and followed me from room to room, as if ready to play.

I reached down to pet her, saying, "Do you want to go for a ride in the car?"

Sophie wagged her tail, then scurried to the front door. I suspected that Sal had taken her for car rides because she knew exactly what I said, and sat waiting for me with anticipation.

Hooking Sophie's leash, I turned back to Irma. "If you change your mind, I'll bring her back."

Irma stared straight ahead with no emotion on her face as Sophie and I departed.

SOPHIE READILY SLID into the back seat of my car and immediately checked out her surroundings. After sniffing the upholstery, she settled herself at the opposite window and gave me a look as if to say, "Let's go." Her expression made me chuckle, even as I replayed the entire conversation with Irma in my head, and still couldn't believe the turn of events.

I drove around the block several times, trying to figure out how to manage the situation. I could find the local animal shelter and take Sophie there, but if Irma changed her mind, I'd have no assurance that Sophie would still be available. Besides, I had taken a liking to the puppy myself, and I hated to see her passed from family to family.

The other issue, of course, concerned the need for dog food and treats. I didn't know how well Sophie would behave if I left her in the car while I ran into the grocery store, nor could I drop her off at home. In any case, Alan would have to help.

Pulling into our driveway, I reached for my phone. After pressing his number, my call to Alan again went to voicemail. I left a cryptic message, then texted, *Please bring home a bag of puppy chow and treats.* I figured that would get his attention.

With John's pick-up still parked out front, I assumed that he'd returned from lunch after taking Deke home, as usual, to continue painting. Rather than risk Sophie knocking over cans of paint, I walked her to our fenced back yard and let her off the leash.

Once the afternoon sun disappeared behind the clouds, it became rather nippy, and I wished I'd worn a heavier jacket while I watched Sophie sniff her way around the yard. As the last of the leaves fell from our trees, Sophie hurdled to catch them, and found it great fun to roll in the piles that Alan had raked, despite my effort to distract her.

Eventually I spotted the rake leaning against the side of the shed and decided to do my share of the yard clean-up. Sophie made it a lost cause since she considered it a new game I played with her. She barked her enjoyment, then scattered every pile I tried to form.

John must have heard the commotion because he opened the back door, stepped out to the patio, and burst into laughter. Sophie sprinted to him, tail wagging and tongue hanging out.

"Don't tell me you got yourself a dog," John chuckled as he bent down to rub Sophie's back and ears.

"I guess I did," I grinned wryly. "Please meet Lady Sophia of Aspen Notch, otherwise known as Sophie."

"She's a friendly pup with lots of energy," John remarked. "She'll keep you stepping, that's for sure."

"I know," I said with a rueful laugh. "It's getting chilly out here. How much damage will she cause if I bring her in?"

"I just finished cleaning up," John noted. "I'll pick up the rest of my drop cloths and check to see that there's nothing on the kitchen floor to hurt her, then I'll take off."

"You're the best. Thanks, John."

Once John left and I could bring Sophie in safely, I filled her water bowl and placed it near the laundry room sink. She lapped at it voraciously, then began to explore the house. She probably searched for food, I thought, since she even sniffed the bag of candy I'd left on the dining room chair.

"You can't have that," I said, moving it to the shelf in the laundry room, and wishing I had something on hand to feed her.

On a whim, I decided to put Sophie back in the car and head to the nearest fast-food place. I couldn't offer her a healthy meal, but I thought it the best option to feed her, and me, since I hadn't eaten since breakfast.

At the drive-through window, I ordered two hamburgers and a diet Coke, then gave Sophie the meat, while I ate the buns, pickles, lettuce, and tomato. Neither of us felt very satisfied, but it would have to do for now, though I hoped that Alan received my text.

"Let's go home, girl," I said, pulling out of the parking lot.

Sophie's tail wagged in response, and I wished I felt as enthusiastic.

CHAPTER 22

While I waited for Alan's return, I dumped the bag of Sal's trash onto the dining room table. Sophie had settled herself at my feet and already fell asleep so, thank goodness, I'd thought to let her play in the yard. I knew a tired puppy made a good puppy.

One at a time, I uncrumpled each paper and flattened it with my hands. With the time of the order pick-up as the one common denominator, I made stacks for each hour of service. As expected, I had more piles of papers for the lunch and dinner times, though I reminded myself that any pages tossed in the trash indicated that the customer had picked up the order.

Some of the papers had no time noted, so they went into a separate stack. At first glance, I thought that they might have identified orders from walk-ins, but I couldn't read Sal's writing, and put them aside.

I studied the pages from Sal's order pad, and thought that I might understand his handwriting if I could figure out how he formed his letters. With the M and Z in Mary Zimmerman's name so distinctive, as well as the P's for the pepperoni pizza, I began to get the hang of it when my phone jingled with a call from Alan.

"Did you receive my text?" I asked as soon as I connected.

"It's why I'm calling," he said. "What's going on?"

"Do you remember your suggestion that we get a dog?" I giggled. "Well, we have one now. She's a black Lab puppy."

"Are you serious?" Alan exclaimed. "You clearly said you wouldn't consider one because of the renovations."

"I'll explain later," I said, "since it's a long story, but we need dog food. Can you stop at the store?"

"Definitely," Alan agreed. "What kind?"

I told Alan the brand of puppy chow that I surmised from the empty bag I'd seen in Irma's trash, then he could pick out a variety of treats and anything else he thought Sophie might like.

"Do you want to postpone our pub date?" Alan asked.

"I think we should, don't you? I mean, we don't know yet how well Sophie will behave if we leave her alone."

"That's probably a good idea," Alan agreed. "Do you want me to also select something for our supper?"

"Sure," I said. "Get whatever you're in the mood for, and add a fresh salad for me because I've had too much junk lately."

"Gotcha. I'll be home shortly."

~

SOPHIE RAISED her head and gave me a questioning look. It made me chuckle to see her so curious about Alan's voice on the phone until I realized that she might need to go out again. At 8 months of age, I didn't know whether Sophie had finished potty training yet, and didn't want to risk having a mess to clean up.

"Do you want to go out?" I asked as I grabbed my heavier jacket from the hall closet. "You can help me rake the leaves."

Whether Sophie understood the word *out* or *leaves* was a mystery to me, but she definitely showed her enthusiasm. As soon as I opened the back door, she sprinted across the yard to revel in her new freedom, so I assumed Irma kept the poor pup cooped up for most of her days.

I found raking the leaves a lost cause, so I began to collect some of the fallen branches in the yard. Occasionally, I'd toss a stick for Sophie to fetch, and she'd bolt after it, then lie in the grass to chew on it, so I could see that we needed to work on basic commands.

With both of us tired after our romp, my satisfaction that Sophie had done her business, and the setting sun, I urged her to come in for some water. I hoped that Alan would soon arrive home with her food and, as luck would have it, he pulled into the driveway as I turned on the living room lamps.

Sophie barked excitedly as Alan entered the front door, then jumped up to see what he had in the bags he carried. Alan and I both laughed when he tried to make his way to the dining room despite Sophie's enthusiastic interaction.

"Down, Sophie," I urged, before reaching out to grab her.

Once Alan placed his wares on the table, he bent down to rub her ears and back. She immediately rolled over so he could tickle her belly.

"Meet Lady Sophia of Aspen Notch," I said with a giggle. "We'll call her Sophie."

Alan glanced at me with a raised eyebrow before asking, "And how did we obtain Sophie?"

"Irma D'Angelo gave her to me," I replied. "I'll tell you about it, but let me feed her first."

Alan handed me the bag of puppy chow, then distracted Sophie while I read the feeding instructions since I didn't know how much kibble a puppy her age should get.

"Just fill the bowl," Alan chuckled. "She's hungry."

Once Alan released Sophie to eat, he began to place our food on the table. I moved my stacks of papers to make room as I explained that I'd found them in Sal's waste basket.

Alan frowned, then said, "You removed evidence from the scene of the crime? Are you crazy? You could be arrested for obstruction of justice."

"It's no big deal," I stated. "I brought them home for you, as well as the order pad near the cash register, but I forgot to tell you about it."

I could see that Alan looked miffed while he removed the lid from the fresh garden salad and put it at my place with a few salad dressing packets. I reached around him with the plates and cutlery as he pulled out a rotisserie chicken with side dishes of green beans, mashed potatoes, and corn.

"Great choice for dinner," I smiled. "I'm starving."

Alan barely grunted as he took his seat. Finally, he looked me in the eye and made a hurtful comment about my lack of good judgment, which served only to raise my hackles. His words annoyed me, though I didn't want to start an argument.

"I'm sorry if I overstepped my boundaries," I said stiffly. "I just wanted to assist you, but I'll mind my own business in the future."

On that note, Sophie began to sniff by the kitchen door, a sure sign that she had to go out. Without another word to Alan, I put on my jacket and stepped into the chilly darkness.

CHAPTER 23

The more I thought about Alan's reaction, the angrier I became, and even pacing the yard didn't settle my emotions. If Alan or the investigators had considered Sal's trash bin important, they should have taken it. In fact, I figured that they hadn't even made the connection that they could identify the killer with the order sheets that Sal had tossed.

Sophie did her business, then explored the yard until she focused on old Abe's cabin, and sniffed all around it. I followed to see what caught her interest, but the corner street lamp didn't provide enough light.

"What is it, Sophie?" I asked as she began to dig near the flower bed by the cabin's side door.

I tried to distract her despite nothing growing in that location except weeds. In the spring, I hoped to plant perennials there, so I thought I'd better nip the digging now, rather than later. Still, I wondered what Sophie had found, and reminded myself to check in the morning when I could look around in the daylight.

Alan opened the back door and called that dinner still awaited me. I thought about ignoring him, but I'd felt a couple of snow flurries which I'd heard could occur in northeast PA, even at the end of October. Besides feeling cold, I wanted to eat.

With a little urging, Sophie followed me into the house and settled herself under the dining room table. Alan apologized for his earlier comment as I removed my jacket, then suggested that we finish our supper in peace. I nodded my agreement, sat at the table, added the dressing to my salad, and silently began to eat. Alan had sliced the chicken and added spoons to the side dishes, which I appreciated, but it didn't make up for his cutting words.

After Alan took another chicken leg and scoop of mashed potatoes, he said, "I looked through the papers from Sal's trash, and I didn't find them helpful. You can't even read his writing."

As much as I wanted to continue my silent treatment, I replied, "If you'd taken the time to listen, I'd have explained how you can determine the identity of the murderer."

"I don't think so," Alan stated, "but tell me."

I reached for the order pad and showed it to Alan, saying, "According to Irma, customers requested these orders, but Sal hadn't yet made them. Did the mayor tell you that he'd placed an order for Stromboli with a 6 p.m. pick-up?

"No," Alan frowned, "but who cares? You found Sal dead when you arrived at 5 o'clock. Besides, how do you know Lou Greene placed the order?"

I pointed to the notation on the order pad, and explained that Irma had read it for me. "Lou G., 1 Stromboli, 6 p.m."

Alan gazed at it, then said, "There might be other Lou G.'s in Aspen Notch or some of the surrounding towns. What's your point?"

"I find it strange that the mayor responded so quickly," I replied, "then pushed his way in as if he belonged there. I mean, maybe he came to pick up his Stromboli."

"No," Alan said with a shake of his head. "As protocol, I called Lou and the county's crime scene investigator on my way to the pizza shop. He arrived on official business."

"Fine," I shrugged, "but I believe the killer interrupted Sal as he made Lou's Stromboli and Mary Zimmerman's pizzas. He had already floured the table for kneading the crust. Did anyone check the oven?"

"I turned it off," Alan noted. "There was nothing in it."

"Right," I said, "because he had to make more dough. Did you find anything in the stand mixer?"

"Yes," Alan nodded, "though only a clumpy mess."

"Someone turned off the mixer before it finished mixing," I said. "Did you check the knob for fingerprints or the floor for footprints?"

Alan shook his head before saying, "I know better than to dismiss your theories because you have a very developed sense of observation, but we didn't find any flour or footprints on the floor. I'll ask if forensics lifted any prints from the mixer."

"Someone cleaned up," I stated emphatically. "Do you recall how flour dusted everything in sight when we returned the money to the safe?"

Alan agreed, then said that he'd take a closer look in the morning. In the meantime, he wondered if I'd made any other conclusions from the papers in Sal's waste basket.

"Not yet," I replied. "Irma told me that Sal tossed the paper to the trash when customers claimed their orders. In my opinion, we can dismiss those from 2 p.m. and before, though we should focus on orders from walk-ins and later pick-ups."

"I suppose so," Alan nodded. "It sounds as if you paid a visit to Irma instead of shopping."

"Yes," I said, reaching for the chicken and veggies. "I felt sorry for Irma, so I stopped by and offered to take in the bags from her porch, which is how I remembered the one with the crumpled papers. Anyway, she helped me decipher Sal's writing until her emotions took over."

"And that's how you got the dog?" Alan queried. "She just gave Sophie to you?"

"Yes," I nodded as I recalled Irma's resolute expression. "I think she considered Sophie as Sal's dog, and she didn't want her. If I hadn't taken the pup, Irma planned to get rid of her."

"Maybe she'll reconsider," Alan said. "Sophie seems like a sweet puppy, but don't get too attached yet."

"I know. I told Irma I'd bring Sophie back if she changed her mind, but she obviously can't care for her while she grieves. I guess we just have to give Irma some time to think about it."

Alan agreed, saying, "Good idea. Do you want to watch a movie tonight?"

"Maybe later," I said. "I want to see if I can determine who might have picked up an order from Sal around the time of his death."

Alan helped me with the clean-up, which mostly involved tossing the containers, though he gave Sophie the leftover bits of chicken before he went in search of the TV remote. It didn't take long for Sophie to settle next to him on the sofa, with her head nestled on his lap.

I had a feeling that Sophie would wiggle her way into our hearts, and the thought brought me comfort.

CHAPTER 24

Sophie exuberantly greeted Deke and John at the front door when they arrived after breakfast the next morning, and we all laughed at her antics despite my insistence that she not jump on anyone. I particularly worried about Deke's unsteadiness when walking, but he skillfully used his cane to distract Sophie until John diverted the pup with his belly rubs.

"Cute pup," Deke said as he took the chair I offered him. "She's going to be big. Look at the size of those paws."

"I noticed that," I replied with a chuckle, "and she's got a hearty appetite."

"What will you do with her today?" John asked. "She can't be in the way when I paint the kitchen and dining room or when they bring in the beam."

Although Alan and I had discussed possible solutions for keeping Sophie occupied, we decided she'd have to stay outside, despite the brisk northerly breeze. Alan had an investigation to conduct, so he couldn't help, which left the task of entertaining her to me.

"I'll let her play in the yard while I rake leaves," I replied. "If we get cold, we can go into the log cabin. Is there any chance that you can speed up the work?"

"Once we secure the beam, it won't take long to finish the kitchen," Deke assured me.

Alan and I expressed our relief because we realized that the renovation chaos caused our frazzled nerves. In fact, we had a long chat on the sofa last night after I put away the papers from Sal's trash. I hadn't cracked the code yet, but I'd decided that it was more important for the two of us to relax together. The conversation gave us an opportunity to rationally discuss our earlier argument, and Alan admitted that he felt conflicted about his responsibilities with the job and his duties at home.

After Alan left for work, I scrambled to straighten up the bedroom while John began laying his drop cloths and moving the living room furniture. Sophie found John's business much more enticing, but it gave me the time to make sure I had the things I'd need for the day.

I double-checked that my set of keys included the one for Abe's cabin, grabbed my purse and the bag with Sal's trash, and picked up Clara's book of riddles, in case I had the chance to read more of them. I took my phone off the charger and put it in my pocket as I called for Sophie from the back door. Her tail wagged with excitement when she saw me putting on my jacket.

As soon as I pushed open the storm door, Sophie sprang past me and bounded to the yard where I let her frolic while I unlocked the side door of the cabin. I'd expected the bolt to be unyielding from rust or lack of use, but it turned easily and, with a mixture of apprehension and anticipation, I stepped over the threshold, wondering what I might find.

The cabin smelled musty and, to my dismay, I saw mouse droppings in every corner. The two side windows had cobwebs, as did the rustic ladder leading to a loft, but I decided to forego an exploration up the steps since I didn't know if the aged rungs could support me.

In addition to the side door I had entered, there was also a front door that appeared original to the structure. When I tried working the old-fashioned latch, it didn't budge, so I figured that someone padlocked the other side since it had direct access to the street.

The hardwood plank floor looked well-worn and in need of repair in some spots. The glass cabinet that Clara used for her candy display seemed in good condition, though it begged a thorough cleaning. I could actually imagine Clara sitting in the rocking chair by the hearth, welcoming patrons and gossiping with visitors.

Sophie joined me in the cabin as I brushed off the seat of a sturdy oak chair near the front entrance. I watched her sniff around the room to explore every nook and cranny, then said, "What do you think, Sophie? We can have our own girl-space."

Sophie gave me a funny expression, and I thought she might have understood my words. We both sat for a while, with me in the chair, musing about the possibilities for using Abe's cabin, and Sophie lying at my feet, though I couldn't decipher her thoughts.

The jingle of my phone alerted me to a call from Evelyn Sandler. I hadn't spoken to her since our discovery of Sal's body, and wondered how she fared after the morbid experience.

"Hi, Evelyn. How are you doing?"

"Better today," she replied cheerfully. "Would you like to get together for lunch?"

"I'd love to," I sighed, "but I'm bound to the cabin and our yard today. I have a new puppy and can't leave her because of the renovations."

Evelyn's laughter made me giggle, as well, and Sophie's tail thumped on the wooden floor. "You have to be kidding!" she exclaimed. "Are you nuts?"

"No," I replied, getting serious. "I'll tell you the story at some point but, basically, Sal's wife didn't want to keep the pup, so I offered to take her, despite the poor timing."

"That was kind of you," Evelyn remarked, "though, if you ask me, Irma D'Angelo has some mental issues, which make her somewhat unpleasant."

I didn't quite know how to respond, so Evelyn's comment hovered in the air. Still, I thought it sad that Irma had no one to turn to while she grieved.

Evelyn must have sensed my reluctance to discuss Irma's quirks. She switched topics, saying, "You know, there's a doggie day-care on the outskirts of town. I can show you its location if you want to check it out."

"I don't know," I replied. "We have a large fenced yard, so Sophie has plenty of room to romp. Besides, she's just getting used to us."

"I don't mean every day," Evelyn stated, "but you might consider it an option when you want some free time. In addition, she'd learn to socialize with other dogs."

Evelyn made a good point, especially with construction work in progress, so it took less than a minute for me to agree. To my surprise, Evelyn offered to come over shortly, and I told her to meet me at the cabin.

"Don't lock up yet," she said. "I've always wanted to see the inside because everyone calls it a local landmark."

"I can definitely see the history here," I replied, gazing around the room, "but it needs a lot of work."

"You can add one more project to your bucket list," she quipped.

"Right," I sighed.

CHAPTER 25

*H*ickory Glen offered the perfect arrangement for Sophie. I liked that the owner, Maggie White, took the time to show us around, introduced the staff, and even called the local vet to see if Sal kept Sophie's vaccinations up-to-date. She explained the day-care and boarding options, and noted that they provided other services, such as grooming and training, as well.

"This is fabulous," I exclaimed, watching a couple of dogs having an agility work-out. "I think Sophie would love it here."

Evelyn agreed wholeheartedly from her seat on a bench, even as she kept Sophie occupied while Maggie and I conducted business. Frankly, I thought Evelyn looked proud of herself for bringing me there.

I handed Maggie my credit card, and arranged for Sophie to stay until 4 p.m. for the next 3 days. After that, we'd stick to an "as needed" basis. I explained that I didn't want to make any commitment for training until I knew if Irma would change her mind about giving me Sophie.

"I heard about Sal's murder," Maggie said as she finalized the paperwork. "I didn't know the wife, but my husband and I often ordered pizza or sandwiches from Sal's Pizza Shop, and we just couldn't believe the news."

"I know what you mean," I nodded. "It was a shock."

"I guess Sal's wife couldn't handle a puppy, what with all of the commotion and everything," Maggie added. "It's too bad, though, because dogs have a way of helping us cope."

"It sounds as if you've experienced something stressful," I replied. "I guess we all have, in some way or another."

Maggie nodded her head in agreement before saying, "My parents died only months apart about 8 years ago, leaving me with their farm. My husband agreed to relocate here, but he didn't want any part of farming, so we came up with the idea of offering doggie day-care."

"You provide a real service to the community," I said.

"Thanks, but I think I'm a better person when I have dogs around me. Besides, we have two golden Labs ourselves, and I wanted to care for my parents' two springer spaniels. It made sense to put some of the land to good use."

"What does your husband do?" I asked.

"He has an accounting business specializing in corporate taxes," Maggie replied. "Anyway, he can work from home, which we both like, and we rent out some of the land to local farmers. It's a win-win situation, and I get to play with dogs all day."

We both laughed, and though Maggie White looked about the age of my daughter, I felt an easy connection with her. I also had no qualms about leaving Sophie with her for the rest of the day, because I had such confidence in Maggie's care. She clearly loved dogs, and knew how to handle them, plus she had taken a lot of time to explain the programs she offered at Hickory Glen, so my instincts told me that Sophie would enjoy her stay.

"I guess we're all set," I said as we returned to Evelyn and Sophie.

Maggie reached down to cuddle Sophie while taking her leash from Evelyn, and said, "Yep. Let me walk her to the field, then you can take off. I'll see you at 4 o'clock."

Sophie didn't even notice our departure.

EVELYN PULLED to the curb in front of Dottie's Café, and though I noticed Alan's police cruiser in front of Sal's Pizza Shop, I didn't mention it to Evelyn. She needed no additional reminder of our experience.

Dottie pointed to a table for two by the counter that she'd just cleared so, with the place filling up with the lunch crowd, I considered us lucky to find seats right away. I already knew that I intended to order the chicken salad sandwich, but Evelyn took a few minutes to peruse the menu.

While Evelyn read, I glanced around the room to see if I knew anyone. I couldn't find one familiar face, a sure sign that I needed to get out and meet more folks from town. By the time Dottie arrived to take our orders, Evelyn decided on a ham and cheese Panini, then we asked for separate checks.

Dottie nodded as she jotted our requests, and I noticed that, like Sal, she scribbled abbreviations another person would find difficult to interpret. When she placed her pad in her apron pocket, Dottie said, "I'll return in a jiffy, but I wondered how you both feel after your devastating experience the other day. I still can't believe it."

Evelyn frowned, then replied, "I felt horrible after finding Sal dead with a knife in his chest. Thank heavens, Marty took me home, because I could barely handle it all."

"You were lucky to have someone with you to talk about it," Dottie replied. "I didn't want Rob to know how frightened I felt. I mean, what if someone targeted all of the business owners on this block?"

Although I'd recently experienced some scary moments of my own, I said, "Alan doesn't consider it a random murder. He thinks Sal's killer had an axe to grind with him."

"That's what he told me," Dottie said, glancing at a couple who just arrived and pointing them to the last available table.

Dottie looked as if she intended to say something else but, instead, she scurried off to take our order to the cook and clear another table. It made me wonder if she had information that would help the investigation, but this was not the time or place to continue the discussion. Besides, Evelyn had a worried expression on her face, so I wanted to change the subject.

"What did you think about Abe's cabin?" I asked, picking out a blue packet of sweetener for when my iced tea arrived.

"It needs a lot of repair," Evelyn replied. "Do you think it has heat?"

"No," I stated, "I guess Clara Whitman used the fireplace to warm the cabin in the winter, because I know that Deke had to chop firewood when he worked for her."

"How about electricity?" Evelyn queried.

"I saw some receptacles and switches," I said, "though I didn't try them. I think I'll hire an electrician to check them out. In the meantime, I hope Dottie's son and his friends can help me clean the place before we do anything else."

"Good idea," Evelyn agreed. "Do you intend to keep it rustic?"

"Yes," I nodded. "I'd like to preserve its history. Other than that, we haven't really decided how we'll use it. The boys think we should turn it back into a candy shop."

Dottie arrived with our lunch platters, and giggled when she overheard mention of Rob and his friends. "They continue to talk about it," she said, "and I can't help but agree with them."

"Time will tell," I smiled. "Do you think Rob can get some friends to help with the clean-up?"

"Sure," Dottie agreed. "They'd love to see the inside. How about sometime this weekend?"

"Wonderful," I said, "and they can play with the puppy."

Dottie looked astonished. "You got a dog?"

Evelyn rolled her eyes, then said, "Sue has Sal's dog. Irma D'Angelo gave it to her."

I expected Dottie to laugh, but she didn't. She seemed to reflect on something else before she noted, "I remember when Sal and Irma first opened their pizza shop, and you couldn't find a happier couple working side by side."

"I've only lived in Aspen Notch a few years," Evelyn said, "but I don't think I've ever seen Irma there except once or twice. She didn't seem very friendly, so what happened?"

"Running a business is pretty stressful," Dottie replied, "and I guess it took its toll. Besides, Irma gained a lot of weight over the years, and she could barely manage to get around, so I doubt she'd want to keep a puppy."

"That's what I assumed," I nodded. "At least, I've tried to do a kind deed."

"That was very thoughtful of you," Dottie replied before she excused herself to wait on another table. "Just don't get too attached because Irma can be somewhat fickle."

CHAPTER 26

hen we left Dottie's Café, Evelyn took me home, and I told her how much I appreciated her help with Sophie and our enjoyable lunch. For the most part, we'd avoided unpleasant topics since I didn't want to discuss Irma's behavior, especially after Dottie's comment about her fickleness. When I reflected on the portrait in Sal's shop that captured the once proud and happy couple, a sharp contrast to the Irma of today, I wanted to know what triggered the change in her, yet preferred not to let the opinions of others color my perception.

Though Evelyn invited me to join her while she did some errands, I begged off. With two hours before I had to pick up the pup, I wanted to check on the progress of the beam's installation and work on decoding Sal's handwriting. When I saw only John's truck and my car in the driveway, I silently speculated that the other workers had finished for the day.

I could barely contain my gasp as I opened the front door to see that the crew had removed the studs between the living room and kitchen, then enclosed the beam behind drywall. John had covered the lime green and gaudy orange walls with the stark white primer, and stood on a rung of his ladder to spackle seams and nail holes.

He laughed when he saw my expression, then said, "Big difference, huh?"

"What an amazing transformation," I gulped. "Deke must have brought an army in here today."

"You haven't seen anything yet," John smiled. "Take a gander under the drop cloth."

To my astonishment, I found a lovely laminated floor in the kitchen, with wood tones that would match perfectly with our cabinets and furniture. "My goodness," I exclaimed. "What a surprise! I can't believe it."

"Before you get all teary-eyed," John chuckled, "Deke said to tell you that he has a crew lined up for tomorrow to install the rest of the flooring throughout the house. You'll no longer have dingy, smelly carpets."

"Wow!" I grinned. "It's all coming together."

"Yep," John nodded. "By morning, once the primer dries and I sand the spackle, I'll add the final coat of paint. After that, Deke can oversee the installation of the cabinets, appliances, and island."

Filled with excitement, I used my phone to take photos, then texted a couple of them to Alan and my daughter, Alexa. The rest would eventually go in a memory book.

While John cleaned up, I told him about taking Sophie to Hickory Glen for doggie daycare. Although he'd heard about the place, he hadn't thought about mentioning it, but agreed that it provided a good option.

"You know," John added, "they might also offer overnight boarding, which you could consider since we need to start early tomorrow. Deke's determined to have your kitchen finished by the weekend."

"I'll think about it," I nodded. "I wouldn't want Sophie to believe we don't care about her."

"She probably loves the attention," John said. "I wouldn't worry about it. Besides, think of the alternative. From what I've heard, Sal's wife doesn't make pleasant company, if you know what I mean."

I ignored the comment, watching John fold the drop cloth and put it in the laundry room with his ladder. While he rinsed the rest of his brushes and rollers, my thoughts stayed on Irma. I decided to check in with her again and, maybe, bring her some groceries. Someone needed to step up to the plate, and I didn't see anyone else lining up to do it.

AFTER JOHN DEPARTED, I spread the papers from Sal's waste basket on the dining room table. Within an hour of quiet time, I'd found a couple of intriguing leads, so I put those in my purse with the hope that Irma would confirm my decoding, then made a quick call to Hickory Glen to ask if Sophie could remain overnight. To my relief, Maggie White had no problem with accommodating my request.

At the grocery store, I selected items that Irma might find appealing. With her weak knees, she probably couldn't do a lot of prep work, so I chose a few TV dinners, canned soup, ice cream, and a coffee cake. None were particularly healthy, and I knew I shouldn't stereotype, but I meant the food as a gesture of kindness, not a lesson in nutrition.

After ringing the doorbell, I waited on Irma's front porch for what seemed an eternity. Finally, she opened the door with a sour expression.

"What's your problem?" Irma grunted.

"None at all," I replied as cheerfully as I could muster. "I brought you some groceries."

"I don't need your charity," she muttered.

"Of course not," I smiled, pulling open the storm door. "Can you manage this bag, while I bring in the rest?"

I didn't give Irma a chance to respond. I handed her the lightest bag, then carried the rest to the kitchen counter. After I put the frozen foods in the freezer, I watched her face while she peeked in the other bags. She seemed to like what I'd chosen.

"How much do I owe you?" she asked.

Given Irma's reference to charity, I gave her the receipt after I wrote my phone number on the back, and told her that I'd gladly pick up anything else she needed at the store.

"Why are you so nice to me?" Irma murmured after she checked off each item on the receipt, then retrieved a twenty-dollar bill from her purse.

"I like you," I lied, "and I had a similar experience with my first husband. After he died, I found out he'd lived a secret life and squandered all our money."

I knew Irma didn't have the same situation with Sal, but she nodded and pointed me to the sofa. She sat in the recliner, then pushed back to raise her terribly swollen legs.

"How's the dog?" Irma queried.

"She's good, though she misses you." I smiled, despite my second lie.

"I couldn't take care of her," Irma sighed.

"I understand," I said. "When you feel up to it, I can bring her to visit."

Irma nodded her head in agreement, although her eyes reflected a deep sadness, which she masked with the tough shell around her. Still, I hoped I could break through.

"I guess you found yourself another man," Irma noted. "How'd you meet the police chief?"

My brief rendition seemed to satisfy Irma's curiosity, and though she didn't need to know all of the gory details, I told her that Alan and I had solved a murder mystery together before we fell in love.

"Are you working with your husband to find Sal's killer?" she questioned.

"Not really," I said. "I don't have any police training."

Irma looked at me intently before saying, "I want you to try. Sal didn't deserve to die like that."

"Will you help me figure out Sal's handwriting?" I asked. "I think the papers from his waste basket may hold an important clue."

"Do you have them with you?" she queried.

"They're in my purse," I nodded.

I thought it a major break-through that Irma agreed to take a look.

After I handed her the packet, and told her what I'd interpreted from the top sheet, she confirmed that Wally S. had ordered two Italian hoagies for 4 p.m.

The second page had me stymied, and Irma squinted as she studied the writing. Finally, she remarked, "There's no order here. Just *Ber C, 4:15.*"

"That's exactly what I thought," I nodded. "What do you think it means?"

"I have no idea," Irma shrugged. "Maybe Sal got busy and forgot to write it, but that's unlikely. He always insisted that we record the order."

"Perhaps the person didn't place an order," I suggested. "Maybe Sal scheduled a meeting, and jotted the information on his pad. I've done that sometimes if I don't have my calendar handy."

"I suppose that's possible," Irma said, flipping to the next page. "Rob B. ordered a pepperoni pizza for 4:05. That might be Dottie's son because he'd sometimes get a pizza if he had band practice."

I'd had a similar thought despite my recognition that any number of persons in Aspen Notch could have the same initials, and I didn't even know that many people in town. Still, I figured that we'd made progress.

To celebrate, I suggested that we open the coffee cake I'd purchased, and Irma agreed before telling me where to find the plates and a knife. As I walked to the kitchen, I reminded her that I'd placed the TV dinners and ice cream in the freezer.

Taking the dishes from the cabinet, I reached for a knife from the butcher's block on the counter, but a gaping slot in the back row indicated a missing large knife.

Before jumping to conclusions, I looked for it in the sink and dishwasher, then the counter and drawers, but I couldn't find it. My stomach churned as I thought the unthinkable.

Did Irma use their own knife to kill Sal?

CHAPTER 27

$\mathcal{I}$ tried to remain calm while Irma and I ate, though my brain kept spinning with threads that could connect Irma to her husband's death. As soon as I could, I made a flimsy excuse for my hasty departure yet, even as I drove home, the coffee cake felt stuck in my throat.

I told myself that Irma would never have asked me to help find Sal's killer if she had committed the crime. In fact, I didn't even know if the missing knife from the butcher's block served as the murder weapon, nor had I thought to take a photo of the handles of the other knives for Alan to see if they matched.

With the sun beginning to set, I turned on the living room and dining room lights, then closed the blinds. Since I thought Alan wouldn't return home for another hour, I retrieved Clara's riddle book from my purse, and sat on the sofa to read it. My pensive mood left me wondering what secrets Clara Whitman hid, and why she spent time crafting dark, mysterious poems.

As I turned the pages, re-reading some of the riddles and focusing on others, I saw no sequence or order to her musings. Clearly, she meant some of the poems for Deke, as she assigned him various tasks for the afternoon, though others highlighted Clara's melancholy, and

I wondered if she used those as a way to express grief after her husband's death in the war.

A broken heart finds no relief,
Absconding joy, like a thief.
The wound a chasm, black as a crow,
Holding sadness, angst, and woe.

Deke told me that Clara, a young woman when she lost her husband, never remarried, nor did she have any children. He remembered her fondly, as a kind and generous person, and people in town spoke highly of her as they shared memories of visiting the candy shop. No one ever mentioned the brooding, despondent figure I saw in her writing.

As I continued reading, I kept coming across depressing and sad poems. Toward the middle of the notepad, Clara began to express her fright, such as the riddle about shadows, and they made me question what she feared. Did she hear sounds in the night, as I had, or did someone stalk her?

I found the next poem similar to the one I'd read for Deke, which he thought referred to the death and burial of Caroline, his daughter. Now, I didn't feel as certain, unless Clara was the child's mother.

No one can know the secret I bear,
Sins of the past, never to share.
Hidden beneath the soil of the earth,
No bed for her head, no crib for her berth.

I mulled over various scenarios until Alan pulled into the driveway with a brief honk to let me know of his return home. I appreciated the comforting gesture, especially after darkness descended, and considered it a reinforcement of his protective nature.

Despite his long day, Alan gave a cheery greeting when he entered, then leaned to kiss me. His jovial mood fit perfectly with my sugges-

KATHLEEN MCKEE

tion that we enjoy an evening of dining and pool at the Black Horse
Pub, especially since I needed to shake off the gloom I'd felt.

"Sounds good to me," Alan agreed wholeheartedly, "but where's
the pup?"

"Sophie's at Hickory Glen," I said. "Evelyn told me about the
place, and we took her there this morning. Actually, I'd only
planned on daycare for a few days, but John told me that he and
Deke want to get an early start tomorrow, so I arranged for her
overnight stay."

"Smart idea to board Sophie, at least for one night," Alan replied as
he gazed at the progress of the renovations. "It looks even more
amazing in here than the photos you texted."

"Deke plans to have the kitchen in usable condition by the weekend," I smiled, "and John will finish painting the walls, though I guess
he'll do the trim next week."

Alan grinned, saying, "It'll be great to get back to normal; at least
our new normal."

While Alan changed into street clothes, I straightened up as much
as I could with our furniture moved to the center of the room. When
I placed Clara's riddles in my purse, I noticed a text from our real
estate agent for my house in Chester County who wrote that she
expected a written offer shortly, and she'd call to discuss it with us
when it arrived. I couldn't help thinking that everything finally began
to fall into place.

"More good news," I said as we donned our jackets. "I'll tell you
about it in the car. In the meantime, prepare to lose your status as the
pool champion of the family."

"In your dreams, sweetie!" Alan quipped.

After Sally, our favorite waitress, took our appetizer order for hot
wings and beer, I noticed the number of patrons gathered around the
bar. Obviously, for a weekday night, the Black Horse Pub attracted a
younger crowd, probably because Aspen Notch didn't have much to

offer as entertainment after their workday, and I enjoyed watching their socializing.

I'd barely taken a sip of my beer when the ring tone on my phone alerted me to a call from our real estate agent. She told me that a couple, impressed with the upgrades on the house, made a very generous offer. They had an interest in the local school district, and even better, wanted a fast settlement.

In the car, Alan and I had discussed what we'd accept as an offer and, with this well above it, I mouthed the figure to Alan, he nodded emphatically, then I gave our approval. Before we disconnected, the agent promised to email the documents for our signature, and asked that I return them as soon as possible.

Alan and I toasted to a successful sale, though he added, "I guess we shouldn't celebrate until everything's signed, sealed, and delivered."

"I think such a wonderful offer gives us a sign that we're meant to live in Aspen Notch," I grinned. "We can bring closure to the old homestead as we make a new start here."

Alan raised an eyebrow, then gnawed on a spicy wing. I knew he thought I had a difficult time with the move but, with things settling into place, I felt more upbeat. We'd soon have a comfortable home, we've made some new friends, and we had a puppy, so all was good.

Of course, Alan had the challenging task of assuring the people of Aspen Notch that he would provide them protection and arrest Sal's killer. If anything, Alan offered his reassurance that no one had anything to fear. He always appeared calm and unruffled in public, and I loved those qualities about him.

As I reached for another hot wing, I told Alan about my visit with Irma. Although he looked surprised, he wondered if she wanted us to return Sophie.

"No," I replied. "Irma admitted that she can't handle the pup, but she seemed happy when I promised to bring Sophie to see her."

"That's good," Alan nodded. "It sounds as if you found Irma in a better frame of mind today."

"Sort of," I agreed. "She definitely has her quirks."

After wiping my hands, I reached into my purse for some of the papers from Sal's trash since I wanted to show him what I'd learned before telling him about the knife.

"She helped you decode Sal's handwriting?" Alan asked.

"Irma confirmed what I suspected," I stated. "Some guy named Wally S. requested two hoagies, while Rob Burkeholder ordered a pizza, and both had pick-up times around 4 o'clock. Also, Bernie Calamito scheduled a meeting with Sal for 4:15, so any of them could be implicated in Sal's death."

Alan's laugh reverberated, which brought a few glances from the bar. "You honestly believe that Wally, Bernie, or Rob killed Sal D'Angelo?" Alan questioned.

"I'm just telling you the facts," I shrugged, "so take it for what it's worth. More importantly, though, I observed a knife missing from Irma's butcher's block."

"Now you have my attention," Alan replied. "What kind of knife?"

"One of the larger ones with a plain black handle," I said.

Alan pulled out his phone and showed me a photo of the crime scene weapon, and my stomach sank when he enlarged it.

"It matches the others in the butcher's block," I muttered, "but I can't imagine that Irma killed her husband."

"Why not?" Alan queried.

"She asked me to help you find Sal's killer," I explained. "Why would she do that if she was guilty?"

"To cover her tracks," Alan shrugged.

Although I recognized such a possibility, I didn't feel that Irma had the capability, so I stated, "Irma can barely walk, nor do I think she could fit behind a steering wheel to drive."

"From what you've told me," Alan sighed, "Irma hated her husband. In my book, she had motive."

Shaking my head, I said, "If that's your theory, why not just kill him at home? Why risk being seen in a public place?"

"Irma's no dummy," Alan contended. "At the very least, she'd have a life sentence in prison for premeditated murder if she did him in at home. On the other hand, she'd have a chance to get away with it if it occurred at the pizza shop."

"Do you plan to bring her in for questioning?" I asked.

"Of course," Alan nodded, "so I'll call her first thing in the morning."

"Please don't tell her how you knew about the knife," I pleaded. "I want to befriend her because she needs help."

To bide time, Alan signaled for Sally to bring us two more beers and place our order for dinner. She mentioned the fish fry special, so we each selected that, though Alan added a basket of fried onion rings for our veggies. Sally laughed; I didn't.

"I'm serious, Alan," I said. "You have to think of a way to discover the missing knife yourself. Bring her a coffee cake or something."

"You drive me crazy," Alan replied.

"That's why you fell in love with me," I reminded him.

CHAPTER 28

*A*lan left for work at the crack of dawn, leaving me to greet Deke and John, then the work crews. I intended to see if they needed me for anything, which I doubted, but thought it polite of me to ask. Then, I'd have breakfast at Dottie's Café, followed by a trip to Hickory Glen to check on Sophie, and I'd spend the rest of my day in the log cabin.

Deke emphatically stated that he wanted me out of the way, since he insisted that the crews needed to have the kitchen in working order by the end of the day. It didn't seem possible to me, but his determination reinforced my confidence that he'd accomplish his goal. I gave him my itinerary, then headed to Dottie's Café.

With the café nearly empty except for a few other early birds, Dottie pulled up a chair to join me after she filled my mug with a fresh batch of coffee. "What has you out and about on this brisk day?" she asked. "I think we may get a little snow."

"Not just flurries?" I questioned. "Are you kidding?"

Dottie chuckled, then said, "We've had major snowfalls in October. After all, we live in the mountains and Sunday is Halloween, but, quite honestly, we might only have a dusting today."

"Ugh," I groaned, "although I appreciate your reminder about Halloween. Will Alan and I get a lot of trick-or-treaters?"

"Probably," she nodded. "You live on the main drag."

"I'm prepared," I said, thinking of the candy I'd bought when I had a meltdown. "Anyway, John wants to finish painting the walls today, and Deke has a couple of work crews lined up, so they wanted me out of the way."

"John who?" Dottie asked, with a strange expression.

"John Calhoun," I replied. "Evelyn Sandler suggested that we hire him to paint the house, then John recommended Deke Hopewell as manager for the renovations. They're both great."

"That's nice," Dottie said. "I don't think I know Deke."

"But you know John?" I questioned.

"I suppose you could say that," Dottie nodded. "We dated for a while, a couple of years after my husband's death, though I broke up with him."

"Why?" I asked. "He's wonderful."

"It's a long story," Dottie said. "Let's just say that I didn't want to get serious because I had to consider my son. After all, Rob had already lost his father."

I nodded, despite not fully understanding. With my kids grown and on their own when their father died, I could have dated, though I had no interest. My children didn't factor into the equation at that point, but my own frame of reference did.

Glancing at an older couple entering the café, Dottie said she'd better take my order. When she returned with my omelet and toast, she refilled my coffee, saying, "By the way, Rob told me that he lined up some of his friends, and they'll help you in the log cabin after lunch tomorrow."

"Perfect," I replied enthusiastically. "I'll stop at the store to buy some cleaning supplies."

"Don't expect perfection," Dottie chuckled. "I think the boys have more interest in viewing the inside of the cabin than scrubbing it."

"Every little bit helps," I sighed.

~

AT HICKORY GLEN, Maggie assured me that Sophie adjusted well, so I arranged for another night of boarding. Maggie thought it best not to disrupt Sophie's routine with my visit since the pup might think I'd come to take her home. Instead, Maggie showed me a video of Sophie's training session, and I knew, without a doubt, that I'd inherited a very smart dog.

From there, I drove to the grocery store. In addition to the cleaning supplies, I picked up a couple of nonperishable microwavable meals and a fruity dessert that looked appetizing. As I walked the aisles looking for healthy food that didn't need refrigeration, I smiled with the recollection of my comment to Alan when he beat me at pool again last night. He just laughed when I blamed malnutrition for my dismal attempt to win.

With no room in our driveway or curbside for my car due to all of the workers' vehicles, I pulled up on the grass near the log cabin which worked fine since I could save time by bringing the buckets, brooms, and dusters directly to the cleaning site. Before I lugged them in through the gate, I took a look at the padlock on the front entrance, and found it old and rusty, but my key didn't open it.

Instead, I unlocked the side door and made several trips back and forth to my car, then placed my wares in an out-of-the-way spot under the loft. With that tedious job finished, I pulled a chair up to the glass counter to use as a work space, though the coldness of the cabin kept me from getting comfortable, or accomplishing anything worthwhile.

I thought about starting a blaze in the fireplace, but knew that wouldn't be wise until we had the chimney checked out. As my second option, I considered driving to the home-goods store to buy a space heater, but I didn't know if the cabin had wiring to support any electrical additions. Besides, I noticed that the occasional flakes of snow had changed to an intense squall and, with visibility limited, I preferred not to drive in it.

With no other alternatives, I pulled my jacket closer to my body, and tried to forget about the cold. To pass the time, I took Clara's riddles out of my purse and began reading. As usual, I found them cryptic and somewhat macabre.

Who goes there? Who traipses at night?
Who crosses the lawn, causing my fright?
What search they, those who are bold?
Is it bones or is it gold?

I felt certain that Clara believed someone stalked her, and I wondered if she had the fence built to keep out unwanted visitors. Its construction could have dated back to Clara's time, though I thought it held up well through the years, so I jotted a memo on the notepad that I kept in my purse to ask Deke if he knew anything about it.

The last line of the riddle had me baffled, and I wondered if Clara had been a wealthy woman. It didn't seem so to me since I wouldn't call the house luxurious, nor could a small candy shop bring much income. Of course, she could have sold off parcels of Abe's land if she needed money but, if she did, she mustn't have used it in a pretentious way. I added it to my questions for Deke.

Skimming through a few more riddles, my eyes caught one that shed more light on Clara's commentary. In fact, it made me think about my father who didn't like to spend money, and often called himself parsimonious. Our family joked about his frugal ways, but he remained proud of the distinction.

Paper and silver in a shallow grave,
No one must know how much I save.
Tins or jars, either are fine,
Safe from those who believe they aren't mine.

Obviously, Clara buried her money instead of banking it. Maybe Dad had done the same thing, although we'd never found any trace of it. Those who lived through the Great Depression often had a distrust of banks, so I didn't consider it unusual for someone of Clara's generation to hide her money.

Still, I didn't understand the last sentence. If Clara buried the money she'd made from selling her candies, who'd not believe it belonged to her? Who'd sneak on her property at night to find it, and why would it concern anyone else?

The thought made me wonder if someone in town knew that Clara buried her money. Maybe history repeated itself with my experiences of the strange noises at night. Had I heard the sound of digging? Surely, I'd have noticed holes in the ground when I raked the leaves or played with Sophie.

I didn't think it possible, and reassured myself that I'd find a rational explanation for the sounds I heard.

CHAPTER 29

*B*y 2 o'clock, I couldn't take the chilly cabin any longer. I'd made calls to set up appointments for a chimney inspector, then a locksmith to replace the padlock at the front entrance, and my stomach growled its hunger. Since the snow squall activity had stopped, I decided to head over to a shopping center, grab some lunch, then have a manicure where I could finally get warm.

When I passed the front of my house, I noticed the truck delivering our new cabinets and appliances, and could barely contain my excitement even as I searched for a place to have my nails done. After a quick hamburger, I could only find a hair salon that advertised a special hair and nail deal, so I pulled in front of the shop, then decided to go in. The stylist who greeted me looked past her prime with black-dyed hair, teased into a chignon that she probably thought looked attractive. It didn't.

"Do you take walk-ins?" I asked, hoping that she'd say no.

"You're in luck, honey. My 3 o'clock cancelled, so you can take my chair."

I settled into the seat after hanging my jacket on a hook by the front door, hoping I didn't make a mistake. The woman draped me in a black plastic cape, talking all the while.

"I'm Rosie," she smiled. "Are you new in town? I don't think I ever saw you before."

"Yes. I'm Sue Jaworski. My husband and I just relocated from southeast PA."

"Wife of the new police chief? Bless his heart, he's got to handle a murder already. What's this world coming to?"

I nodded, then shook my head accordingly. Not knowing quite how to respond, I changed the subject, saying, "I'd like to get a trim and a manicure. Is that possible?"

"Of course, dearie," Rosie replied, "but those roots need a touch-up. Let's do the whole works since we're not busy this afternoon."

Rosie handed me a color chart as I weighed my options. It wouldn't hurt, I thought, to enjoy some pampering. Besides, I found the warm shop a nice alternative to the cold cabin.

"That sounds like a good idea," I smiled, then explained my preferred color and cut.

Rosie looked thrilled, while the only other patron, a gal under the dryer, winked at me. Her stylist must have taken a break, perhaps in the back room, which made me wonder about the success of the business with only two customers.

As Rosie mixed the concoction for my hair, she suggested that I select my nail polish, and she'd do the manicure while my color set. I looked through the collection displayed on the wall, picked one I thought might look good, then returned to my seat.

"I guess you're still getting settled," Rosie said, while she spread the goop on my roots. "Word around town says you guys bought the old Whitman place. I have pleasant memories of Mrs. Whitman. You know, she used the cabin for a candy shop."

"So I've heard," I nodded. "Folks must have considered Clara Whitman a pillar in the community. If anything, everyone tells me they liked her goodies."

"She was my mother's best friend, God rest them both."

My ears picked up on Rosie's comment, so I said, "Really? Then you must have known her well."

Rosie laughed, saying, "I knew her even as a toddler, and I'm sure she babysat me at least a time or two."

"How would you describe her?" I questioned.

"Clara? I'd describe her as kind-hearted and generous. She loved children, which is probably why she opened a candy shop. Kids always stopped by on their way home from school."

"Was she about the same age as your mother?" I asked.

"I suppose so," Rosie replied. "Mama said she felt sorry for Clara because her husband died in the war, leaving her all alone."

"She never had any children?" I queried.

Rosie looked at me strangely, then nudged me to follow her to the manicure counter. She filled a bowl with soapy water and instructed me to soak my hands before she finally replied, "That's what they say, but Mama thought differently. I heard her mention Clara's pregnancy to my father though, when I asked her about it, she told me to mind my own business."

"But you never saw any child?" I asked while Rosie began filing my nails.

"No," Rosie replied, "and Mama never mentioned it again."

"How old were you when you overheard it?" I asked.

"Old enough to know about pregnancy," Rosie chuckled. We had six kids in my family, and I was probably about 11 years old at the time."

I tried to calculate when Clara could have been pregnant, without knowing Rosie's current age. Even a random estimate made me realize the impossibility that Clara conceived the child prior to her husband's deployment to Korea. Apparently, Clara bore a child out of wedlock, and given Clara's riddle, he or she may have died and she buried the bones in the yard. The thought made me shiver.

While Rosie painted my nails, I asked if her mother had ever mentioned that Clara acted depressed or had weird fears.

Once again, Rosie eyed me, and said, "What makes you ask that? Did someone in town spread malicious rumors?"

Shaking my head, I wondered if I should tell Rosie about Clara's booklet of riddles. Quite honestly, I didn't know if I could trust her ability to keep a confidence, but luckily, I didn't have to reply because the other stylist returned and greeted me with a friendly welcome.

We chatted for a moment until she brought the other patron to her chair, then Rosie pulled my color through while my nails dried. After she washed my hair, Rosie began to chatter again, but this time she focused on Sal's murder.

"I sure hope they find the person who did it," Rosie said with scissors in hand. "His poor wife must be in shock, bless her heart."

"Do you know Irma?" I asked.

"I used to style her hair all the time," Rosie nodded. "The poor thing hasn't been back since she became stuck in one of our chairs."

"I heard she's put on a lot of weight," I replied.

"You would, too, honey," Rosie sighed. "Let me tell you, if my husband ever spoke to me the way her husband did, I'd have used these scissors to castrate him, God rest his soul."

I hated to give it more than a passing thought, but Irma D'Angelo definitely had a story to tell. No doubt, at one time she became involved in the community, and did normal activities such as having her hair done. It saddened me to think that she retreated into the shell of the woman she had become.

CHAPTER 30

I pulled into my driveway next to John's pick-up truck at close to 5 p.m. to see that none of the other work vehicles remained, which indicated that the crews had made good progress. With great excitement and anticipation, I turned off the engine, took my purse, and practically sprinted to the house.

As I walked through the front door, John flipped all of the hallway switches to bathe the house in light. Deke coordinated the big reveal by turning on the living room lamps, then both of them smiled at seeing my tears of joy. The place looked amazing but, best of all, I could now use the kitchen.

"As you can see," Deke began, "we didn't finish the island or the molding, but we'll get to those next week before we do the bathroom."

"I can't believe how much you've accomplished today," I gasped, my eyes darting from the new flooring to the cabinets. "You must have called in a lot of favors."

Deke laughed, then invited me to check out the stove and refrigerator while John finished cleaning his brushes. I even ran the water in the double sink, a luxury I'd always wanted, and I couldn't find anything that lacked perfection.

"I'm glad you like it," Deke said, retrieving his cane from the back of a dining room chair. "John and I will happily serve as your first dinner guests."

"That's a deal," I chuckled. "Give me time to practice my culinary skills because I haven't cooked anything in the kitchen for quite a while."

John joined Deke and me at the front door. "We'll hold you to it," he smiled. "Anyway, we'll see you on Monday. Let me get Deke home, since his bedtime approaches."

They'd no sooner backed out of the driveway before Alan pulled in. I excitedly called to him, even before he had a chance to honk, then ran to greet him, foregoing my jacket in the brisk evening air. The two of us sauntered hand-in-hand along our front path while I shared my enthusiasm for the work that Deke and John had done.

"Prepare to be surprised," I said at the threshold. "Close your eyes."

Alan complied while I led him to the sofa, facing the new kitchen. When I finally allowed him to peek, I totally enjoyed his priceless expression.

"Wow," he exclaimed. "This calls for a celebration!"

"I agree," I grinned. "Where shall we go?"

"You don't want to spend the evening cooking a fabulous dinner for two?" Alan quipped

"Very funny," I panned. "Let's go to that Italian restaurant and share a bottle of wine."

ALAN CALLED in a reservation at La Traviata, then we both changed our clothing. I chose a dressy pair of black slacks with a crimson floral top that matched my nail polish. As I applied my makeup, I noticed Alan standing at the bathroom door watching me.

"You look gorgeous," he grinned. "What's different?"

Still gazing at his reflection in the mirror, I had to laugh at his backhanded compliment. For someone trained in tactics of observation, he hadn't even noticed my new hairdo or nails.

"I took some time for myself this afternoon," I smiled. Pampering at the local beauty salon does wonders for a girl's spirits."

"Good idea," Alan said. "You probably found the cabin too cold to hang there all day, so I guess we should hire someone to inspect the fireplace."

I nodded my agreement and said, "The inspection will be done on Monday morning. Do you happen to have a key for the padlock on the front entrance of the cabin?"

"I thought our key opened both doors," Alan said.

"It doesn't," I replied, "so I also arranged for a locksmith on Monday to change the locks."

"That's wise," Alan nodded. "Are you almost done? We need to go now or we'll miss our reservation at the restaurant."

"I'm ready," I agreed, turning off the lights except for the lamps in the living room. "Would you make sure Deke locked the back door?"

In the car, Alan asked if anything had happened to make me skittish enough to have the locks changed. I assured him that I just wanted a routine precaution for the historic log cabin, probably no different from his decision to change the locks at Sal's shop. With the glare of a passing light, I noticed the concern on Alan's face, and thought he didn't need anything else to worry about.

The hostess at the restaurant led us to a private table for two in a corner by the tall window with a view of the beautifully landscaped courtyard. When Alan pulled out my chair, I noticed Lou Greene with a woman I presumed to be his wife, and it looked as if they'd prepared to leave.

"Isn't that the mayor over there?" I whispered.

Alan peered in the direction I indicated, then nodded and waved them over. I really didn't care to meet the mayor's wife since it seemed strange to me that we'd lived in Aspen Notch for almost a month and she'd never reached out to welcome me.

"Good to see you both," Lou said with a broad smile. "Sue, I'd like to introduce you to my wife, Mildred."

"Nice to meet you," I replied with as much enthusiasm as I could garner.

"Likewise," Mildred said in a tone that defined her status as Aspen Notch's First Lady. "I apologize for not calling on you, but trying to rearrange my calendar is a nightmare."

"I can only imagine," I nodded. "Alan and I plan to invite you and Lou for dinner, now that we have a working kitchen."

"That would be lovely," Mildred smiled, nudging Lou that they needed to depart. "We'll look forward to it."

Alan commended me for a good save when they were out of earshot. He knew that Lou, as mayor, didn't impress me, and now I could say the same about his wife. Still, Alan reported to Lou, so I thought it better to build communication, not hinder it.

When our waiter arrived, Alan ordered a bottle of their house wine and fried calamari as an appetizer, then he passed me the basket of crusty rolls from the center of the table. While we waited, I decided to tell him my theory about Clara Whitman.

"I've just about finished reading all of Clara's riddles," I said, "and I feel she definitely had something to hide."

Alan raised his right eyebrow. "Have you figured out the last of her riddles?" he asked.

"I think she had a child out of wedlock and buried it in the yard," I replied.

Trying to contain his laughter, Alan shook his head, then queried, "How do you come up with these things?"

I told Alan that one of the riddles actually mentioned bones in the ground, then explained that Rosie, the hairdresser, heard her mother say that Clara was pregnant. Putting two and two together confirmed that Clara bore a child, who must have died, though it occurred after her husband was killed in action.

"It's pretty far-fetched," Alan noted as the waiter poured our wine, "but it's easy enough to search birth records."

We clinked glasses before I replied, "That's what I plan to do, though Clara might not have recorded the birth. Anyway, I think she also buried money."

"That's what a lot of folks did in the old days," Alan said. "Maybe we'll be rich if you can find it."

"You're mocking me," I sighed.

"Not at all," Alan smiled. "If there's anything I've learned about you in the past year, it's that you're like a dog with a bone. Speaking of, how's Sophie?"

"I went to see her this morning, but Maggie White—she's the owner—thought it better that I just watch a video of her in a training session. You should've seen how smart she looked."

"Good," Alan grinned. "Sophie can help you solve your mysteries."

After we placed our orders, I asked Alan about the crime investigation, especially since I wanted to know if he'd matched the murder weapon with Irma's missing knife. Alan didn't give me much information, but admitted that he'd met with Irma. In fact, he couldn't understand her openness with me because she barely gave him any decent responses.

Although I didn't know why Irma clammed up with Alan, I told him about the discussion I had with the hairdresser, who knew Irma fairly well. Alan listened intently when I shared what Rosie told me about Irma and her relationship with Sal.

"It sounds as if your visit to the salon reaped more than a bit of pampering," Alan said. "Now you're beautiful *and* you got an earful."

"I'll bet you say that to all of the girls," I teased.

"What? The beautiful part?" Alan grinned. "I reserve that only for you."

"You're such a charmer," I said. "So, tell me the facts. Was Irma's missing knife the murder weapon?"

"You know I can't tell you that," Alan sighed.

"Thank you, officer," I smiled smugly. "Now I'm sure that it was."

"And how, pray-tell, do you make that deduction?"

"You're so predictable," I said with a giggle. "If it wasn't the weapon, you'd say so to shut me up. By evading the question, you confirmed the answer."

Alan raised his eyes to the ceiling and said, "You drive me crazy."

"You still love me anyway," I nodded.

Alan lifted his glass as in a toast. "With all my heart!"

CHAPTER 31

$\mathcal{A}$s planned, Rob, Cole, and Dylan met me at the side door of the cabin after lunch on Saturday. The sunny day took off some of the chill in the drafty structure, though I still advised the boys to keep their jackets on while we worked. After I explained that we needed to remove the spider webs and sweep the debris, I promised that it wouldn't take long if we worked together.

"What a cool place, Mrs. J.," Rob exclaimed. "My mom told me some of the history, so I know that the founder of Aspen Notch built this cabin."

"Yep," I said. "Can you imagine living in just one room?"

"He must have slept in that loft with the ladder," Rob remarked. "Can we go up there?"

"Definitely," I nodded, handing them each a duster. "You can tell me what it looks like."

"You haven't seen it yet?" Cole asked, investigating the sturdiness of the ladder.

"I didn't know if the ladder would hold me," I replied. "Do you want to try it first?"

Cole gave the first few rungs a tug, then shrugged, "Sure, it looks fine."

"Be careful," I advised. "I don't know about the sturdiness of the floor boards up there."

Once he made his way up to the loft, Cole peered over the side with a silly grin. He assured Rob and Dylan that they could come up safely, then he sat on the edge with his legs dangling. I laughed when the other two joined him because they looked like three marionettes waiting for their next gig.

"Come on up, Mrs. J.," Rob said, "but you'd better bring a flashlight. It's kind of dark along the back wall."

"I can use the app on my cell phone," I said, making sure I had it in my jacket pocket before taking the first few steps.

Once I climbed high enough to peer to the back of the loft, I turned on the flashlight, then handed my phone to Dylan, and asked him to shine the light for me to see. I had expected some kind of bed or mattress, but the loft contained nothing, not even many cobwebs, which I considered unusual.

"Take some photos," I said. "I want to show my husband."

Rob snapped a few pictures for me, then the boys pulled out their own phones to capture more images for themselves. When I asked why they didn't use their own flashlight apps, Rob reminded me that it used up their batteries too quickly, which made me smile about the ingenuity of teens.

Satisfied that we found nothing needing disposal in the loft, I stepped off the ladder, then sprayed glass cleaner on the display cabinet. When the boys finished upstairs, they worked on the main floor with me to dust, sweep, and wash windows. After a little more than an hour, pleased with the results, I gave them each a $20 tip and signed their service vouchers.

"Thanks, Mrs. J.," Rob said as he pocketed his money. "We like helping you, especially here in the cabin. I've decided to make this place the focus of my history term paper, but I'll have to do some research about Abe Whitman."

"That's a great idea," I said. "Maybe the library has some good resources."

"I hope so," Rob nodded. "I'll try to go there tomorrow afternoon."

Cole and Dylan started teasing Rob about working in the library on Halloween, so I asked what they planned to research. Neither of them had a clue, but agreed that they'd like to learn more about the founder of Aspen Notch.

"Can you all have the same topic?" I asked.

"Not really," Dylan replied. "At least not the same person. Maybe I could study the lady who sold her candy here because my dad still talks about her."

"I suppose you could count Clara Whitman as a person in history," I nodded. "You could also consider her husband an interesting character since he was Abe Whitman's grandson and died in the Korean War."

"I like war stuff," Cole said, "so I'll do him. Besides, they all have this cabin in common."

"That's true," I agreed. "I hope you'll share with me what information you discover because I've wanted to know more about each of them myself."

I briefly considered telling the boys about Clara's riddles, but decided that they'd only divert them from their studies, and their instructors wanted them to do history research, not solve puzzles. In addition, if Clara had actually done anything sinister, I wouldn't want her misdeeds on display, so I thought it better to keep the knowledge to myself. Of course, I had to first figure out what, if anything, she hid.

Before they departed, Dylan asked if we might permit the three of them to camp in the cabin some night. I remembered how my kids, especially Michael, enjoyed camping, but that was different. He'd set up a tent in the backyard and invite a couple of his buddies to spend the night. I honestly didn't want to take responsibility for three high school students on my property, no matter how much I trusted them.

"I don't think so," I said, shaking my head, "at least, not as we move into the winter months. We can revisit my decision next summer and, maybe by then, I'll have had time to do some of the necessary renovations."

"It's OK, Mrs. J.," Rob assured me. "The cabin needs a lot of work. I noticed that you need to replace some of those loose floor boards in the loft."

"Good to know," I noted, mentally adding it to my list of things to do. "You're each welcome to visit, especially since you might need more photos for your projects."

"That's cool," Dylan stated. "Do you and Officer Jaworski plan to accept trick-or-treaters tomorrow night?"

"Definitely," I smiled. "Do you intend to wear costumes?"

The three of them nodded, then burst into laughter. None of them would divulge what they considered so funny, though I felt sure it had something to do with their outfits.

I'd just have to wait and see.

CHAPTER 32

*W*ith a few hours to myself before having to pick up Sophie at Hickory Glen, I lugged in the groceries that I'd left overnight in the cabin, then Alan called to tell me that he'd pick up a bottle of wine and the fixings for dinner after he met with the crime scene investigator. He wanted something special for our first time cooking in the new kitchen and, by the tone of his voice, I gathered that he intended to surprise me, so I had no idea what he planned.

I returned a call to our real estate agent to make sure that she'd received the documents we'd signed, then clicked Trudi's number in my contacts. Other than an occasional text message, I hadn't touched base with my dear friend since we moved, but I hoped she'd understand once she heard about all of the goings-on around here.

She picked up immediately, saying, "It's about time! I didn't want to bug you during your move, but we haven't spoken in almost a month."

"I know," I replied apologetically. "The days fly by, then I'm exhausted at night. Frankly, I don't feel settled yet, but we'll get there."

"A move is difficult in any circumstances," Trudi noted. "Did you find a painter to tackle the lime green living room?"

I had complained to Trudi about the horrible décor when she helped me pack, so she now seemed pleased to hear about the remarkable transformation of our home, though we still had the upcoming construction of an *en-suite* bathroom. Of course, I told Trudi every detail of the renovations, and she expressed her delight in the progress we'd made.

"How's Aspen Notch?" Trudi asked. "Have you made any friends yet?"

"One or two," I said, "though I'd say that Evelyn Sandler has probably helped me the most. She and her husband moved here just a few years ago, so she knows what it's like to be new in town."

"Is she our age?" Trudi asked.

"Yes," I replied. "Her kids are grown and on their own."

"Good. Then you have some companionship."

"I suppose so," I said, "but the one time we did something together, we found a dead body in the pizza shop."

"Are you kidding me?" Trudi gasped. "You found another dead body?"

Trudi's surprised expression made me laugh, especially since I had to tell her of a similar situation last year when Alan helped clear my name in a theft that turned into a murder probe. Now, in Sal's case, I tried to stay out of Alan's business. After all, he had a reputation to uphold as the town's police chief.

When I relayed all of the relevant details of the gruesome discovery Evelyn and I made, Trudi clicked her tongue. I knew she probably shook her head, and wondered how I managed to get myself involved in such sinister activities, so I wanted to set the record straight.

"Alan's working on the investigation," I assured her, "and he has everything under control. Besides, I need to train the new puppy."

"What new puppy?" Trudi questioned.

"Sophie," I explained. "She belonged to Sal, the dead guy, but his wife asked me to take her because she couldn't handle the pup."

Trudi gave a rueful chuckle, then said, "It sounds as if you're still involved, at least with the wife."

"Her name's Irma D'Angelo," I remarked, "and I feel sorry for her. I'd like to help in some way, but Irma's a challenge."

"She probably needs to grieve," Trudi suggested, "but I'm sure she'll appreciate any kindness you can show her."

Though I agreed verbally, I didn't want to reveal Irma's many quirks. Instead, I switched topics, and asked Trudi about her activities since our move.

"Same old stuff," Trudi said. "We've raked the leaves, and cleared out the garden. In fact, I actually had enough zucchini to whip up a few batches of zucchini bread."

"Save a loaf for me," I pleaded. "We'll drive down there for settlement in a couple of weeks."

"Your house sold?" Trudi exclaimed. "That's fabulous!"

"Contingent on the inspections," I replied, "so pray that everything goes smoothly."

"I'm sure it will," Trudi said. "Have you made plans for Thanksgiving?"

"Alan and I haven't talked about it yet. Now that I have a kitchen, I'd like to host. Would you be able to come?"

"No," Trudi said, "but thanks. Our kids and their families plan to come here, although we want to visit you and see Aspen Notch, perhaps in the spring. Winter will arrive soon and, as you know, those mountain passes get treacherous."

"I remember," I said, thinking of the frightening pile-up I experienced last year.

In the end, we decided to play it by ear. I promised to let Trudi know our settlement date and told her that we'd stop by at some point during our trip. Our conversation ended before I realized that I'd forgotten to tell her about Clara's riddles. Since Trudi always enjoyed puzzles, I'd intended to ask if she had any helpful insights, but it would have to wait until our next phone chat since I needed to pick up Sophie.

After texting Alan that I went to get Sophie, I grabbed my purse and jacket, then decided to turn on the lamps in the living room to make the place welcoming for Alan. As I glanced out the front window, I noticed an older model blue sedan at the curb across the street. I thought it odd because the church had its own parking lot and the driver had pulled up near a fire hydrant.

The driver, whom I couldn't identify, wore a ball cap that concealed his or her eyes and hair, and the tinted car windows made it difficult to see the interior. Nonetheless, the person seemed interested in the log cabin.

Shrugging off my curiosity, I proceeded with the drive to Hickory Glen after making sure that I'd securely locked the back and front doors of the house. I told myself that the lurker just wanted to check out old Abe's cabin, but I thought it better to be safe than sorry.

I had second thoughts after stopping at a traffic light, because I noticed the same blue sedan two cars behind me. Was it coincidence or did the driver follow me?

CHAPTER 33

*S*ophie provided good company for the short trip home from Hickory Glen. Happy to see me, she readily hopped into the back seat of my car, and I chatted with her all the way. I occasionally glanced in the rear-view mirror to check her reaction, as well as to determine if anyone followed me, but I no longer saw the blue sedan.

When I pulled into our driveway next to Alan's vehicle, I noticed the western sky with its streaks of crimson and gold intertwining among the billowy clouds. It still amazed me to watch the sun disappear so quickly behind the mountains, and I hated the thought of adjusting the clocks back to standard time in just a few days. Despite the inevitable early sunsets, at least I'd have Sophie's company while Alan finished his police duties.

Before heading to the house, I checked the mailbox at the curb and permitted Sophie to water the nearby bush. Why Alan never retrieved our mail remained a mystery to me, though he admitted he just never thought about it. It seemed like a flimsy excuse, I thought as I stuffed everything into my handbag, then led Sophie through our front door. I'd barely unhooked the leash before she bounded to Alan in the kitchen.

"Good to see you, Sophie-girl," Alan chuckled, releasing her from the harness. "You, too, Mrs. J."

While Sophie explored, I gave Alan a smooch, discreetly observing the counters and sink with a quick glance. It appeared that Alan decided to prepare his seafood specialty, because he had jumbo shrimp defrosting in a colander, and he'd emptied a pound of lump crabmeat into the mixing bowl.

"Stuffed shrimp?" I asked. "Yum!"

Alan grinned his pride, saying, "We'll have crab cakes and scallops to accompany it. The only thing you need to do is set the table and show me where I can find the baking pans."

"Gladly," I replied, searching for the box under the dining room table that contained kitchen ware, "though it appears that you already explored."

"I needed the bowl and colander," Alan quipped. "What's a guy to do?"

I laughed until Sophie decided to search the cartons with me. Apparently, she found cardboard more entertaining than her toys, so I pushed her aside. To distract her, I filled her water bowl, then prepared another with kibbles, but it didn't take long for her to devour her food, return to the boxes, and tug one to the living room.

"She's going to make a mess," I said in dismay.

"She's a puppy," Alan chuckled. "That's what they do."

In the end, I decided to let Sophie have her fun. With the open floor plan, I could watch her capers while I assisted Alan, though he eventually suggested that I pour the wine while he butterflied the shrimp, which I recognized as his polite way to tell me he didn't need my help. After we clinked glasses, I moved to the sofa and retrieved the mail from my purse.

I set aside the monthly bills, already beginning to arrive, then glanced at the ads and flyers before making a pile on the coffee table for the trash. The final piece of mail, enclosed in a sealed, unmarked business envelope, looked like a bill for trash services until I opened it to find a death threat written in red crayon with large upper-case lettering.

MIND YOUR OWN BUSINESS OR U WILL DIE

With shaking hands, I showed the letter to Alan. His brow furrowed and his eyes darkened as he asked, "Who's this from?"

"I don't know," I gulped. "Was it meant for me or you?"

"Who's it addressed to?" Alan questioned.

"There's no address or stamp," I replied. "Someone must have left it in our mailbox."

"Place it in a freezer bag," Alan advised. "I'll submit it to forensics tomorrow."

"My prints are all over it," I sighed.

"Don't worry about that," Alan stated, "but we need the envelope, as well."

I hurriedly grabbed the envelope and bills before Sophie got to them, although she already had strewn the flyers and ads across the living room floor with bits of cardboard intermingled. I didn't laugh.

"Bad girl!" I scolded with my voice louder than necessary.

"She's just a playful puppy," Alan reminded me. He wiped his hands on a towel, then took the envelope from me. "I'll take care of the matter later."

"I need to know if someone's out to get me," I said.

"What have you done?" he asked.

Staring at Alan, incredulous about his insinuation, I did everything to hold my tongue, knowing that I'd regret anything said in anger. Instead, I grabbed Sophie by the collar and led her to the back door. Her tail wagged with anticipation while I put on my jacket. Testily, I told Alan that we'd be in the yard until I cooled down.

Oblivious to my mood, Sophie romped while I paced after I made sure the work crew had firmly closed the gate. I had no doubt that someone meant the letter for me. Worse, Alan acted as if it were no big deal, and his assumption that I could have done something to warrant a death threat made me furious.

Alan gave me 10 minutes to seethe, then came to find me. Sophie brought him a stick that he tossed for her to fetch before he tried, unsuccessfully, to put his arms around me.

"I'm upset and frightened, Alan. Someone cased our place this afternoon, then followed me to Hickory Glen. Now, we get a threatening letter and you make it seem as if I'm to blame!"

"I'm sorry for my poor choice of words, but what do you mean that someone followed you?"

"I noticed an older model blue sedan parked across the street, but I couldn't see the driver's face. Anyway, the person followed me when I went to pick up Sophie."

"Did you get a license plate number?" Alan asked.

"No," I sighed.

Alan slowly shook his head, then reached to embrace me. This time I let him, and he comforted me with his calm words of assurance that he'd handle the situation. Finally, he suggested that we go inside.

Alan's whistle to call Sophie coincided with the screech of tires from the street, then the sound of glass shattering. My scream pierced the air while Alan sprinted to the gate. Sophie cowered in fear at my feet.

"Let's go in, girl," I said, trying to put on a brave front for the puppy. "Everything's fine."

Even I didn't believe my words.

CHAPTER 34

*A*lan returned to the house carrying large shards from a broken bottle, which he wrapped in the shredded flyers before placing them in the trash. He put to rest my fear that someone may have broken the side window in the log cabin, and assured me that we had no damage to our property, though I still didn't like our place targeted with vandalism.

"It's mischief night," Alan reminded me. "I caught sight of the car with teens smashing bottles on a joy-ride, so I'd better cruise the neighborhoods. Give me 20 minutes, then you can put the baking trays in the oven. We'll eat when I return."

I nodded my agreement, and watched Alan don his police vest and jacket. Only a month ago, I encouraged him to accept the position of police chief, but now I regretted that. If anything happened to Alan, it would devastate me, and I'd rue the day that we ever decided to relocate to Aspen Notch.

"Be safe," I said, almost in a whisper.

Alan kissed me, then said, "I'll be fine. Please keep an eye on the stuffed shrimp and scallops because they get rubbery if they're overcooked."

I locked the door, then tidied the living room. Sophie, not happy that I removed her piles of torn cardboard, nipped at my heels as I tossed them into the trash. With time on my hands, I emptied a carton containing kitchen items, and placed everything into the dishwasher except a serving platter and bowl. After rinsing and drying those, I set the oven to pre-heat.

I poured another glass of wine, then sat at the table with the threatening letter. Sophie laid at my feet, asleep in no time.

What had I done to deserve such a warning? I discovered a dead body and, as my civic duty, I called Alan, the police chief. I emptied Sal's trash can, which I probably shouldn't have done, but I had good intentions. Then, I visited Irma, merely as a kind deed. Did someone construe it as something else?

The scrawl in red crayon appeared child-like, obviously meant to mislead. Most adults didn't have crayons lying around, unless they had children or grandchildren, though anyone could easily purchase a box.

Most people, including me, probably kept a pack of the ordinary loose-leaf paper, so its use didn't surprise me. I tried holding it up to the light, but I didn't detect any indentations of previous writing. Of course, forensics might have better tools to determine such clues.

I really couldn't think of any person who had anything against me. Though not particularly fond of Lou Greene or his wife, since he stuck his nose in Alan's business and she was a snob, I hadn't done or said anything to upset them. Irma may not have seemed pleased with me for barging into her house with groceries, but she liked me well enough to ask me to take Sophie.

I shook my head in frustration, wondering if the note was merely a childish prank for mischief night. Cole, as a jokester, surely had access to loose-leaf paper for his assignments. Maybe he also had an old box of crayons. I could see him thinking it fun to tease me, not realizing that I wouldn't find it amusing.

After I safely stored the letter and envelope in a zip-lock bag and placed it on top of the refrigerator for safe keeping, the oven beeped its readiness for Alan's gourmet medley. I placed the tray in the oven, set the timer, dished up the container of coleslaw Alan purchased, then waited for him to return home for dinner.

SOPHIE SLEPT at our feet while Alan and I enjoyed a glass of wine after our feast. Alan told me of the stern warning that he gave to the teens responsible for causing the ruckus, then mentioned that he'd also kept his eyes out for an older model blue sedan. He found no vehicles matching my description.

"I'm probably over-reacting," I said apologetically. "It's possible that I merely saw a tourist looking at Abe's cabin and, maybe, just coincidence that the person ended up behind me at the light."

"Could be," Alan nodded. "What about the letter?"

"I've racked my brain to find a rationale for it," I said, "but I can't think of anything, unless someone played a prank on us for mischief night."

Alan raised an eyebrow while I explained my theory. He agreed with the possibility that someone sent it as a joke, but he didn't intend to dismiss it. It wasn't funny, and the person who sent it needed a strong reprimand, so he'd still drop it off at forensics in the morning.

"How's the investigation going?" I questioned.

"We have nothing conclusive," Alan sighed. "They found only Sal's prints on the knife; otherwise, the weapon was clean."

"Did you ask Irma about her missing knife?" I asked.

"She didn't cooperate very much," Alan replied, "though she told me it went missing a long while ago. She assumed Sal took it to work."

"It's hard to get anything out of her," I nodded. "Irma's a tough cookie."

"You seem to have a knack," Alan said. "Do you want to try again?"

I grinned, saying, "Are you asking for my help?"

Alan took a sip of his wine, then said, "I guess I am."

"Good answer," I replied, dividing the last dregs of the bottle between the two of us. "You can deputize me."

"Let's not get too carried away," Alan chuckled. "Just see what you can get out of Irma."

"OK," I nodded, "but don't forget that we still have Sal's trash."

"It's inconclusive," Alan shrugged. "Without a full name, anything we guess is pure speculation."

"It's more than you currently have going for you," I said.

"Granted," Alan agreed, "but conjecture wouldn't hold up in court. We'd need something or someone to corroborate, and I don't believe that will happen."

Alan's statement ended the discussion. He carried our dinner plates to the sink, while I put leftovers away. We'd once made a deal that whoever did the cooking didn't have to do the dishes. At least, that's how it worked when Alan served as the chef, though not so much the other way around.

Alan settled himself in the recliner with the TV remote while I loaded the dishwasher. Sophie awoke and moved herself to the kitchen, obviously looking for scraps. As I washed the counter, my thoughts returned to the papers from Sal's trash can and the money in his safe. What if someone wanted to meet Sal for some kind of payoff? Could Sal have operated money laundering or a blackmail scheme that led to his death?

Alan, already asleep in his favorite chair, opened an eye when I took Sophie for the day's last visit to the back yard. After checking that Alan had securely latched the gate, I let her do her business. With a full moon casting shadows among the trees, I wouldn't allow my imagination to run away with me. Instead, I called to Sophie in a clear voice, and made sure that any invisible lurkers heard me praising my dog.

I didn't know how much of a watchdog Sophie would become, but her presence consoled me.

CHAPTER 35

*A*fter brunch on Sunday at Dottie's café with Evelyn and Marty Sandler, Alan and I decided to go our separate ways. He wanted to drop off the threatening letter at the county's forensics department since they always had someone on duty, then cruise the neighborhoods. I needed to go grocery shopping to stock the empty pantry and refrigerator.

Alan took me home first, pulling into the driveway and reminding me to touch base with Irma D'Angelo when I had a chance. He preferred that I go sooner, rather than later, since he felt that Irma may have additional pertinent information that she hadn't realized would help the investigation.

"Do you want me to talk about the money in Sal's safe or the knife?" I questioned.

"The money was clean," Alan replied. "It's not a factor."

I gave Alan one of my looks, and said, "Are you kidding? It's pretty incriminating."

Alan shook his head. "Irma didn't even know about the amount of cash until she opened the safe. She may have been angry about the stash after the fact, but it wouldn't give her a motive for murder."

"I guess you're right," I nodded. "So, what do you want to know?"

"Ask her if Sal had any enemies," Alan suggested, "things like that."

"Anything she says to me would be hearsay," I frowned, "and it wouldn't hold up in court."

"True," Alan agreed, "but you can use your phone to get a digital recording."

I rolled my eyes. "Come on, Alan. Get real. I can barely find the flashlight app, let alone one to do an audio recording. What am I supposed to do? Say, 'Wait a minute, Irma. I need to record you.'"

Alan laughed. "OK. Forget the audio. Just get her to open up to you. If anything raises a red flag, I'll bring her in."

That suited me fine. After waving him off, I went in to see if Sophie had done any damage while we left her alone. I planned to let her have a run in the yard, then finalize my shopping list, and I'd buy a few items for Irma so I had a reason to visit her.

I didn't want to get to Irma's house too late since I had a feeling that she disliked Halloween, and probably wouldn't even answer her doorbell. Sophie had a disgruntled expression when I cut her romp short, but I promised to make it up to her later.

SOPHIE GREETED me with gusto when I brought in the groceries. I looked around for evidence of puppy mania, but found nothing out of the ordinary. I let her out in the yard while putting away the perishables, and watched from the kitchen window every few minutes to make sure she did her business. When I called her in, she dragged a stick, struggling to fit it through the door.

Laughing at Sophie's antics, I decided to permit the stick in the house. If anything, it would keep her content while I took two bags of food to Irma. When I put on my jacket, she gave me a look that made me feel guilty for leaving her again. I'm not sure she fully understood my promise to return home soon, but she resumed gnawing the stick and spitting out bits of wood on the kitchen floor.

Once again, Irma took a long time to answer her door. I understood her difficulty moving around, but I figured she also needed to process if she wanted visitors. No doubt, she arranged her chair to have a view of anyone standing on her porch, so I sighed my relief when she finally responded.

"What do you want?" Irma muttered, eyeing the bags I carried.

I pulled open the storm door and let myself in, saying "I picked up a few things for you at the grocery store. Maybe one of these days you'd like to come with me so you can make your own choices."

Irma didn't bar me from full entry so I brought the bags to the kitchen counter and began to unpack them. She followed, then carefully observed each item I removed.

"How much do I owe you?" Irma asked, reaching into her pocketbook.

I gave her the receipt only because I knew she wanted to pay and wouldn't accept charity, then I loaded the ice cream and TV dinners into the freezer. I left the box of donuts and bag of Halloween candy by the sink.

"I can only stay a few minutes," I said, hoping that she'd invite me to sit in the living room. "They tell me that we'll get a lot of trick-or-treaters tonight."

"Don't turn on your porch light," Irma shrugged. "That's what I do so they don't ring my doorbell."

"I'm tempted," I replied, "especially since I found a death threat in my mailbox yesterday, but you and I both have treats on hand in case we change our minds."

Irma's face turned ashen. She hobbled to the pile of mail on her dining room table and showed me a similar piece of loose-leaf paper with the crayoned message. Each of us had received the same warning.

"Geez," I exclaimed. "Did you call my husband? The police need to know about this."

"Why bother?" Irma queried. "I'm pretty sure the chief thinks I killed Sal. When he visited me, he kept asking about our missing knife."

"I received the exact same note," I remarked, "right down to the crayon's red color. He took it to forensics for examination today."

Shuffling to her chair, Irma told me to take a seat. I left the letter on her table and sat across from her. Although she hid her emotions well, I knew that Irma must have felt the same fear I did to receive such a threat.

"What's it mean, Sue?" Irma questioned. "Mind my own business? That's all I ever do. Maybe someone knew that I spoke to you, and you're the wife of the police chief."

"I don't know what it means," I sighed. "Quite honestly, I wondered who I could have angered in town, then I thought it might be a mischief night prank."

Irma shook her head. "No. It's somehow tied to Sal. I feel it in my bones. Maybe it's about all that money in our safe. How'd Sal get hold of that much cash?"

"I'm probably not supposed to tell you this," I replied, "but Alan said that the money's clean. Did Sal gamble?"

Again, Irma shook her head. "Sal thought that anyone stupid enough to risk losing their hard-earned money deserved to land in the poor-house. He'd never have done that."

I hated to offer other alternatives but Irma seemed ready and willing to talk. Taking a deep breath, I asked if Sal could have been involved in money laundering.

"What's that?" Irma asked.

"When someone has dirty money, like a person who sells a lot of illegal drugs, he can't deposit the cash in a bank without raising red flags. Sometimes a foreign bank will accept it, but the feds stay vigilant, so it's easier to use a legitimate business to cleanse the money."

"Would Sal have known about that?" she asked.

"Probably," I nodded.

Irma used another expletive about her husband. I tried to deflect some of her anger by explaining my theory that Sal may have agreed to meet someone for either a drop-off or pick-up of cash. Maybe they argued. Perhaps Sal threatened to turn the person over to authorities. Unless we determined who had an appointment with Sal, we'd never know.

"Do the cops think someone killed him with the knife from our butcher's block?" Irma questioned.

"The murder weapon matches your other knives," I said.

A tear fell to Irma's cheek, and she stated, "As much as I'd thought about leaving Sal, I didn't kill my husband."

"Did Sal have any enemies?" I asked.

"If he did," Irma replied, "he didn't tell me about them. He hardly spoke to me unless it was in anger."

"Did Sal abuse you?" I queried.

"He never raised a hand to me, but he had a nasty tongue. Sal didn't let me forget that I caused our son's death."

"It wasn't your fault," I replied softly, reaching for Irma's hand. "You have to believe that."

Irma shook her head, pulling away to reach for a tissue. As she composed herself, I could see that Irma again began to put up barriers and close down, so I knew I wouldn't get more information at this point. I gathered my purse and asked if I may visit her again in a day or two.

"I don't care," Irma shrugged, with her face a mask, "but give that horrible letter to your husband. I want it out of the house."

CHAPTER 36

While I backed out of Irma's driveway, I had a weird sense that someone watched me. I didn't know if I felt paranoia or a real threat, but didn't want any chance that a menacing person would follow me home. I headed away from my house, and watched through the rear-view mirror. Sure enough, I saw the old blue sedan a block behind me, and when I turned right, its driver did the same.

Reaching for my phone, I pressed Alan's number. Thank heavens, he answered on the first ring. I tried to keep my voice calm when I said, "The blue sedan's behind me, so I need help."

"Where are you?" Alan questioned.

"On Elm Street, approaching the park with Abe's statue. Are you still cruising?"

"Yes, I'm just a few blocks away. Pull over and stay put," Alan advised.

Hands shaking, I swerved to the curb, then slowed to a stop, as I kept my eyes on the other vehicle the entire time. The driver initially slowed, then sped past me, so I only caught the first three digits on the license plate. Within minutes, Alan's police cruiser appeared.

Rolling down my window, I waved for Alan to follow the sedan, but instead, he pulled behind me. In frustration and with a split-second decision, I gunned the engine and took off in pursuit of the jerk who did his or her best to frighten me.

I heard Alan following behind me with his sirens blaring, though I finally had to give up in the center of town. Too many people milled about to risk a high-speed chase, so I pulled to the curb in front of the library, then waited for Alan, as if I anticipated a speeding ticket. As he approached my car, I could see that he didn't look very happy.

"What were you thinking?" he asked in a stern voice, yet his eyes showed deep concern.

"I thought I could catch the creep," I explained, "but I lost sight of the vehicle."

"Are you crazy?" Alan sputtered. "You didn't know if the perp had a weapon, and you could have been killed."

"I'm sorry," I sighed, "but I tried to tell you to follow the jerk."

"I needed to see if you were all right," Alan stated, "then you pulled that stunt."

"I know," I muttered. "I said I was sorry. Please see if you can find the vehicle. I think it was a Chevy, and the license plate started with Y9P."

Alan frowned, shaking his head. "I'd like you to go home, and don't open the door for anyone."

I watched Alan return to his vehicle, then pulled out into the town traffic. By the time I reached our driveway, I could see a string of early trick-or-treaters emerge on our street, so I knew what I intended to do.

I flipped on the lights at our front door before Sophie met me with wet kisses. After I gave her a few minutes in the yard, I brought a bucket of candy bars to the entry hall, then she and I waited to greet the Halloween revelers.

I had no intention of allowing myself to be a victim.

∽

SOPHIE and I sat watching TV when Alan arrived home about 9 o'clock. Although he frowned to see the porch light still on and a nearly empty bucket of candy on a chair next to the open front door, he seemed in a better frame of mind. Nonetheless, he said, "You don't listen," as Sophie and I greeted him.

"Sometimes I do," I sighed, "but it's our first Halloween in Aspen Notch, and I couldn't ignore the trick-or-treaters."

"I only wanted you to stay safe," Alan replied.

"I know," I nodded, "and I appreciate your concern, but I can't let that person in the blue sedan intimidate me. Anyway, you should have seen Rob, Dylan, and Cole, all in costume. They dressed as mountain men, with fake pelts thrown over their shoulders."

"Like the town's founder?" Alan queried.

"Yes," I nodded. "They wanted me to vote for which one best represented Abe Whitman."

"Who won?" Alan questioned.

"I called it a tie," I smiled, "then gave them each a few extra candy bars. I also asked if any of them played a prank on me yesterday."

Alan frowned. "You told them you had a death threat?"

"Of course not," I sighed. "I just mentioned that I received 'a mysterious letter in the mail.' They obviously didn't know what I meant."

"I'm not sure if that should relieve me or not," Alan said. "We still don't have many leads."

"Any luck finding the car?" I asked, thinking I should hold off before telling Alan about Irma's death threat.

"No," Alan replied. "I'll run the description through the division of motor vehicles tomorrow. Did you eat?"

"Just a Snickers," I replied, "but I have an Italian sausage and ziti casserole in the oven. Do you want some?"

"Sure," Alan nodded. "I'm famished."

Sophie moved to her spot under the table while Alan and I ate. He served himself a large portion, then placed a napkin in his collar so he wouldn't mess up his uniform tie. The maneuver always made me giggle.

"You look tired," I said, dishing a smaller serving for me. I almost forgot that I had bought a small loaf of Italian bread, so I quickly cut a few slices and brought out the butter dish.

"I'm OK," Alan said. "I had a long day, but I'm glad we had no incidents other than yours tonight. Did you have a chance to talk to Irma?"

I reached for my purse on the chair next to me and took out the death threat that Irma had received. Alan gawked at it with a look of disbelief on his face, then exclaimed, "Cheese and crackers! Are you kidding me? She received the same letter?"

I nodded, saying, "Irma seemed pretty upset about it. We had a good conversation before she put her guard up again, but I'll tell you one thing. She didn't kill Sal."

Alan listened intently while I told him all that Irma and I talked about. Even as he sopped up his Marinara sauce with the last slice of bread, he occasionally nodded his approval of what I'd said to her. When I finally finished, he asked what made me think about money laundering.

"I don't know," I said. "I guess I remembered something I'd heard on the news about the indictment of a government official for laundering money. Do you think it's possible?"

"Anything's possible," Alan replied. "It's a long-shot, but we're located not far from syndicated crime. Do you remember your friend, Earl? He had ties to the mob."

"Don't remind me," I said, thinking back to the murder investigation in Dunmore last year. I had gullibly fallen for Earl and almost died because of it.

While Alan cleared the table, I reminded him that the papers from Sal's trash contained a clue about whom Sal met. In addition, I felt certain that the person feared identification by Irma and me.

I rinsed our plates and put them in the dishwasher, then said, "Did you tell anyone that I had looked through Sal's waste basket?"

"I mentioned it to Lou," Alan replied. When he noticed my expression, he quickly added, "He's the mayor, for God's sake, so I had to keep him informed."

"Therein lies our answer," I stated. "Either Lou Greene hired someone to threaten Irma and me, or he blabbed to the murderer."

Alan's loud guffaw woke Sophie, who then mistakenly thought she could counter-surf while I put the leftover casserole into a plastic container. I gently pushed her down before putting a few pieces of sausage in her bowl.

"Sorry," Alan said when he saw my frown. "I don't know what you have against Lou Greene, but the mayor deserves our respect."

"Evelyn Sandler told me to be careful whom I trust in this town," I said, "so I'll give you the same advice. If I were you, I'd also look into Bernie Calamito's business dealings because he was the last person to see Sal D'Angelo alive."

"Says who?" Alan questioned.

"Says me," I replied with finality.

CHAPTER 37

*N*ovember rolled in with a cold northerly wind blowing most of the remaining brown leaves off the trees. Alan left shortly after breakfast to take Irma's warning letter to forensics, then John and Deke arrived while I tidied the bedroom. I could hardly wait for them to begin working on the *en-suite* bathroom and walk-in closet, so Alan and I could soon return to the master bedroom.

Deke showed me the construction plans for the remodel, as well as pictures of the vanity, sink, and toilet he'd selected for the space. He handed me a catalog with the shower and fixtures, and suggested that I choose styles that I'd like, then John said he'd match the color of the bedroom, if that's what I wanted. It all seemed a bit overwhelming, but nothing I couldn't handle.

When the demolition crew arrived, Sophie acted like the welcoming committee. She excitedly jumped up on each of the guys, and they responded with belly rubs. I made a mental note to reinforce the meaning of *"Down!"* since she obviously lacked proper manners.

Deke directed the men to the back room, then reminded me that they needed to remove walls and flooring. I assured him that I intended to take Sophie out to the cabin while we awaited the locksmith and chimney inspector.

Deke stopped short, saying, "Why a locksmith?"

"We don't have a key for the rusty padlock on the front door of the old cabin," I explained, "so I'll have him change the locks on both doors. Besides, it'll give us added security."

Deke shrugged, then agreed that I made a wise decision, though his eyes said otherwise. I figured he thought of the added cost for something not necessary, but it didn't matter. Changing the locks gave me a sense of well-being.

John placed drop cloths in the hall to begin painting the trim as I retrieved my heavy winter jacket from the closet and, though we both laughed when Sophie dragged one of the tarps across the living room floor, I knew she kept him from his work. I scolded Sophie, then said, "I'm sorry, John. We'll be out of your way in just a second, but I need to find my gloves."

"No problem," John chuckled. "She sure is a frisky pup. In fact, she reminds me of a dog I had as a kid. I thought it the worst day of my life when she crossed over the rainbow bridge."

"I know what you mean," I nodded. "We had a family dog during my kids' youth. I swore I'd never go through it again, but look at me now."

John smiled, saying, "The puppy part's a challenge, but once she settles down, you'll like having her around."

"I guess so," I said. "Would you ever get another dog?"

"Definitely, if I had a family. I thought I'd be married with a couple of kids by now, but it wasn't in the cards for me."

"You never met the right gal?" I questioned.

John turned away, busily unfolding another drop cloth, and I kicked myself for not minding my own business. Finally, I located my gloves in my jacket pocket where they had probably stayed since last winter. My "aha moment" coincided with John's response.

"I thought I'd met the right woman," John remarked, "but she didn't want to get serious and broke up with me, so I felt like a fool."

"Dottie Burkeholder?" I asked.

John's eyes opened wide. "What makes you say that?"

"I told Dottie about you and Deke," I explained, "because she asked about our renovations. She said she didn't know Deke, but had dated you awhile back."

"What'd she say about me?" John quipped.

"She spoke of you fondly," I grinned. "You know, Dottie hasn't dated anyone else. You should take yourself over to her café and have a cup of coffee or something because she might have more interest now that Rob's older."

"I'll think about it," John replied, busily opening his can of paint.

Smart enough to know that our conversation ended, at least for now, I told Sophie to come to the cabin with me. It made me smile to think that I may have reignited a spark of interest, and I wondered how Dottie would react if John paid her a visit. Time would tell.

SOPHIE GREETED the chimney inspector with the same gusto as all of our guests. While he gave Sophie her expectant belly rubs, I explained that Alan and I needed his assurance that we could safely use both the house fireplace and the one in Abe's cabin. I let Sophie play in the yard while I learned the intricacies of older chimneys.

When the locksmith arrived, I told him that I wanted new keyed deadbolts on both doors of the cabin. Although he showed me samples of electronic fixtures, I insisted on ones that would reflect the historic value of the place. He had the perfect solution in his truck and, after my approval, he immediately began the installation.

After checking on Sophie, I returned my attention to the chimney inspector. He assured me that we had no blockage in either chimney and the flues worked properly. Because of the age of the chimney in the old cabin, however, he suggested that I might consider a wood stove insert in the hearth or use an electric space heater.

"Both are great options," I replied, "but I'm not sure if the electrical wiring is up to code."

"Have an electrician check it out," he advised. "Here's the card for a guy I know who can get you a good deal on a wood-burning stove, so give him a call."

I promised to follow-up, then wrote out a check for his services. In my opinion, peace of mind was well worth the cost. By the time he left, the locksmith grabbed my ear.

"I considered you and Officer Jaworski lucky to get this place. I had my eye on it, but my wife nixed the idea because she thought it'd cost too much to make the house livable. Still, its history amazes me."

I nodded my agreement, but silently thought that he had a very smart wife. When I asked if he'd known Clara Whitman, he shook his head as he explained that he and his wife moved from New York City about 10 years ago. They thought Aspen Notch would provide a safer environment to raise their kids, though they now had doubts about their decision.

Remembering that he'd changed the locks on the pizza shop after Sal's murder, I tried to offer reassurance, saying, "From what I've heard, Aspen Notch has no crime. It was just a freak incident last week."

"Who told you we had no crime in our town?" he asked. "The mayor and his cronies? Why do you think I have a booming business? I'm just saying, be careful."

I offered a party-line reply when I said, "Of course, the mayor highlights the virtues of living in Aspen Notch. He told us that our town needed only one cop when he hired Alan."

"Think about it," he replied. "No offense intended, but what town hires a stranger passing through to serve as the chief of police? I know your husband had plenty of experience and the right credentials, but like most things in Aspen Notch, only a few chosen ones have a say in any of the important decisions around here."

I thought it better to keep my mouth shut about my own opinion of Lou Greene. Instead, I asked how he'd improve safety in our town.

"If I were your husband, I'd insist on a few more officers, maybe part-time, at first, until the manager could realign the budget. No one wants to see taxes go up, but I'd suggest at least one cop on foot patrol in the town center."

"It makes sense to me," I agreed. "In fact, I'll mention your recommendation to my husband. Maybe he can make a case for a larger police force to the mayor."

"With this town council, I doubt it will fly, but there's still a chance if the police chief stands his ground. Anyway, I'm done here. Do you want the old padlock for posterity's sake?"

"Sure," I said, writing out a check, "and I appreciate your candid advice."

I tested the keys in both locks, and gave a thumbs-up as the locksmith backed into the street. With a sense of relief, I felt that I'd accomplished two important tasks and still had the day ahead of me. I just had to figure out what to do with Sophie for the afternoon.

Though I had checked on Sophie from the cabin window several times earlier, I'd focused my attention elsewhere for at least the past half hour. Still, each time I looked, Sophie seemed content in the far corner of the yard.

Finally, after the chimney inspector and the locksmith departed, I took the time to see what captured Sophie's interest. Upon closer inspection, I found that she had dug a huge hole, at least a foot deep.

"No, Sophie!" I said firmly. "No digging."

Sophie ignored me despite my unsuccessful attempt to distract her by tossing a stick. With dirt flying everywhere, she continued to paw the ground.

Suddenly, I thought about Clara's riddles. Did Sophie find something buried? My heart thumped as I gazed into the hole to see the corner of a wooden object.

I prayed it wouldn't contain bones.

CHAPTER 38

*G*rabbing a trowel from the shed, I got down on my knees to help Sophie widen her hole. Once I could maneuver my fingers under the outer edges of the box, I tugged to release it from its tomb, wedged between two woody stems that Sophie must have tried to reach. It made me chuckle to realize that she merely dug for tree roots, yet discovered something much more important.

Finally, the earth released its grip and I brought the box to the light of day. After brushing off the dirty exterior with my hands, I thought it looked like a man's plain wooden jewelry box with a simple metal latch that had rusted over the years. In order to examine it more carefully without Sophie's attempt to grab it from me, I carried it to Abe's cabin, though I called for her to follow me.

I knew at a glance that the box was too small to contain bones, which gave me the confidence to open it without the fear of making some gruesome discovery. Using the old cabin key from my keyring as a wedge, I carefully pried the latch open and stared at the contents. Inside were Abe's grandson's dog tags, an army knife, two silver medals with their citations, a couple of letters addressed to Clara, a faded photo, a man's watch, some gold cufflinks, and an envelope containing $100 in small bills.

Pulling out my phone, I texted Alan. *Sophie found a buried treasure. It must be Clara's silver and gold.*

Alan responded with just a thumbs-up emoji, so I figured he probably didn't even remember Clara's riddle.

The photo, a wedding picture in sepia tones, showed a smiling couple I assumed were Clara and her deceased husband. The love letters, short and sweet, came from a young soldier who promised to return home soon. My heart ached for Clara, knowing that her dreams went unfulfilled, and she buried all that remained of her dear husband.

I returned the contents to the box, wondering if I should put it back in its resting place, though I wanted to show it to Alan first. I thought Deke might also find it interesting, though he had too much to manage today to give it more than a passing glance, and I couldn't take it to the house because of the chaos. Instead, I decided to put the box in the trunk of my car.

After locking the cabin, I told Sophie we'd go for a ride, so she readily hopped into the back seat, anticipating a new adventure. We shared a fast-food hamburger as I relished the heat of the car, then I drove to the pet store since she could come in with me. To Sophie's delight, I purchased a bunch of toys to keep her occupied, doggie treats, and a Frisbee for the yard.

Still too early to return home and too cold to stay outside, I cruised the streets to search for the blue Chevy, to no avail, so I figured the creep probably kept the car hidden in a garage. When I approached the police station and saw Alan's vehicle in front, I decided to see if he'd made any headway with the search.

Alan, seated at his desk when Sophie and I entered, stared intently at the computer, with his brow furrowed as it often did when he concentrated. I hated to disturb him, but Sophie pulled on the leash, then greeted him with a bounding leap. Alan's surprised grin assured me that he didn't mind the intrusion.

"Sorry to bother you," I apologized. "We need a place to hang until the work crew finishes the demolition. Do you mind?"

"No problem," Alan replied. "What did you mean when you texted about a buried treasure?"

"Our puppy's a digger," I chuckled. "She likes to chew on tree roots."

"What did she unearth?" Alan queried.

"A man's jewelry box," I said. "It's in the trunk of the car, but I'll get it if you can keep an eye on Sophie."

When I returned with the box and opened it to show Alan the contents, he gave a soft whistle. Sophie thought he meant it for her, and she stopped her exploration of the police station to return to Alan.

"This is really cool," Alan smiled. "Good job, Sophie. Do you plan to donate it to the historical society?"

"I don't know," I said. "I thought about burying it again. What do you think?"

"I'd give it to the town," Alan said, "unless you decide to keep it as an artifact in the cabin if you ever wanted to open up for tours or something."

"That's a good idea," I nodded. "By the way, the locksmith replaced the locks on the cabin, and the chimney inspector gave his approval to use the fireplaces, but I want to ask Deke to have an electrician determine if we could use space heaters, rather than heat the cabin with a fire in the hearth."

Alan agreed, then said, "It sounds as if you accomplished a lot, but I can't say the same about me."

"No luck with the motor vehicle registration?" I asked.

"I'm still working on it," Alan sighed. "Are you sure it had Pennsylvania tags?"

I shook my head, saying, "Not really. I only focused on the numbers."

"Y9P is just not enough to go on," Alan noted. "There are thousands of vehicles with those first three digits, so trying to find it will take time."

I nodded my understanding, then asked, "Any news from forensics about the warning letters?"

"They're working on Irma's," Alan replied. "Since our fingerprints are in the data base, they determined that you and I held the loose-leaf page, but otherwise, it's clean."

Still, I pressed, "Did they find any trace of indentations on them? Maybe they noticed previous writing from the pad."

"No," Alan replied, "though they might catch something from Irma's letter."

My sigh came from frustration more than anything else. Every aspect of the investigation led to a dead end. Alan needed a little luck on his side because his reputation rode on his ability to find Sal's killer.

I noticed the stack of papers from Sal's waste basket on the corner of Alan's desk, though it didn't appear that he'd done much to sort through the pile. I began to ask his impression of them when Bernie Calamito walked in, and of course, Sophie ran to greet him.

"I just stopped by to chat," Bernie chuckled as he reached to pet Sophie. "It's good to see you again, Sue, though it looks as if you got yourself a dog."

I hadn't seen Bernie since his introduction to us a month ago, yet he remained friendly and outgoing. I watched for any signs of guilt or nervousness, but saw nothing of the sort.

"Have you been away?" I asked. "I thought I'd see you in town and, in fact, I hoped to meet your wife."

"Gladys has felt under the weather," Bernie replied. "She insisted that I give her some peace, so I went to Jersey to visit the kids."

"Sorry to hear that," I remarked. "Did you leave before or after your meeting with Sal D'Angelo?"

Bernie reacted immediately, as did Alan. For that matter, they both had shocked expressions after my flippant question, although Bernie composed himself quickly.

"What meeting?" Bernie questioned. "I don't know what you're talking about."

Alan's eyes urged me to cease and desist, but I blindly ignored his silent message, and stated, "As you probably know, Evelyn Sandler and I discovered Sal's body at 4:45 p.m. on that fateful day. I've pieced together who may have entered the pizza shop prior to our arrival, and according to Sal's records, you had a meeting there at 4:15."

Bernie glanced at Alan, evidently wondering if he should reply. Seeing no response, he glared at me, and said, "First of all, you have no right to stick your nose in police business. You're out of line and I intend to file a complaint with the mayor, but I also want to make it perfectly clear that I was out of town when Gladys told me of Sal's death."

I held my ground, saying, "We'll need corroboration in order to verify that you missed your meeting with Sal."

Bernie expressed his anger with an expletive then, in a firm tone he stated, "I had no meeting with Sal D'Angelo on the day he died. If you don't believe me, ask my wife or call my kids."

Still, I pressed, "Did you order a pizza for 4:15 on the day Sal died?"

As angry as a disturbed hornet, Bernie stormed out of the police station, slamming the door behind him. Alan stared at me, then shook his head as if he couldn't believe my gall.

"I guess that didn't go so well," I commented. "You should probably call his wife and kids, but if you ask me, Bernie was the last person to see Sal alive."

CHAPTER 39

Still annoyed with me when he arrived home for supper, Alan barely spoke a word, despite my peace offering of his favorite stuffed peppers meal. Even Sophie's antics with her squeaky hedgehog on the living room floor did nothing to lift his mood.

"Do you want to talk about it?" I questioned, passing the stewed tomatoes.

With a frigid gaze, Alan stated, "You were out of bounds, interfering with a police investigation."

"Excuse me?" I queried. "You asked for my help."

"Not to interrogate a member of town council," Alan said. "What was that all about?"

I took a deep breath before saying, "We needed to know why Bernie's name appeared among the papers in Sal's trash."

"You assume that 'Ber C.' implied Bernie Calamito," Alan remarked, "though it could have meant Bernadette Calhoun or Bernard Cooper."

"Do they live in Aspen Notch?" I asked.

Alan groaned. "I have no idea. I'm saying you jumped to unwarranted conclusions that made Lou Greene furious."

"It seems to me that the mayor should keep his nose out of police business, as well," I shrugged.

"I report to the mayor," Alan argued. "He had every right to confront me after Bernie filed his complaint."

"If you ask me," I said, "we have way too much cronyism in Aspen Notch, and you've played right along with it. How many people are on town council?"

Alan exhaled slowly, running his hands through his hair. "Five, including the mayor. Why?"

"Who are they, besides Lou, Bernie, and Marty?" I asked.

"Wally Southwick and Herman Crowe."

"All men, no doubt all handpicked by Lou Greene," I said, nodding my head for emphasis.

"What's your point, Sue? The town elected each of them."

"Voting can be rigged," I sighed. "I'm suggesting that you have a responsibility to fully investigate evidence, and you don't back down just because a member of town council goes crying to the mayor."

"Don't twist this, Sue," Alan replied firmly. "It's not your place to stick your nose where it doesn't belong."

Shaking my head, I took my plate to the kitchen sink with a clear signal that we had no more to discuss. Alan left the table, apparently not in the mood for dessert, retrieved the TV remote, and plopped in the recliner.

Sophie went to the back door while I put the leftovers in the refrigerator, so I let her out before rinsing the dishes. As I wiped the counters, I thought to call her in.

From the patio, I whistled, then yelled, "Come on, Sophie. Let's go." Sophie didn't respond, nor could I detect her presence due to the darkness and deep cloud cover. I walked to the far corner of the yard to see if she had returned to her hole then, in a panic, I checked the gate and found it wide open.

Sophie had escaped.

I sprinted to the front yard and, despite my numerous calls and whistles, I heard no bark in reply. Could Sophie have tried to find her way back to Irma's house? My guess seemed the only reasonable answer.

I quickly returned to the house to grab my jacket, purse, and keys. Alan glanced up from the world news, obviously still angry with me, though he said, "Where are you going?"

"Sophie's missing," I explained. "I have to find her."

"How'd she get out?" Alan questioned.

"Someone opened the gate," I said in a rush to leave.

As I shut the door, I heard Alan's glib reply, "I guess you forgot to close it this afternoon."

Was that possible? I thought as I revved the engine.

No. I distinctly remembered making sure that the latch had caught before I put Sophie in the car when we'd gone to the pet store earlier. Still, I couldn't believe that I forgot to check it before letting her out after dinner.

As I slowly made my way down Church Street, I kept my eyes on both sides of the street. Occasionally, I'd pull to the curb and call to Sophie, and pray that she merely decided to explore the neighbors' yards.

Finally, with a sigh of relief, I spotted Sophie on the lawn in front of Irma's house. Not sure if she'd stay put or continue her adventure, I didn't dare take my eyes off her, and as I drove forward, I watched her sniff the bushes near the porch.

Out of nowhere, a car appeared in front of me, careening at high speed. I screamed as I swerved to avoid a collision, but lost control and smashed into the corner telephone pole. Just before the air bag deployed, I had the distinct awareness that the offending vehicle was the blue Chevy.

CHAPTER 40

The paramedic who helped pull me from my car spoke in a calm and gentle tone while she cuffed my neck and took my blood pressure. Several residents stood by, telling each other what they'd heard or witnessed, and one woman held Sophie by the collar. I didn't see Irma among the onlookers.

Within minutes, a police vehicle appeared, lights flashing in the darkness. I began to weep as Alan reached to embrace me.

"I'm OK," I assured him, despite my tears.

"What happened?" he asked.

Before I could answer, one of the men in the crowd spoke up, saying, "I saw the whole thing, Officer. I'd just arrived home from work and went to get my mail. It wasn't this lady's fault."

A couple of the others said they came outside when they heard the crash. Another guy stepped forward to say, "I saw it, too. An older model sedan appeared out of nowhere, and the driver must have been high or drunk. If the lady hadn't swerved, she'd have died in a head-on collision."

"The lady's my wife, folks," Alan stated, "so we appreciate your concern. After the paramedics examine her for injuries, I'll take statements from those who witnessed the accident, and the rest of you are free to leave."

The woman holding Sophie remarked that she believed the dog belonged to Irma D'Angelo, but no one answered when she rang the doorbell. Alan explained that Irma couldn't care for Sophie after Sal's death, and she had asked us to take her. As he reached for Sophie's collar, he added, "This little pup must've decided to go on an adventure, so my wife went looking for her. We appreciate that you could grab hold of Sophie."

The paramedics offered to take me to the hospital, but I declined. Other than a bruised chest from the air bag and a sore right knee, I felt fine. Of course, I had frazzled nerves, but a nice glass of Chardonnay would have me sleeping like a baby.

I added my thanks to Alan's as neighbors disbursed. The ambulance returned to base while I took stock of the damage to my car. The crumpled right front and flat tire disheartened me, and I thought if it weren't for the stupid telephone pole and curb, I wouldn't have to anticipate an increase in our insurance rates.

Alan urged Sophie and me to wait for him in the police cruiser while he finished taking statements. Sophie must have sensed my emotions, because she kept licking my face and arms. Honestly, we probably actually bonded at that moment and, as weepy as I felt, I embraced her.

ALAN'S ATTENTIVENESS when we arrived home brought relief to my nerves. He helped me to the recliner, covered me with a throw from the den, then wrapped ice in a towel for my knee. I had no problem accepting the glass of wine he offered, and watched as he poured one for himself.

"I'm sorry," I said, once more feeling the tears in my eyes. I reached for a tissue and blew my nose.

Alan paced before sitting across from me on the sofa. "It wasn't your fault, Sue, but I found the thought of almost losing you too much to bear."

"I'm like an old penny," I teased. "You can't get rid of me."

"I love you," Alan sighed, "more than you can imagine."

"I love you, too," I said, reaching for another tissue, "and I'm sorry that I caused you so much trouble today."

"Don't worry about it," Alan smiled tenderly. "You're cute when you're feisty."

Sophie settled herself next to me on the recliner, ignoring her new toys. Occasionally, she'd stare at me, as if she wanted to assure me of her allegiance. When I reached down to pet her, I forced myself to hold it together for her and Alan.

"Did any of the witnesses get the license plate numbers?" I asked.

Alan shook his head, saying, "No, but they identified it as the same car you've seen trailing you. This time the person was out for blood."

"Someone's very nervous about my involvement in your murder case," I said, taking another sip of wine. "I don't want to kick a dead horse, but I can't help wondering what kind of a car Bernie Calamito drives."

I expected Alan to roll his eyes or grunt. Instead, he gave a simple response, "A black Lexus."

"Wow," I said, raising my eyebrows. "Pretty pricey for a retired guy."

"If you recall," Alan replied, "Bernie told us he worked as a car salesman. He probably knows how to find a good deal."

"No doubt, he does," I nodded. "I'm just saying."

Alan refilled our glasses, then asked if I wanted more ice for my knee. I shook my head, handing him the soggy towel with half-melted ice, saying, "I've had enough. Thanks."

As I watched Alan dump the ice in the sink, I asked if he'd ever regretted taking the job as interim police chief. He turned to face me with a somber expression, and said, "Every day since we came here. How about you?"

I tried to carefully word my response. "When I watch you deal with so much stress, I worry about you. You look tired and haggard, and I believe the job involves too much for one person to handle."

"I'm just as concerned about your safety," Alan replied solemnly. "My job puts you in harm's way."

"I just have a knack for finding trouble," I quipped.

With a rueful chuckle, Alan agreed. I told him about the conversation I'd had with the locksmith and suggested that he make a case with town council for hiring additional recruits, at least on a part-time basis. I made sure that Alan understood that I felt proud to be the wife of Aspen Notch's chief of police but, in the end, I'd support whatever decision he made about the job.

"I'm not a quitter," Alan replied with conviction.

"No, you're not," I agreed, "but you *are* a stubborn old mule, trying to do everything yourself."

"I should learn to listen to your intuition," Alan said. "If it makes you happy, I'll call one of my old retired buddies from the NYC police department in the morning. He lives in New Jersey, and I think he might be willing to snoop into Bernie Calamito's background."

"Now you're talking, pal," I smiled.

CHAPTER 41

*E*very bone, muscle, and tendon in my body made itself known the day after my run-in with the telephone pole. After helping me struggle into my clothing, Alan explored the previous day's work in the master bedroom, then returned to tell me his impressions of the demolition.

"I don't understand Deke's plan of operations," Alan said. "It's like a war zone in there. Do you know what he's doing?"

"He told us that the crew needed to tear out the walls and rip up some of the new flooring to prepare for the bathroom and closet, but they'll replace it."

"Down through the subfloor?" Alan questioned. "I can see the concrete pad in some spots."

I hobbled my way past Alan to see what he meant. Sure enough, more activity had taken place in our bedroom than what seemed necessary, at least in my uneducated opinion. I promised to ask Deke about it when he arrived, since I knew Alan wanted to get an early start on his investigative work.

"Make sure he sticks to his original budget," Alan said as he put on his jacket. "I don't want any unnecessary work done."

"I'll remind him," I nodded. "Would you double-check that the gate is closed before you leave? I plan to let Sophie out the back door."

Alan gave me a parting kiss, then said, "No problem. Will you call the insurance company?"

"Yep," I nodded, "I'm on it."

With a few moments of peace before Deke, John, and the work crew arrived, I made a cup of hot tea and fed Sophie. After I let her out, I popped a bagel into the toaster, then watched her from the kitchen window while I ate my breakfast. It didn't surprise me that Sophie returned to her hole, and the digging kept her occupied, which gave me time to make the bed.

After I called her in, Sophie settled on the kitchen floor while I unloaded the dishwasher. I told her that we'd stay in the den today, mostly because my car went to the repair shop. She tilted her head as if she actually listened to me.

When John and Deke arrived, I asked for an update. Deke walked me through what they'd accomplished, explaining that they'd found evidence of moisture in the subfloor, possibly from the laundry room. He scheduled the plumber for later in the day to install the pipes for the bathroom and make sure we'd have no future leaks.

I nodded my understanding, saying, "Luckily, you found the problem. When will the electrician arrive?"

"In the next day or two," Deke replied, "after they put in the new subfloor and studs. Why?"

"I'd like the wiring in the cabin checked," I said, "since I'd prefer to use space heaters in the winter, rather than a fire in the hearth. We may need a new circuit breaker."

"That's not in your budget," Deke advised.

"I know," I said. "Have them send me a separate invoice."

"We can do that," Deke agreed. "Did the inspector find anything wrong with the chimney?"

"No. I just don't want to risk a fire because the cabin's a treasure I want to protect."

Deke agreed, then reminded me that he'd done a lot of work for Clara out there. I told him that the place looked good, especially after the boys helped me clean it on Saturday and, maybe, when he had a moment, he'd want to take a look inside the cabin for old time's sake.

"I'd like that," Deke nodded wistfully.

"Wait until John or I can walk with you through the yard," I remarked. "Sophie likes to dig for tree roots, and she already made an interesting discovery."

Deke's eyes widened with surprise. "What did she find?" he questioned.

"Clara must have buried her husband's war memorabilia in his jewelry box," I replied. "I brought it to the police station to show Alan, but forgot to bring it home."

Deke's eyes had a faraway look when he stated, "I recall digging the hole. Clara sobbed when she covered that box with dirt and said her final goodbye to him."

"She must have been heartbroken," I sighed. "You know, she wrote a riddle about gold and silver that she buried, and I suppose she meant the silver medals and gold cufflinks."

"Probably," Deke said, shaking off the past. "You'll need to take the puppy out again today. Besides the new bathroom, we also plan to work on the island for the kitchen."

"I can't," I replied. "I wrecked my car last night."

John gasped audibly, and stopped entertaining Sophie to ask what happened.

"One of the workers must have left the gate open," I said. "Sophie escaped and I drove around to find her, but some jerk ran me into a telephone pole."

"Ouch," John stated. "Are you OK?"

"Yes," I nodded. "Anyway, Sophie and I will work in the den today because I have to call the insurance company and get estimates on the car repair."

"Do you know who did it?" John asked. "Your husband needs to arrest the guy."

"None of the witnesses got the full license plate numbers, but we know it was an older model blue Chevy."

"I've seen that car around here," John noted, gazing out the front window. "It's often parked in front of the church. If you ask me, whoever's been watching your place opened your gate, because none of Deke's workers left by the back yard."

"Maybe that's another reason for me to stay in the den today," I said, "since I have a good view from that window."

"The problem is," John remarked, "you can't read the tags from that angle and the car windows are tinted, so you can't see the driver."

"I know," I agreed. "I saw it parked out there once, though I didn't realize the person staked out as often as you say."

"I'll tell you what," John replied emphatically. "You let me know if the car shows up, and I'll meander out to my truck. We'll get the numbers on those tags today."

"You're a lifesaver," I sighed.

And I meant it literally.

CHAPTER 42

*I*t took all morning to work out details with the shop where they towed my car and our insurance company. The haggling didn't involve the cost, but rather the determination of whether or not to declare my vehicle a total loss, which sounded ridiculous to me. The damage appeared minimal, at least in my mind, but the repairman assured me that I had done a job on the axle.

While on the phone, I constantly watched the cars on the street, with the hope that the creep would return during John's work day. Sophie occasionally snoozed at my feet, then played with her toys, and I considered it remarkable that none of the commotion from the work crew seemed to upset her.

Finally, just before noon, the blue Chevy appeared. With a nervous twitter, I called to John, "The car's out there."

Without a word to me, John sauntered to his truck as if he needed to retrieve something he'd forgotten. I watched him take his time, with a ball cap shielding his eyes, then grab his step stool to place it on the driveway. He even acted as if he had to test his weight on it, which made the entire scenario rather amusing.

My heart sank when the driver of the Chevy took off, obviously to avoid John's attention, and I doubted that John had a good vantage point to view the license plate. Sophie joined me to greet John at the front door, and I had a gloomy countenance because, once again, I felt thwarted.

Imagine my surprise when John announced his success, saying, "Pennsylvania tags, Y9P 4386L."

I couldn't help but yelp in excitement, grab his shoulders, and give him a kiss on the cheek. Sophie thought my happiness gave her an invitation to pounce on John.

John grinned. "Call your husband. We've got the jerk."

Ecstatic, I could barely control my shaking fingers while I wrote the license plate number on a slip of paper, then pressed Alan's number on my phone, but my call went right to voicemail. I figured Alan had probably reached out to his buddy to request background information on Bernie, so I left a message asking Alan to return my call.

"Everyone's taking a lunch break as soon as the plumber finishes," John reminded me. "Do you want us to bring anything back for you?"

"No, but thanks," I replied. "I have leftovers in the fridge."

"I don't like the idea of you staying here alone," John said. "You could come with us."

"I'll be fine," I assured him. "By the way, you should have lunch at Dottie's because I think she'd enjoy seeing you."

John laughed as he moved his paint cans to the counter. "You must be psychic," he said. "I told Deke about Dottie and he insisted that we go there today as his treat."

"Great!" I smiled, "and if you see Alan, tell him to call me."

"Definitely," John agreed.

THOUGH I RELISHED the tranquility after the workers left for lunch, I couldn't settle my unease. With my typical second-guessing, I regretted my decision to remain home alone. Of course, Sophie kept me company, but I didn't think she could provide much help if the creep returned with a vengeance.

The thought of taking Sophie outside didn't appeal to me, but I had to make sure that the gate was still securely latched. I watched the street from the front window while I put on my jacket, but didn't notice anything odd that caught my attention. In fact, Church Street seemed relatively quiet.

Sophie followed me out to the yard, immediately nosing her way to the hole. I hobbled to the gate, relieved to see it still secure, then checked the doors on the cabin. Nothing seemed out of place, but it annoyed me that some kook could make me feel so frightened.

I learned by experience that I couldn't control the actions of anyone with a vendetta. Last year, someone almost killed me because I knew too much, or so he thought. I vowed never to put myself in that horrible position but, once again, I faced danger.

After I let Sophie enjoy the brisk November chill for a few extra minutes while I tried to reach Alan, I whistled for her to come in. At least, the pup responded, though Alan didn't. I had critical information to relay, but no way to deliver it.

While I waited for my leftover stuffed pepper to warm in the microwave, I meandered to the master bedroom to inspect the plumber's work. He'd made the connection to the pipes in the laundry room, with additional PVC pipes, valves, drains, and fittings in place for the sink, toilet, and shower, and it all looked good to me.

Sophie sniffed around, and her attention on the concrete pad brought my eyes to it, as well. I saw no evidence of the water damage that Deke explained as the reason to remove some of the subfloor, so it made me wonder if Deke told the truth.

As we returned to the kitchen for my lunch, I glanced out the front window again. To my relief, the Chevy hadn't returned. My thoughts focused on Deke as I poured a glass of iced tea. We didn't know much about him, nor did we check references. Yes, we felt pleased about the quality of work in the kitchen, but I often didn't stay home during the demolition. Could Deke have searched for something in the walls or floor of our home?

As a teen, Deke had worked for Clara, and even helped her bury the items belonging to her deceased husband. He knew of her riddles, though he hadn't expressed much interest in having me read them all to him. Of course, I'd often left the booklet on the dining room table, so I thought he might have taken the time to read it when I went out.

I wondered why Deke had shown so much interest in the renovations we planned. Had Clara told him that she'd hidden additional treasures in the house? The project management job we offered Deke may have given him the perfect opportunity to search, especially when he encouraged me to leave the chaos to him.

When I told Deke that I wanted the locks changed on the cabin, he had a strange expression. Did Deke find the missing key to the padlock? If so, perhaps he feared losing the chance to explore Clara's shop, or he may have already done so.

With my imagination in high gear, my stomach churned, and I could barely swallow the last few bites of lunch. Sophie had the honor of finishing it, while I checked the street again. I knew I'd better get a grip, especially if the driver of the Chevy actually intended to unravel me.

The ringtone on my phone snapped me back to reality. I hoped to see Alan's caller ID, but stared at an unknown number. Seconds away from not responding, I changed my mind in case one of the work crew had called. I picked up to hear Irma's voice, shrill and loud.

"Stay away from me, you evil woman!" she yelled.

CHAPTER 43

$\mathcal{A}$ lan found me on the sofa, with my arms wrapped around Sophie for comfort. I felt such a relief when he walked through the door that I could have cried but, perhaps due to my frazzled nerves, I acted like a petulant child.

"Why didn't you answer my calls?" I asked.

"I was on the phone all morning," Alan replied patiently. "Besides, I'd planned to stop by and see how you felt today."

"Lousy, if you must know," I grumbled.

Alan pushed Sophie aside and sat next to me, then placed his arm around my shoulder. "I'm here now," he said in a gentle tone. "Do you want to talk about it?"

"The creep came back, staking out the place again," I said, reaching for the scrap of paper in my side pocket. "John got the license plate number."

"Geez," Alan exclaimed. "Why didn't you text it to me or something?"

"I didn't want it floating around cyberspace," I shrugged. "Who knows what that jerk has in store for me?"

Alan transferred the number to his phone while I read it aloud, then he said, "I'll run the tags as soon as I return to the station, so don't worry. We'll get this kook."

"I don't want to stay here alone," I sighed.

"The work crew will return from lunch soon," Alan noted.

"I don't want to stay with them either," I stated.

Alan looked into my eyes and, perhaps, he saw my fear because he said, "You can come with me. I have to bring Irma to the station for further questioning, but I have to remind you not to interfere with the investigation."

"I won't," I assured Alan, "but I doubt Irma will want to see me there." After I told him about her earlier phone call and volatile outburst, I asked, "Why would Irma think I'm evil?"

"Irma's call to you might have resulted from mine to her," Alan remarked. "Get whatever you want to bring with you, and gather a few toys for Sophie, because I have one of the county cops holding down the fort for me at the station and don't want to keep him waiting too long."

"I'll leave a note for John and Deke," I said.

"Fine," Alan nodded. "Do that, then we'll go."

FROM THE CRUISER, Alan called Sergeant Mark Matthews to give him a heads-up about my arrival. Alan told him that I had the license plate numbers for the car that ran me off the road, and asked Mark to search the department of motor vehicles' roster when he went to pick up Irma.

Sergeant Matthews put me at ease while he gave Sophie her belly rubs. Tall and brawny, the young cop seemed familiar with the murder case, as well as my situation with the person who trailed me. It made me wonder if Alan had taken my words to heart and intended to groom Mark Matthews to serve as an additional Aspen Notch police presence.

While Mark worked at Alan's desk, I settled myself on a wooden chair by the table with the coffee pot and fax machine since it afforded me a good view of the front entrance and an area for Sophie to play. While we waited, I pulled Clara's riddle book from my purse, and searched for one that referred to any other items she could have hidden.

I re-read the riddles that Clara wrote about bones, silver, and gold, and her mention of a shallow grave led me to believe that she'd buried other things, not just her husband's memories. Another riddle gave me pause.

> *Too many secrets for a woman, now old.*
> *They must go to my grave, never to be told.*
> *Falling prey to desires with only a boy,*
> *It wasn't a ploy, nor did it bring joy.*
> *Sorrow and regret are all I have left,*
> *My heart is heavy, my soul bereft.*

I tried to connect the dots, remembering that Rosie, the hairdresser, believed Clara had been pregnant. I knew that too much time had elapsed for Clara's deceased husband to have fathered the child yet, as a young woman, she surely had hopes and desires, which may have led her to a liaison with someone in Aspen Notch.

Sophie looked up from her play when I gasped with the new image that took shape in my brain. Although Clara was 10 years older than Deke, he was a mature teen who'd helped her every day through his high school years. Had there been more than that? Did they both fall prey to sexual desires and have trysts that resulted in her pregnancy? Did he even help to bury the child?

I tried to wrap my head around my imaginings that took shape since Clara specifically wrote that she had desires for a boy. I'd seen similar situations posted on the news, and always wondered how a woman, old enough to know better, could rob a young man of his innocence. I knew I shouldn't judge, though I often formed an opinion.

In Clara's case, I didn't consider her a cougar because I couldn't imagine that she'd schemed to seduce the boy, whom I believed may have been Deke. I recognized that familiarity could breed deep feelings for another. After all, Alan and I fell in love when we worked together to solve a crime last year. Things like that can just happen.

Once again, I felt sorry for Clara Whitman because I knew her secrets weighed heavily on her. Perhaps she realized that their love could never be brought to light, I thought and, maybe, she ended the relationship with full regret for her error in judgment.

I wondered if Clara's morose thoughts through the years were tied to her fears that someone would reveal her secret. Did she worry that people would brand her as a predator who had sex with a teenager? Did she hold any guilt in the death of her child? I'd never know exactly what happened, but I felt sure that it resulted in a lifetime of grief, regret, and sadness.

I knew one thing: only Deke could answer my questions.

CHAPTER 44

$\mathcal{I}$rma struggled with her walker while Alan helped her through the front entrance of the police station. Sophie, alerted by the noise, caught Irma's scent and bounded toward her, though I tried to grab her collar. Luckily, between Alan's firm command to Sophie and my frantic dash to take hold of her, we averted disaster.

Irma glared at me with an expression of disgust, and said, "Get that mutt out of my face. What are you doing here?"

"Police protection," I replied, trying to stare her down. "I was the person whose car hit the telephone pole in front of your house last night."

"I heard the commotion," she muttered. "You should be more alert when driving."

I had no doubt that Irma watched the proceedings from behind her drapes. Alan may have thought the same thing since he asked if she witnessed the event or saw the car that ran me off the road.

Irma shrugged her shoulders. "I'm not a busybody, nor am I in the habit of watching the goings-on outside. My parents taught me to mind my own business."

"Witnesses described an older model Chevy," I persisted, despite my promise to Alan that I wouldn't interfere. "Are you positive that you didn't see it?"

We all waited expectantly for Irma's response, although it looked as if she wanted to weigh her options. When she asked if she might sit first, Alan offered her one of the larger chairs.

"Is this why you brought me here?" Irma queried, once she got settled. "It's not how they do it on TV crime shows."

Alan gave a quirky smile, and said, "I can take you to the interrogation room, if that's what you'd like, but I didn't bring you here because you're a suspect. I think you can help bring Sal's killer to justice."

"Why didn't you tell me that?" Irma asked, reaching for a tissue in her purse. "You got me all riled up."

"I'm sorry," Alan replied, pulling up a chair next to hers. "We believe the driver of the blue car may have sent you and Sue the death threats. He or she is getting volatile and might try to hurt you, as happened with Sue last night."

On that note, I took Sophie back to our spot, trying to stay out of the way. Still, I watched as Irma dabbed at the corner of her eyes, then said, "I saw a blue car parked in front of my house, but didn't realize it was a Chevy."

"Do you know who might own that car?" Alan asked.

"No," Irma replied, "but I think I've seen the car before, maybe in town. I just can't remember."

Alan simply nodded, and assured Irma that she could let him know if she thought of it later. In the meantime, he noted, Sergeant Mark Matthews would record their conversation, then waited for the signal to begin. Irma nervously fiddled with her tissue until Alan said that he wanted to discuss the missing knife and Sal's connection with anyone in town, particularly one with whom she didn't approve.

"You mean like if he had an affair?" Irma glared.

"No," Alan reassured her. "I'm talking about his business dealings. You found a lot of money in your husband's safe. Did Sal meet with someone on a regular basis, maybe as a partner of sorts?"

"I don't think so," Irma replied. "Sometimes he'd say he planned to go fishing with Bernie Calamito on his day off. They were friends, but he knew I didn't like the wife because Gladys Calamito has a nasty disposition."

I had to stifle a smile as I busied myself with Sophie and her toys, although I recognized that we often possess the same irritating traits we see in others. I figured that Irma might not realize that she, too, had an unpleasant streak.

"Did you and Sal ever have the occasion to entertain the Calamito's at your home?" Alan asked.

Irma squirmed in her seat, most likely trying to get her expansive hips in a more comfortable position. She locked eyes with Alan, then muttered, "Once, and that was enough. Don't get me wrong. I didn't typically mind if Bernie came to our house, since he was friendly enough. Sometimes, he even made a fish dinner for Sal and me with what they had caught."

"He didn't take any home for his wife?" Alan queried.

"Maybe he did," Irma shrugged. "I don't know for sure."

"Could he have borrowed the knife from your butcher's block?" Alan questioned.

Irma's brow furrowed, as if she reflected back on those days. "I never thought about that," she murmured. "Do you think he might have used it to kill Sal?"

"We don't know," Alan replied, shaking his head, "but we guess that Bernie may have been the last person to see Sal alive."

"Did you ask him?" Irma pressed.

"Yes," Alan stated. "He told me he went out of town."

Alan's comment clearly had a definite impact on Irma's demeanor. She turned to me, and asked if that information had come from the notes in Sal's waste basket because she recalled our discussion about "Ber C. 4:15."

"It's a long shot," I replied, "and I know you mentioned that Sal could have forgotten to record the order, but Bernie was adamant that he went to visit his family in New Jersey."

Irma paused, with a wisp of a smile, then stated, "You're helping me, like you said you would. I'm sorry for not believing you."

Once Irma's comment brought me into the conversation again, I told her that the only clues the police had were papers from the waste basket, the knife which had no fingerprints other than Sal's, and the cash in Sal's safe. Someone had cleaned up any evidence, including footprints from flour on the floor.

Alan must have decided that he couldn't keep me out of the discussion, so he added that he'd interviewed anyone who had an order to pick up on the afternoon of Sal's death. They all confirmed Sal's presence when they arrived and departed with their hoagies or pizza.

"Did you check to see if there are any other Ber C.'s who live in Aspen Notch?" I asked.

Sergeant Matthews chimed in, saying, "I did a directory search and found a few people identified by first initial and last names beginning with C. but, other than Bernie, none of those first names began with B-e-r."

"Oh, great," I sighed. "We have another dead end."

"Not really," Matthews replied with a sly grin. "The 1996 blue Impala Chevrolet is registered to Bernard A. Calamito."

CHAPTER 45

*A*ll eyes turned to Sergeant Matthews, and my gasp sounded loud in the quiet room as I considered that I may have solved the case. Alan's and Irma's faces both registered surprise, but for different reasons. After all, Alan knew that Bernie drove a black Lexus, while Irma, on the other hand, thought of Bernie as a friend of Sal's, not his killer.

Alan, as the first to speak, remarked, "Double-check that, Sergeant. Bernie serves on the town council, and is the mayor's right-hand man. I don't want to make any false accusations."

"I did, sir," Matthews nodded. "The roster listed Bernie Calamito's current address."

"I've never seen him drive a blue Impala," Alan noted.

"It could be his wife's car," Matthews replied. "Do you want me to bring him in for questioning?"

Alan nodded pensively as he told Sergeant Matthews that they should first have additional county police assistance. Alan reached for his phone, then suggested that Mark take Irma home after he dropped off Sophie and me at our place. When the two additional officers arrived, they'd pick up Bernie and Gladys and bring them to the police station. No doubt, he wanted Irma and me out of the picture.

"That Gladys is a cagey character," Irma noted. "She'll lie to protect Bernie."

"Would she be vindictive enough to run me off the road and send death threats?" I asked.

Irma nodded, saying, "I wouldn't put anything past her."

After making arrangements with the county cops, Alan peered over Sergeant Matthews' shoulder to view the computer screen. They spoke in a muted conversation while I gathered the toys and put Sophie on her leash. Irma put her tissue away, then struggled to stand with her walker.

Finally, Alan turned to me, and said, "You don't have to worry now. We'll have Bernie and Gladys at the station, so you'll be safe."

"I'm fine," I replied with an encouraging smile. "In fact, I'd like to get home and talk to Deke about a few things."

I suspected that Alan thought I referred to the bathroom remodel, not my suspicion that Deke and Clara Whitman had a love affair at one time. I also planned to ask what he searched for in the walls and floor of our home, but I needed time to figure out how to bring up the conversation with Deke without causing any tension between us.

Sergeant Matthews helped Irma to the police cruiser, and I followed behind with Sophie, relieved that Alan would soon bring closure to Sal's murder. I could see that he felt stressed about having to question Bernie and Gladys though, even worse, he'd have to inform the mayor.

I knew Alan would find that task a challenge.

I DIDN'T BOTHER BRINGING Sophie into the house. Instead, we went directly to the back yard and I let her off-leash. While she darted toward her hole, I unlocked the side door of the cabin. Though chilly inside, Abe's place afforded some protection from the cold northerly breeze.

I stood inside the doorway, trying to imagine Clara in the very same spot while she decided how to set up her candy shop. I pictured a distraught young woman, wondering what she'd do to support herself. Did she have no family to return to after her husband's death? Was she originally from Aspen Notch? If not, had she wanted to remain in the home she'd shared with her dearly-departed husband, perhaps close to friends they'd made during their brief marriage?

Deep in my thoughts, the ringtone on my phone alerted me to a call from Evelyn Sanders. "Are you busy?" she asked when I connected. "Would you like some company?"

Although I honestly didn't, I pleasantly responded, "Sure. I'm just trying to imagine what I might do with Abe's cabin, so come on over."

"I'll be there in a jiffy," Evelyn replied, "but don't close up. I want to see it now that the boys helped you clean it."

While I waited, I tossed a stick for Sophie several times until she tired of playing fetch. Within minutes, I saw Evelyn's car pull up to our curb, so I met her at the gate.

"Where's your car?" Evelyn asked after a cheery greeting. "I passed by earlier and thought you went out."

"It's in the shop," I said morosely, "probably totaled. I'm waiting to hear."

"What happened?" Evelyn questioned.

"Somebody ran me into a telephone pole last night," I sighed. "It happened right on Church Street."

"Are you OK?" she pressed.

"Just bruised."

"Geez," Evelyn exclaimed. "How awful! You know, Marty told me he heard about an accident near Irma D'Angelo's house, but he didn't mention your name."

"I'm not sure, but maybe Alan didn't release it," I replied with a rueful grin. "Anyway, let's go in the cabin and get out of the cold air."

I left the door ajar, since I thought Sophie would realize that she missed Evelyn's arrival. Though I considered it strange that she didn't come running to see Evelyn, I felt relieved not to have to deal with her antics for a while.

Evelyn settled herself in the rocker by the hearth while I told her about the chimney inspection. She agreed that a heater could provide a better alternative than a fire to warm the place, but it all depended on what I planned to do with the cabin.

"I'm not sure yet," I said, glancing around the room. "Rob Burkeholder and his friends want me to have a candy store, as in the old days, and Alan suggested that we open it for tours."

"And you?" Evelyn queried.

I giggled, saying, "Quite honestly, I wouldn't mind having a small garden shop. I need something to keep busy while Alan works, and I love gardening."

"That's a fabulous idea," Evelyn smiled, "especially since we have nothing like that here in Aspen Notch."

"I know," I agreed. "I could stock it with decorative pots, garden décor, and handcrafted flower arrangements."

"You could have seasonal themes," Evelyn suggested. "Can't you just picture the place decorated for Christmas?"

"Believe it or not, I can," I nodded. "Then, in the summer, I could even sell some of my fruits and vegetables because my friends often told me I have a green thumb."

"And I could make pies or jelly," Evelyn chuckled.

I found Evelyn's enthusiasm contagious, and delighted in sharing ideas with a friend. Within the hour, we had planned our visions for *Sue's Garden Shop*, although I laughingly agreed with Evelyn that I should come up with a catchier name for the place. Of course, I needed to discuss everything with Alan, though he'd often mentioned that we could use the cabin for a business.

Evelyn glanced at her watch, then explained that she had to leave since she promised to make Marty an apple crisp for dessert. As she gathered her purse and scarf, she remarked that Sophie must have fallen asleep in the yard, and I might need to check on her. Frankly, I'd totally forgotten about the pup, and as we rushed outside, I told Evelyn that Sophie escaped the night before, and my search for her led to the crash.

To my relief, we found Sophie in the center of the yard, digging another hole. Totally engrossed in her task, she didn't hear my call, or she ignored it, and I thought I'd better look to see what held her focus. Once Evelyn knew that Sophie hadn't escaped again, she mouthed her farewell to me and departed.

With Sophie's head deep into a new hole, I knelt down to examine her bootie. Although she'd managed to remove most of the dirt around it, an old mason jar with a rusted lid protruded, so I gave it a tug, and freed it from its burial place.

Sophie had found more of Clara's silver and gold.

CHAPTER 46

S ophie leapt to grab her prized possession from my hands, but I quickly enveloped it within the front of my jacket. She nearly knocked me over twice as she pounced on me, determined to retrieve the jar. Laughing, I made it into the house before she did, and hurriedly placed it far back on the kitchen counter.

"Whatcha' got there?" John asked from the laundry room sink as he finished up for the day.

"Sophie found a buried treasure in the yard," I chuckled.

"Lucky you," John smiled. "How much did she find?"

"I have no idea, but I'll have to leave it out of her reach until she's distracted. Are you guys done?"

John nodded, saying, "We'll leave soon. Deke's checking the crew's work in your bedroom."

"Good," I said, "because I want to talk to him. Can you give us a couple of minutes?"

"Sure. I have a few more brushes to wash."

"If you don't mind," I said, "please keep an eye on Sophie since I have a feeling that she'll try to counter-surf."

I heard John's laughter as I made my way down the hall. I had no idea how I'd discuss the difficult topic I'd planned with Deke, though

I felt it necessary. As I approached, I saw that Deke leaned on his cane while he inspected the new bathroom floor.

Deke glanced up with a smile, then said, "I'm glad you're back because I need to show you a few things."

"Why are you here, Deke?" I questioned abruptly.

With a quizzical expression, Deke asked what I meant. I should have heeded the adage: *"Be careful of your thoughts. They can turn into words at any time,"* but I didn't. My words tumbled out of my mouth as I stated, "You're looking for something here, in Clara's home. Is it something you left with her or something she took from you?"

"I don't know what you're talking about," Deke replied.

Close to losing my courage, I requested that Deke follow me to the den. He needed a place to sit, and I wanted a moment to gather my thoughts. Once Deke took a seat on the futon and I sat on the desk chair, I felt able to continue.

"You didn't need to tear up the subfloor," I stated firmly. "I inspected it when you went to lunch and found no sign of any water damage. Please tell me why you're here."

Shoulders humped, Deke stared at the floor as if he tried to decide whether or not he should tell me the truth. After a few minutes of silence, he looked into my eyes with resignation, and said, "I didn't intend to mislead you. When John told me that you needed a project manager, I knew I could do the job for you, but I also wanted to find what once belonged in my family."

"What's that?" I questioned.

"My grandmother's gold wedding band," Deke replied. "I gave it to Clara long ago, but she lost it."

Deke's words confirmed my guess about his relationship with Clara. I could imagine a young Deke, not much older than my age when I became involved with the boy who invited me to the senior prom. What I'd considered true love dissipated soon after we went off to different colleges. Still, I would never forget my first romance.

"You and Clara were lovers?" I asked gently.

Deke nodded. "I pilfered my grandmother's ring from my mother's jewelry box, since I figured she wouldn't miss it. I gave it to Clara when I asked her to marry me."

"Did she turn you down?" I questioned.

"Clara told me that she'd think about it," Deke replied.

"Did you know about Clara's pregnancy?" I asked.

"Yes," Deke stated in almost a whisper. "The baby never came to term, and Clara felt devastated when she miscarried."

"She had a little girl?" I pressed.

"How did you know?" Deke queried. "It was our secret."

I explained that I surmised the truth from Clara's riddles and my conversation with Rosie, the hairdresser. Deke merely nodded, then expressed relief to know that he could now openly search for the ring. He wanted closure for a time in his life that he needed to put to rest.

"Clara took the miscarriage as a sign that we shouldn't marry," Deke sighed.

"Do you think the age difference between the two of you factored into her decision?" I asked.

"Yes," Deke agreed. "Clara thought we shouldn't see each other, so she terminated my employment and requested that I no longer visit the candy shop. I respected her wishes, though she broke my heart."

I could clearly see, despite all the years that had passed, Deke never forgot his first love. Clara hurt him deeply when she put an end to their relationship, yet I understood her rationale. Fortunately, Deke fell in love again, and he enjoyed a long and fulfilling marriage with another woman.

Remarkably, Clara stood among those who grieved with Deke and his wife after they lost their only child, sweet Caroline. Clara must have re-lived the memory of her own loss, especially knowing that Deke had fathered two children, and both had died. What sadness for all of them.

I had no doubt that, despite his ulterior motive of finding the ring, Deke wanted to restore Clara's home as his final gift to her. In my mind, that had significance, and his lasting testament had meaning for me, as well.

"Would you like to keep Clara's book of riddles?" I asked.

Deke shook his head. "No. Clara would want you to honor her memory. I have no doubt that she's watching over you."

"I've had that feeling," I said. "I wish I'd known her."

"You're so much like her, it's uncanny," Deke noted.

"Maybe it's why I've enjoyed trying to solve her riddles," I stated. "Even Sophie's getting into the act. She's already dug up two of the items that Clara buried, and I have a feeling that we'll discover more."

Deke smiled, saying, "What did Sophie find now?"

"A mason jar with money," I noted. "I'll show you."

Deke followed me into the kitchen, and John played with Sophie to distract her while I handed Deke the jar. Though most of the currency looked to be in small denominations, we heard a distinct rattle of coins.

"Clara always liked to bury her money," Deke chuckled. "She didn't trust the banks. Do you want me to try to open it?"

"Of course," I said, handing him a rubber jar opener. "The lid's pretty rusted."

Despite his struggle to open the jar, Deke gave the lid one final twist, then dumped the contents onto the counter. Amidst the silver coins that spilled out, we saw one golden object.

Deke found his grandmother's precious ring.

CHAPTER 47

*A*lan looked exhausted when he arrived home for dinner. I'd had time to make meatballs with marinara sauce and a garden salad, but waited to drop the pasta into boiling water until he walked through the door. I had set the table earlier, and made Clara's jar the centerpiece, which I considered quite clever of me.

After giving me a kiss and Sophie some belly rubs, Alan hung his uniform jacket in the hall closet, then pulled out his chair at the table. He didn't say anything about the jar until I put the steaming bowl of spaghetti and meatballs in front of him.

"Everything looks good," Alan smiled. "What's with the money in a jar?"

"Sophie found it today," I said, giggling while I brought in the salad and dressings. "It's another of Clara's treasures buried in the yard, and the jar contains $112.75."

Alan laughed. "Our little digger may help pay for all of our renovations. Good going, Sophie."

While we ate, I told Alan about Deke's confession that he had searched for his grandmother's ring in our walls and floor. Alan listened intently, then said, "Did you fire Deke for breach of contract?"

"No," I replied. "I felt sorry for Deke, and he assured me that he won't charge us for any unnecessary work."

"You're a softie," Alan muttered, although I detected that he may have agreed with me.

"It's why I'm so lovable," I quipped.

"True," Alan admitted. "So, why did Clara Whitman have Deke's ring."

"When I read all of Clara's riddles," I replied, "I began to wonder if Deke and Clara had a serious relationship. Then, after your comment about the extensive work in the bathroom, I took a closer look and agreed that Deke had no good reason to go into the subfloor unless he searched for something."

"I gather you put two and two together," Alan said.

"Exactly," I beamed. "Everything became clear to me as I recognized Clara's tendency to bury things, so I confronted Deke once I put the pieces of the puzzle together."

Alan shook his head, reaching for a few more meatballs. "You have an amazing brain," he said. "You make connections from things most people wouldn't think twice about. Maybe I really should deputize you."

"Are you asking for my help again?" I teased.

"I guess I am," Alan nodded. "We're at another dead end."

"Did Bernie and Gladys skip town?" I queried.

"No. I questioned both of them with their lawyer present. He vouched that Bernie had visited his son in Jersey and Gladys had a doctor's certificate for her illness."

"What about the car?" I asked.

"Technically," Alan noted, "it's Gladys' car, though Bernie put both of their vehicles in his name. Anyway, it's been in the shop for repairs."

"That should be easy to verify," I remarked.

Alan sighed. "I did. The mechanic assured me that no one could drive the car, since it needs a new transmission."

While I cleared the table, I asked if Alan's police buddy in New Jersey had found anything regarding Bernie's business dealings. Alan again shook his head, saying, "Except for a couple of traffic violations, Bernie's as clean as a whistle."

"What's your gut telling you?" I questioned.

Alan took a moment to reflect, then said, "I think Bernie's telling the truth, but I don't know about Gladys."

"Could Gladys commit a murder?" I asked. "I suppose she could have felt jealous of her husband's friendship with Sal, and I don't really know her, though I can't imagine such a motive."

"Me either," Alan replied. "I guess it's possible, but not plausible. Do we have any dessert?"

"I have orange sherbet in the freezer," I stated. "Do you want some?"

"Yes," Alan grinned. "I'll get it if you want to take Sophie out since she's sniffing around the sofa."

"Caught in the nick of time," I chuckled as I retrieved my jacket. "Let's go, Sophie."

Sophie lurched ahead of me as soon as I opened the back door. While she went to a far corner of the yard, I checked the gate and saw it securely latched. As I walked to Abe's cabin to make sure I'd locked it, the sound of screeching tires at our curb startled me.

Suddenly, an ear-piercing explosion tossed me off my feet, and I landed hard on my back. Just before everything went black, I knew one thing for sure: I caught a glimpse of the blue Chevy as it raced away, and the driver intended to kill me.

CHAPTER 48

J gained consciousness in the back of an ambulance, though my head throbbed and the noise in my ears left me all but deaf. The same EMT woman as the night before checked my vital signs, and tried to speak to me, but I couldn't make out her words. Finally, the ringing sounds began to dissipate.

"Your husband's meeting you at the hospital," the EMT lady remarked as she flashed a light into my eyes. "It seems as if you're having a bit of bad luck these days."

"I'm not dead yet," I sighed, "so I guess it's good luck."

The paramedic gave a wry chuckle, then took my blood pressure again. "You're very fortunate," she said. "I saw the hole made by the pipe bomb inside your fence, and if you'd taken one step closer to your gate, you'd have received the full impact."

"I had just checked the latch," I explained, "then turned to make sure that I'd locked the cabin. I guess it's a miracle that I stepped away from the fence in time. Is my dog OK?"

"Yes," the woman smiled. "The pup took good care of you with plenty of licks until we arrived, then Officer Jaworski put her in the house."

Closing my eyes, I moved various parts of my body to see if it caused pain. Except for my headache, everything seemed in working order, which relieved some of my fears, but the jarring of a speed bump, though the driver had slowed, indicated that I had a few more days of soreness ahead of me.

When the ambulance came to a stop, I opened my eyes. The paramedic spoke her report into a Bluetooth device as her partner opened the rear door, and I found Alan waiting for me with the emergency room personnel.

"I don't need to go in," I said as they removed me on the gurney from the ambulance.

"Yes, you do," Alan replied softly. "You'll need x-rays and a thorough exam to see if you have a concussion, because I found you totally unconscious."

They whisked me into a cubicle, where a nurse met me and again took my blood pressure. With a worried expression, Alan explained what occurred, saying, "I ran to the yard when I heard the blast and found you on your back about 25 feet from the bomb crater."

"The force of the explosion must have thrown your wife away from any shrapnel, probably saving her from more serious injuries," the nurse remarked as she snapped an oxygen counter on my index finger. "I'm sure the doctor will order x-rays."

Alan nodded his approval while the nurse asked me basic questions about my medical history. As she entered the details into her computer, I realized that my brain had cleared and I considered the focus on me a waste of time. Alan needed to find the person responsible for the havoc occurring in Aspen Notch.

When an aide arrived to take me to the x-ray department, I assured Alan that he needn't follow. Instead, he could begin to track down the origin of the pipe bomb.

"Mark Matthews and the forensics team are working on it," Alan replied while he continued to walk by my side. "They'll update me through the night."

"The driver of the blue Chevy tossed the bomb into our yard," I stated, picturing the scene still etched in my brain.

Alan did a double-take. "Impossible," he exclaimed. "The mechanic told me it wasn't drivable."

"You'll need to send someone to the auto repair shop," I said, "because I'm positive that I saw the blue Chevy."

Alan didn't even get a chance to respond before the doors swung open to Radiology, where the technicians waited for me. One of them positioned me for each of the x-rays, then moved out of range, while the other took the pictures and made sure to have clear images. I cringed to see the clock on the wall indicate the time as 11:15 p.m.

When the aide transported me back to the cubicle to wait for the attending physician, I noticed Alan pacing in the waiting area, deep in conversation on his phone. He signaled that he'd join me for the doctor's assessment and, thank goodness, we didn't have a long wait.

Just before midnight, to my relief, the doctor told me that I could go home since, other than scrapes and bruises, I had no serious physical injuries. He instructed me to take two Tylenol for my headache and drink plenty of water before bed. Other than that, I just needed to rest for the next day or so.

While Alan went to get the car, the aide helped me into a wheelchair and transported me to the hospital entrance. As I sat waiting for Alan, I couldn't help but think about a very different outcome had I not turned away from the fence when I did, and I had no doubt that the person responsible would continue until we found him or her.

ON THE DRIVE HOME, Alan didn't want to discuss the investigation, but I insisted since someone targeted me with two threats on my life. I felt it important that we determine the identity of the blue Chevy's driver, and I thought that we should take a closer look at the letters sent to Irma and me.

"Irma got another one," Alan muttered. "She called 911."

"Geez," I sighed. "Whoever's doing this must be nuts."

"As you can imagine," Alan said, "Irma's scared. I called her when you had your x-rays, and she's decided to stay with a relative, though she didn't say where."

"In Aspen Notch?" I asked.

"I assume New York," Alan replied. "She gave me her cell phone number in case I need to reach her."

"That's probably a good idea," I nodded. "The kook could target the next pipe bomb for Irma. What about the auto repair shop?"

With the light of a passing car, I saw Alan shake his head. "Mark Matthews met the owner at the shop," Alan stated, "who showed Mark the Impala on the lift with no transmission. Sorry, honey, but you didn't see the blue Chevy."

I closed my eyes as Alan maneuvered into our driveway, and the scene just before the blast remained vivid in my mind. Without a doubt, I saw the same car that ran me off the road. How would that be possible? Suddenly, it came to me.

I grabbed Alan's arm as he turned off the engine. "Check the license plates," I urged.

"What do you mean?" Alan questioned.

"The vehicle on the lift with no transmission should have tags registered to Bernie Calamito. I'll bet you a million dollars that someone switched the plates."

"Do you actually think we'd find another blue Chevy in Aspen Notch?" Alan asked.

"I do," I stated firmly, "and I've no doubt it has Bernie's license plate on it."

CHAPTER 49

$\mathcal{A}$lan sent out an all-points-bulletin to search for the older model blue Chevy as soon as we got into the house. I, on the other hand, received an impressive greeting by Sophie. As I made my way to the recliner, flipping on the hallway lights and taking off my jacket, my eyes caught sight of the massive wads of toilet tissue strewn from the bathroom to the living room.

"What's all this?" I asked Sophie in my sternest voice.

She put her eyes to the floor, her tail thumping, with guilt written all over her face. Alan glanced up from his phone, and gave a hearty chuckle, though I stifled my own grin, grateful that Sophie hadn't had the impulse to do any serious damage while we went to the hospital. She had focused on only one objective, and we could easily rectify that.

In between his calls, Alan picked up the mess and offered to make me a cup of decaf tea. He even took Sophie out while he inspected the fence and crater resulting from the pipe bomb. Not yet ready to go to bed, I kicked back in the recliner and pondered why someone would want to hurt me.

Not many people knew that I'd gone with Alan and Irma to Sal's shop after his death, and even fewer realized I'd taken the contents of

Sal's waste basket. The locksmith had seen me there, and may have noticed my nosing around, but I doubted it since he'd focused on changing the locks.

Lou Greene, the mayor, may have known of my meddling with the investigation because Alan, for some reason, seemed to believe that he had to tell him everything. Lou could have held a grudge against me since I accused Bernie Calamito of being the last to see Sal, but that happened well after the death threat. Lou just annoyed me, and I couldn't imagine that he'd try to kill me.

I didn't think I'd ever discussed any details of the murder case with Evelyn Sandler. First of all, I never wanted to add to Evelyn's distress because our gruesome discovery of Sal's body upset her so much. More importantly, though, I considered her my friend, and knew she had nothing to hide.

By the time Alan returned with Sophie and my tea, I'd not thought of anyone who'd want to harm me. Sophie plopped to the floor by my side, while Alan described the size of the hole made by the bomb and the minor repairs we'd need in order to fix the fence.

"It could have been worse," I said, trying to sound upbeat and worry-free.

Alan nodded, looking exhausted. "I've decided to notify Lou of my resignation in the morning," he remarked. "You're in too much danger, and I can't risk losing you."

I took a sip of my tea, gathering my thoughts, then stated, "That won't solve this problem or make it go away. Aspen Notch needs you."

"Mark Matthews can step in," Alan said. "He's young, but he's a good cop. I'd gladly hand over the reins to him."

"I agree that he'd be a great addition to the Aspen Notch police force," I replied, "but you have the experience required to serve as chief of police. You can groom him as your successor."

"I don't want to put you in harm's way," Alan countered.

I nodded my agreement, saying, "I know. I'll lay low for a few days. Besides, John and Deke will keep an eye on me here."

Alan rubbed the stubble on his chin, a sure sign that he needed to mull over his options. I understood his conflict since someone murdered his first wife in a botched robbery, and he spent years hunting down her killer. I certainly wouldn't want Alan forced to relive the experience.

"This would be the perfect time for a smoke," Alan noted with a quirky grin.

"You gave up cigarettes almost a year ago," I said.

"I know. I'm just saying."

We both laughed until Alan took my mug to the sink, then helped me from the recliner. I put my arms around him, leaned into his strength, and kissed him lovingly. He returned my kiss passionately before he led me to our bedroom.

Sophie would just have to get used to it.

CHAPTER 50

*E*velyn called the next morning to ask how I felt since she heard about the pipe bomb incident and my injury on the local news. She wanted to visit me in the hospital, but thought it better to call first.

"I'm home," I said, trying to reassure her that I felt fine. "You're welcome to come over, but we have to stay in the den."

"That's a relief," Evelyn sighed. "I'll be your nurse for as long as you can put up with me. Marty decided to go hunting, so I have time on my hands."

"I'd appreciate having your company," I said, "especially since workers will install all of the bathroom furnishings today. We can play cards or something, as long as we stay out of the way."

"I'll arrive shortly," Evelyn noted, "and we'll have fun."

I rummaged through the desk drawer for a notepad and the deck of cards as I told Sophie that her friend would join us. She wagged her tail in anticipation, though I didn't know if she really understood my words. Regardless, I felt sure that she'd relish the extra attention.

I had just finished telling John that Evelyn Sanders would come for a visit when my phone jingled with a call from Alan.

"How do you feel?" he asked. "I'm sorry I had to leave so early this morning, but I didn't want to wake you."

"Worse than after my first attempt at skiing with you last winter, but better than after giving birth to Alexa," I panned.

"It's good to see you haven't lost your sense of humor," Alan chuckled. "You're a real trooper."

"Actually, you're the trooper of the family," I teased. "I'm just along for the ride."

"Very funny," Alan said. "Have you followed the doctor's orders?"

"I haven't done much of anything," I remarked. "Evelyn's coming over to play nursemaid."

"That's great. I won't hold you, but I wanted you to know that you made the right call. Someone stole Bernie's tags from the Impala."

"I knew it!" I exclaimed.

"You can gloat later," Alan replied. "Promise me that you won't leave the house today. I've advised the county and state police to search for the blue Chevy with Bernie's license plate, and I'll question Gladys further since she drove the Impala."

After I gave my word, Alan noted that no one informed the news media of my release from the hospital because their security director suggested the extra precaution for my safety. I agreed that their plan eliminated some of my fear, and I'd let Evelyn, John, and Deke know the necessity of their discretion.

"Be safe," I said. "I'll keep the home fires burning."

"I hope you're joking," Alan replied with a hearty chortle. "Bad things come in three's, so you're on shaky ground. We don't need a fire on top of everything else."

"Don't even think about it," I laughed. "I meant to say that I love you and look forward to your coming home."

"Right back at you, pal."

～

EVELYN BROUGHT enough food for an army. In addition to ham and cheese sandwiches for lunch, she had a bag of chips, a container of onion dip, a package of sticky buns, a 2-liter bottle of soda, and her lasagna specialty that Alan and I could have for supper. Touched by her thoughtfulness, I welcomed her warmly.

As she placed her bags on the kitchen counter, I put away the things needing refrigeration, while John gathered the rollers in the laundry room that he needed for the day. Since Evelyn had suggested John for our house-painting project, I told her how much we admired his work, loud enough for him to hear my praises, and his face beamed with pride.

"It looks fabulous in here," Evelyn said. "Well done, John."

"I appreciate your endorsement," John replied, joining us in the kitchen. "In a few more days, we'll finish the job here, and we've enjoyed working for the Jaworski's."

"Not so fast, John Calhoon," I chuckled. "We intend to fix up Abe's cabin so I can open a garden shop."

John's face lit up. "That's great news. Everyone in town has speculated what you'll do with the place."

"I haven't discussed my ideas with Alan yet," I said, "so please keep it to yourself for now. I'll also let Deke know since we'll want him to oversee any necessary renovations, and he understands how I want to preserve the historic look."

Evelyn and John both nodded their agreement. Despite all of the turmoil during the last few days, I had a good feeling about using Abe's cabin as a business. I had no concept of the start-up involved, but if Clara Whitman could do it, so could I. Besides, I considered it another way to showcase the town's history.

"Speaking of keeping quiet," I added, "Alan and I would prefer that no one divulge my presence at home."

John's questioning gaze required my retelling about the pipe bombing, which shocked him since he hadn't watched the news on TV, and he suspected the same for Deke. Of course, he wondered if the driver of the blue Chevy instigated the incident and, though I thought it probable, I assured him that the police had everything under control.

"Your husband has the license plate numbers," John said. "What's the holdup?"

"It's complicated," I stated. "Anyway, I don't intend to fret about it since county and state police are searching for the car. I'd appreciate it if you would tell Deke about the need for total discretion until the cops find the creep."

"Of course," John nodded, "and I'll keep an eye out, as well. Don't worry about a thing."

I expressed my thanks and suggested that Evelyn open the box of sticky buns. I didn't want either of them to sense my unease, so I tried to keep our conversation upbeat, even as I gave Evelyn a knife and plates.

"By the way," John noted as he took a bite, "I forgot to tell you about lunch at Dottie's place yesterday. She said she'd go out with me."

"That's fabulous," I grinned. "Did you make plans?"

"Yep," John smiled. "We'll see a movie on Saturday night. Actually, her son doesn't know it yet, but we'll go with him and a few of his friends."

"Won't he be surprised?" I teased. "You'll like Rob and his buddies. They're nice kids."

"I'm just glad I listened to your advice," John replied. "All these years, I considered Dottie the woman for me. It's probably why I never found anyone else who left me weak-kneed like she does."

"Take your time and don't push it," I advised. "I think the two of you would make a great couple."

Evelyn agreed and joked about my role as a matchmaker, which brought a chuckle from John, and I recognized that it felt good to play a part in another person's happiness.

As we carried our plates to the den, with Sophie nipping at our heels, I thought about the impact we had on others. A kind word and selfless concern for others made life so much more meaningful, and I intended to do more of that in Aspen Notch.

That is, of course, if the crazy lunatic who tried to get rid of me would leave me alone.

CHAPTER 51

*E*velyn and I gazed out the den window as we enjoyed our sticky buns. She had no idea that I unobtrusively watched for the blue Chevy, while she had her focus on the weather. Although I saw nothing other than a few wispy clouds in the sky, she noted that we'd probably have a measurable snowfall before Thanksgiving, which I considered much too early in the season.

I'm not sure how the conversation switched to my recent accidents, but I really didn't want to give any details to Evelyn. I skirted around the issue, trying to make light of my bad luck, but she didn't seem to buy it.

Evelyn put her plate of crumbs on the coffee table, which Sophie considered her reward for staying by our side. "Sorry," she smiled, shooing Sophie away. "Marty and I spoke about this after we saw the news last night."

"Spoke about what?" I asked as I moved our plates to the top shelf of the bookcase.

"Honestly," Evelyn admitted, "I felt frightened since you and I found Sal's body. What if his killer comes after us?"

"Have you had any strange occurrences?" I queried.

"No," Evelyn stated with a shake of her head. "I suppose that sounds paranoid because Marty thought it did. Anyway, he figures that someone's trying to divert Alan's concentration on the murder case. What better way to keep the police chief from snooping than to make *you* a distraction?"

"Marty has a point," I said with a rueful chuckle. "Do you want to play Hearts?"

"Sure," Evelyn agreed, "but you'll have to remind me of the rules since I haven't played in years."

My ploy to redirect Evelyn's attention worked, because she turned her focus to our card game. After our first round, I added up the scores while Evelyn watched two burly guys from the window when they carried in the new toilet. We heard them traipse down the hall, which caught Sophie's interest, and she pawed at the door.

Sophie's restlessness made me realize that she hadn't gone out since John and Deke arrived. When I commented about that, Evelyn immediately offered to take her to the yard.

Once she and Sophie returned, I dealt the next hand. As Evelyn organized her cards, she remarked that she saw several cops measuring the crater from the pipe bomb and looking for evidence. It was no wonder, I thought, that the driver of the blue Chevy had kept his or her distance.

On a whim, I asked Evelyn about Gladys Calamito, saying that I'd never met her. It still seemed odd to me that neither she nor the mayor's wife had ever welcomed me to Aspen Notch.

"She's all right," Evelyn replied. "You have to understand that she's kind of an introvert. Bernie's the talker in the family."

"I heard that she's not feeling well," I remarked.

"That's interesting," Evelyn said, leading with the two of clubs. "I saw her at the mall last week, and she didn't look sick."

"Maybe I heard wrong," I stated. "Was Bernie with her?"

"No," Evelyn replied. "She told me that he was busy."

"Out of town?" I questioned.

"I didn't get that impression, but we didn't talk that long. Like I said, she's a quiet one."

I took time to reorganize my cards, wanting to ask more questions about Gladys, but afraid that I'd overstep my bounds. I knew Evelyn well enough to suspect that she'd have told me anything negative about Gladys right away since she didn't keep her opinions to herself.

We finished our hand just before John gave a light tap to the den door, then entered. He wanted us to know that the work crew intended to take their lunch break, and that he and Deke would leave shortly for a quick bite themselves. Before they left, though, Deke wanted to show me the bathroom arrangement.

While I went to see Deke, John took Sophie out again, and Evelyn put away our morning snack and prepared our lunches. If it weren't for my stiff and achy muscles, I'd have jumped for joy with such attentiveness from my friends.

I found the bathroom vanity even more beautiful than the brochure had pictured. It fit perfectly in the space allotted, and had wooden organizers in each drawer to keep everything in its place. I particularly liked the built-in electrical power strip with holders for my curling iron and hair dryer, and it even had a space for Alan's electric razor.

"I love it," I exclaimed to Deke. "I can't believe how well you can read my mind."

"The plumber will arrive after lunch to hook everything up," Deke noted. "The electrician will finish up tomorrow, and he'll also take a look at the cabin's electrical box. I have a feeling you'll need to upgrade it."

"That's what I figured," I said. "Besides, I've decided that I should use the log cabin for a garden shop, so I'll need plenty of electrical outlets.

Deke didn't look overly surprised, but his expression told me that he liked my plans. Frankly, the more I heard myself talk about starting a business, the more eager I felt.

"Clara would be proud of you," Deke replied with a broad smile, "and I can help you design the shop."

"I hoped you'd say that. I wouldn't know where to begin."

EVELYN and I feasted on her sandwiches and chips at the dining room table. Sophie laid at our feet, probably hoping to catch any morsels we dropped. Besides, I'd given her a chewy bone, so that kept her busy while we chatted.

After she took a sip of her soda, Evelyn remarked that she'd decided I should get to know Gladys Calamito. She wanted to host a dinner party for Bernie and his wife, as well as the mayor and his wife, with Alan and me as the guests of honor. I tried to show a little enthusiasm, but Evelyn picked up on my reserve.

"What's the matter?" she asked, taking a long look at me. "We can have an enjoyable meal while you make new friends."

"I don't know," I shrugged. "I met the mayor's wife, but didn't take to her attitude, as if she's so busy with her social calendar. Also, I'm not that interested in meeting Gladys since I've heard she has a nasty streak."

Evelyn gazed at me, then said, "Mildred Greene does have a lofty opinion of herself, but she's OK. I mean we're not close friends, but she's a good mayor's wife. On the other hand, I think you'd like Gladys once you got to know her."

After reflecting for a moment, I stated, "I guess if I want to start a business, I should build a social network, so Alan and I will gladly come to your party."

"Good," Evelyn smiled. "I'll talk to Marty about it and get back to you with a date."

As we ate our lunch, we chatted about some of the people I should align with in Aspen Notch. They could help spread the word about the garden shop and provide a lot of support for our start-up. It made me smile to hear Evelyn chat about *our* grand opening, as if she were a partner, though I'd have to give that further consideration.

Munching on one of her chips, Evelyn asked if I'd heard when Irma D'Angelo planned to have a funeral for Sal. Though she admitted she had no particular fondness for Irma, Evelyn told me she'd want to attend.

"I don't think she'll have one," I replied.

"Why not?" Evelyn questioned.

I shrugged my shoulders, not really knowing the answer. "She's still distraught, I guess. I don't think she has any friends, and she's never mentioned any family. She and Sal had a son, but he died of meningitis."

"Wow," Evelyn exclaimed. "I didn't realize they'd lost a child. That's terrible."

"Yes," I nodded. "His death caused a great deal of grief, as you can imagine. Irma told me that Sal blamed her for not bringing Frankie to the doctor soon enough."

"Geez. What a horrible thing for her husband to say. That must have devastated Irma."

"I'm sure," I agreed, "and she had no family to turn to. Her parents and Sal's parents are deceased."

Evelyn's concerned expression turned to a frown. "She's got family, right here in Aspen Notch."

"I don't think so," I replied, shaking my head.

"I know so," Evelyn said emphatically. "A cousin, I think. He's an auto mechanic, employed at Joe's Garage. He worked on my car the last time I needed an oil change."

I swore my heart skipped a few beats as I pondered what Evelyn told me. My brain swirled, making connections I didn't want to consider. Still, they loomed larger than life.

"Are you OK?" Evelyn asked. "Your hand is shaking."

"I need to call Alan. Can you take Sophie out?"

"Sure," Evelyn said, "but maybe I should call 911."

"No, I'm fine. I just need to talk to Alan."

As soon as Evelyn and Sophie went outside, I pressed Alan's number, and prayed that he'd pick up the call. I breathed a sigh of relief when he answered on the first ring.

CHAPTER 52

*A*lan barely finished his greeting before I interrupted. I tried to keep my voice steady while putting words to my thoughts since every part of my brain exploded with snippets of conversations and observations that came rushing to the forefront.

"What's the name of the auto repair shop where the blue Impala's getting a new transmission?" I asked.

"It's on the lift at Joe's Garage," Alan replied. "Why?"

Incongruent as it sounded, I blurted, "You need to arrest Irma D'Angelo for the murder of her husband."

Alan paused, then reminded me that he had no evidence of Irma's involvement in Sal's murder. When I disagreed, maybe more vehemently then necessary, Alan took the time to hear me out.

Gathering my thoughts, I stated, "You always tell me that a crime against someone needs motive, opportunity, and means. I now realize that Irma meets those criteria."

"I'm listening," Alan said.

"Irma had come to hate Sal," I remarked. "He reminded her constantly of the death of their child, berating her verbally. He accumulated a huge sum of money, yet they hardly had any food in the house."

"I'm not sure that's motive for murder, but go on."

Taking a deep breath, I continued, "Obviously, the means was the knife from their butcher's block. Irma lied when she said she didn't know where it was, then tried to make us think that Bernie had taken it."

"Do you think she tried to set up Bernie?" Alan asked.

"Maybe, at first," I replied, "though I'm not sure because she liked Bernie. It makes more sense that she tried to implicate Gladys Calamito."

"You reminded me that Irma could barely get around," Alan noted. "How did she have opportunity?"

"That's the key," I said. "Evelyn just told me that Irma has a cousin who lives in Aspen Notch. She may have asked him to drive her to the pizza shop, and prevent anyone from going in while she killed Sal with the knife that went missing from their butcher's block. Then he took her home so she could act like the bereaved widow."

"Honey, that's a bit far-fetched," Alan sighed. "Who's this cousin?"

"I don't know his name but he's a mechanic who works at Joe's Garage," I replied. "He had opportunity to switch the tags on the Impala and, maybe, make the bomb from some kind of metal pipe used in auto repairs."

"What about the death threats?" Alan questioned. "Irma received two of them."

"I wouldn't be surprised if Irma wrote them herself, then had her cousin deliver mine. I totally forgot about it, but when Irma checked the receipt for food I brought, she used a red crayon."

"Do you think Irma knew enough to make sure she left no fingerprints?" Alan asked with skepticism.

"She watches crime shows on TV," I stated. "Remember, she asked why you didn't take her to the interrogation room at the police station."

"This is all circumstantial," Alan remarked. "We can talk more about it when I get home."

"No, we can't," I all but yelled into the phone. "Irma said she intended to leave town, so search her house, give her a lie-detector test, and arrest her. While you're at it, find that cousin of hers who tried to kill me."

I PACED the floor in the living room, with the phone still in my hand, when Evelyn returned with Sophie. My entire body ached and my head throbbed, but I knew I needed to muster some grit to get through the rest of the afternoon.

"Is everything OK?" Evelyn asked.

"I guess I had a panic attack," I replied, willing myself to calm down. "Alan talked me through it."

"That's understandable," Evelyn gently remarked. "Why don't you go into the den and take a rest? I'll clean up here and Sophie can stay with me."

"That would be wonderful," I sighed. "Thank you."

In the hall bathroom, I took two extra-strength Tylenol and downed them with a sip of water before heading to the den. After closing the door, I took a deep breath and settled myself among the pillows on the futon. I knew I wouldn't fall asleep, because I kept thinking about Alan, and prayed for his safety.

I heard Evelyn chatting with Deke and John in the kitchen when they returned from lunch. I surmised that the plumber and work crew would also soon arrive, but I welcomed more of the distractions to keep my fears at bay.

My friend, Trudi, sometimes reminded me that I could be gullible. Despite my awareness of the trait, I hadn't changed. I fell for Earl's deceit last year as readily as my first husband's lies for years during our marriage. Now I felt that Irma D'Angelo had duped me again. Would I ever learn?

My mother once told me that she considered trust one of my best qualities. She meant it as a compliment, I felt certain, though I couldn't help wondering if I would have been better off with something like beauty or brains. Still brooding about my naiveté when

Evelyn tapped on the door, she announced that she brought me a cup of freshly brewed tea.

"I wasn't sure if you fell asleep," she said with a warm smile, "but I wouldn't be doing my job if I didn't fulfill your every need and want."

I reached for the mug, grateful for her thoughtfulness. It took everything in me to hold it steady when Sophie pounced on my lap, though we both laughed when Evelyn pulled her away.

"Just what the doctor ordered," I said, "but I'm not a very good hostess. Shall we get back to our card game?"

"I hate to say this," Evelyn replied, "but Marty just called. His buddy didn't feel well, and they decided to make a short day of hunting, so I'd better go home."

"That's fine," I said, trying to decide if I felt disappointed or relieved. "I'm really grateful for all of the time you spent with me today."

"I enjoyed it," Evelyn grinned. "Don't get up because I can let myself out."

"Before you go, can you tell me the name of Irma's cousin who changed your oil at Joe's Garage? I thought I might ask him to give me an estimate on the repairs for my car."

"Let me think," Evelyn paused. "I've got it. His name's Ben Cirillo, but I doubt he gives estimates since he works for Joe."

"OK," I nodded. "Thanks for everything. You have no idea how much you helped me today."

"That's what friends are for," Evelyn smiled.

CHAPTER 53

*S*ophie and I dozed in the den until John tapped on the door. Glancing at my watch, I saw that the time approached for Deke and John's departure, and realized that the house, now quiet, indicated the work crew must have already left.

"Your new bathroom's ready for use, if you want to take a look," John said, opening the door a crack.

"Are you kidding?" I asked.

John laughed, saying, "It's ready as long as you don't need light or privacy. I just meant that the plumbing works now."

Sophie and I followed John to the new *en-suite*. Deke told us that the crews would install wallboard and door frames in the morning after the electrician finished the wiring. I couldn't help thinking it all came together faster than I imagined.

"It looks good," I said, especially approving the size of the walk-in closet. "Now, go on home and get some rest."

"Do you want me to take Sophie out before we leave?" John questioned.

"I'd appreciate it," I nodded. "If you don't mind, toss her a few sticks so she gets a chance to run."

Deke and I walked to the living room where we could sit while waiting. He looked especially tired, which had me a little worried, and I wondered if he'd have the stamina to oversee the renovations to Abe's cabin. I didn't share my misgivings with Deke because, in the end, he'd have to make the final decision.

"Are you OK here until your husband gets home?" Deke questioned.

"Sure," I nodded. "I won't go out and I'll lock the doors. Besides, I have Sophie as a watchdog."

Deke gave a quirky smile, perhaps thinking that the pup wouldn't do well as my protector. He may also have detected my false bravado which, admittedly, wasn't very convincing.

"I have another question for you, Deke," I said, hoping I didn't sound too intrusive. "You know Sophie's a digger and I'm afraid she might find bones hidden in the yard. Can you tell me where Clara buried the child she bore?"

Deke nodded, with a sad cast to his eyes. "In the flower bed by the old cabin. Clara told me that the tiny fetus fit into a cookie tin, and she buried it deep, so I don't think Sophie will find it."

With a rue chuckle, I said, "I wondered why Sophie kept snooping there. I intend to plant a perennial garden in that area, so I'll make it off-limits to Sophie as we preserve Clara's legacy."

"It would mean a lot to Clara," Deke said softly, "and to me. Thank you."

Relieved to know the location of the burial plot, I assured Deke that I saw no reason to dredge up the past, and he could trust me with his and Clara's secret. Deke nodded, then took my hand and gave it a squeeze. We needed no additional words.

My phone rang just as John returned from the yard with Sophie. Seeing Alan's name on the caller ID, I excused myself to answer. John and Deke both nodded.

"Any news?" I asked.

"Turn on channel 6," Alan said. "I'll be home shortly."

Alan disconnected the call as I pressed the TV remote. The local news anchor, standing in front of the Aspen Notch police station, interviewed Alan. While the camera scanned Sal's Pizza Shop and numerous state and county police vehicles, Alan announced that Ben Cirillo, identified as a first cousin to Irma D'Angelo, had ties to a drug cartel and killed Sal D'Angelo. He also admitted responsibility for the pipe bombing at the police chief's residence.

Almost simultaneously, John and Deke let out a whoop. I felt my eyes dampen and relief spread to every part of my body. With great pride, I heard Alan's statement of appreciation to the men and women in blue who helped bring a speedy close to the investigation. Lou Greene, the mayor, stepped forward to praise Alan's tenacity to restore confidence and security in the town of Aspen Notch.

"Your husband's one sharp cop," John noted as I turned off the TV. "I'll bet the guy who did it is also the person who ran you off the road."

"Probably," I agreed, "and you helped identify him. The two of you can go now since I don't have to worry anymore and Alan's on his way home. Besides, I intend to have a celebration dinner in his honor."

CHAPTER 54

$\mathcal{E}$velyn called as I put her lasagna in the oven, and I knew, even before I answered, that she must have seen the early news. No doubt, she'd have lots of questions for me to field.

"Irma D'Angelo's cousin killed Sal!" Evelyn exclaimed.

"I just heard about it," I said. "It's unbelievable."

"Tell me all the details," Evelyn pleaded.

"I don't know any more than you do," I sighed, "because Alan's not home yet."

"It must have devastated Irma when she learned that her cousin did it." Evelyn continued. "I felt sorry for her, especially after you told me that her young son died."

"I've always felt sorry for Irma," I said. "She was a victim of grief and emotional abuse, and I guess we'd never know what effect that has on a person unless we've experienced something similar."

"Well, I hope she can get over this and move on with her life," Evelyn remarked. "Promise you'll call me tomorrow. I can't wait to hear how Alan figured it out."

I gave my word of honor, though I knew I'd keep some things to myself. Since I still needed to set the table and prepare a salad, I cut our conversation short.

Slicing a tomato when Alan arrived, Sophie surprised me with her insistent bark, which made me wonder if she actually could serve as a guard dog. As soon as she recognized Alan's scent, she ran to him, then pounced as he hung his jacket in the hall closet.

Laughing, Alan pushed her away, then embraced me. I nestled in the curve of his shoulder before reaching my lips up to meet his. If the oven timer hadn't dinged, we may have had to put dinner on hold.

"You're amazing," Alan said, breaking away from me.

"I just had a hunch, though it wasn't quite correct. You're the one who had to do all of the dirty work."

"I couldn't have done it alone," Alan remarked. "You put us on the right track, and Mark Matthews provided tremendous assistance. Did you watch the press conference?"

"I did," I nodded. "I'm so glad you thanked the other cops, and I considered the mayor's recognition of your talents a very nice gesture."

Alan agreed, then said, "Lou seemed pretty relieved to have the case closed."

I suggested that Alan get comfy while I put dinner on the table. He didn't argue the point, a sure sign of his exhaustion. I turned off the oven, placed the lasagna in the center of the table with the salad, and opened a bottle of Cabernet Sauvignon.

It made me smile to see Alan padding to the dining room in his sweats and slippers, with Sophie trailing behind. I knew she waited for the perfect opportunity to pilfer a slipper, but I distracted her with a bowl of kibbles. After I poured us each a glass of wine, I raised mine with a hearty "Cheers!"

Alan followed suit and pulled out a chair. "I intended to take you out to dinner. Honest."

"Another night," I promised. "Evelyn brought the lasagna and I just needed to heat it in the oven."

"That was nice of her," Alan said. "Did she provide good company today?"

"Evelyn helped me see the connections," I explained. "If she hadn't told me Irma had a cousin in town who worked as an auto mechanic at Joe's Garage, I'd never have found the missing piece of the puzzle."

"You didn't even know the cousin's name," Alan noted.

"I asked Evelyn after I spoke with you," I said. "When she identified him as Ben Cirillo, it all became clear to me."

"How's that?" Alan asked.

"Sal had horrible handwriting, and I needed Irma's help to decipher it. She told me it said *Ber C.* on the piece of paper from his trash, and I gullibly believed her. After I learned her cousin's name, I realized that Irma had duped me."

"Do you think she tried to throw you off by misleading you with the letters in the name?" Alan queried.

"Yep," I nodded. "She knew that the paper could identify her cousin as the person meeting Sal at 4:15, so she transposed the lower-case letter *n* in Ben to throw me off-track."

"Irma's no dummy," Alan stated, "but if it makes you feel any better, I also thought it looked like an *r*, not an *n*."

"Irma was definitely clever," I agreed. "She considered me a threat to the cover-up, and must have warned Ben to scare me off."

"Obviously," Alan nodded as he scooped a large square of lasagna to his plate, "and divert your attention by giving you the pup."

"She probably also wanted me to think that she couldn't get around well enough to care for a puppy. It worked but, if you ask me, it was *her* loss."

"And our gain," Alan chuckled, "especially if Sophie finds any more of Clara's treasures."

After I added lasagna and salad to my plate, I asked, "How did you know that Ben, not Irma, killed Sal?"

"That made an interesting turn of events," Alan said. "You might just say that we got lucky."

"Tell me!" I pleaded.

"Later," Alan promised. "Let's just enjoy our supper for now because I'm famished."

CHAPTER 55

fter supper, Alan took Sophie to the yard while I put the plates in the dishwasher and the leftovers in the fridge. By the time they returned, I had brought our wine to the living room and already sat under the throw on the sofa, though I made room for Alan to join me.

"It feels as if it wants to snow out there," he noted as he slipped under the coverlet with me.

"Cuddle time," I smiled, nestling closer. "Now will you tell me how you got Irma's cousin to confess?"

"You're like a dog with a bone," Alan teased. "What part do you want to hear?"

"All of it," I sighed.

Alan explained that the hospital security director called him shortly after my earlier call since their parking lot cameras picked up a blue Chevy with Bernie's tags. A security officer met the driver at the hospital entrance and asked to see an ID. It identified him as Ben Cirillo, and he had a syringe in his jacket pocket.

"Who was that for?" I questioned.

"Guess," Alan quipped.

"What was in the syringe?" I asked.

"I sent it to the lab for analysis," Alan noted, "although I'd suppose a large dose of crystal meth, enough to kill."

I shivered with the realization that he had gone to the hospital to finish the job and kill me. Continuing, Alan noted that he sent Sergeant Matthews to place Cirillo under arrest, then put out an all-points-bulletin for Irma.

"Had she already left town?" I queried.

"No," Alan replied. "Ben Cirillo crumbled when Matthews hand-cuffed him. He told Matthews the entire story, and accused Irma of masterminding everything. Basically, he sold her down the river."

"So, where did you find Irma?" I asked.

"She holed up in Ben's apartment," Alan stated. "Believe it or not, he lived right above the pizza shop."

"Weird," I said with a shake of my head. "He could watch the place and inform Irma of the goings-on. Hey! I wonder if he was the one who'd taken cash from Sal's register."

"Yep," Alan nodded. "I got him to admit it."

"Interesting," I remarked. "So, where did he keep his car, the other blue Chevy?"

"That's even weirder," Alan replied. "He found the same make and model as the Calamito's second car on eBay, and kept it in a garage in the next town. Apparently, Irma promised to pay him for it from the stash in Sal's safe, along with a hefty fee for his services."

I ran my fingers through my hair as I thought about the planning that went into Irma's scheme. Alan went on to say that, with the help of county police, he brought Irma to the station. Within an hour, he managed to get a search warrant signed by one of the county judges and sent a team to the D'Angelo home. They found the loose-leaf pad, a red crayon, and a box of nitrile gloves. The pad had the indentations from her death threats.

By the time the search team informed Alan about the findings in her house, Sergeant Matthews arrived at the station with her cousin. Irma knew she was cornered, especially when Ben Cirillo faced her and snarled that he had only followed her orders. They got into a shouting match, each accusing the other of murder.

"Are you sure that Ben wielded the knife that killed Sal?" I asked.

"Yep," Alan replied. "As you suspected, he had a meeting with Sal at 4:15 that day, and we now know that Sal D'Angelo laundered cash for him. Cirillo has a rap sheet for selling drugs."

"I guess they went to the back room to exchange money and the deal went bad," I said, musing aloud. "With no sign of a fight, though, maybe Cirillo planned to stab Sal and take all the money in the safe. Do you think Irma knew about Sal's business dealings with Ben?"

"No," Alan said. "She admitted to having a huge argument with Sal the night before. Irma called Ben the next morning and told him to get rid of Sal. She swears she didn't mean that he should kill Sal, but he swears that she did. A good lawyer's going to have to sort that out."

"Did Irma give him the knife from her butcher's block?"

"No. Ben picked it up from the table in the prep room. Sal must have taken it to his shop to replace one of his knives, and it didn't have Cirillo's prints because he wore gloves."

"So," I murmured, "It really did shock Irma to hear that Sal had died."

"Exactly," Alan nodded. "When she saw so much cash in the safe, she put two and two together. Of course, then you entered the picture, and showed her the papers from Sal's trash. When you told her your theory about Sal and money laundering, she informed her cousin that you posed a threat."

I nodded, wondering how I could have been so stupid to trust Irma. She figured that I'd share what I knew with Alan, so she plotted ways to distract me. Each time that I'd returned, showing her additional information, she had to come up with a new plan.

"Do you think Irma cleaned up the crime scene before you had the locks changed?" I asked.

"No. Ben did that. He swept the flour from the floor, but never thought about checking Sal's waste basket."

""I'll bet Irma had a fit about that," I noted. "Where are they now?"

"The county prison," Alan said. "Ben will stand trial for murder, and Irma gave us enough evidence to indict her as his accomplice, at least in the attempted murder of you."

The whole situation troubled me. I still felt sadness for Irma, knowing we'd never understand how bleak her world had become as she lived in darkness. I didn't have as much pity for her cousin, and considered him pond scum, destroying others. I told Alan my opinion of Ben Cirillo, then said that I hoped he'd enjoy the rest of his life in jail.

Alan took my fingers, intertwining them with his. "I spent my entire career trying to protect our citizens. It still surprises me when someone turns to a life of crime because I think of it as such a waste."

I nodded my agreement, then turned to look into Alan's eyes. "Have you decided if you want to stay on as Aspen Notch's chief of police?"

"Not if I put you in danger again," Alan remarked.

"You can't safeguard me from every hazard in life," I said, "and I can't shield you from harm. It's not part of the equation."

"Then I suppose I'll continue," Alan stated. "Lou Greene wants to make the job permanent, not interim."

"What do *you* want?" I pressed.

"I'd like to keep my options open. I told Lou that we need a larger police presence in Aspen Notch. He didn't disagree that Sergeant Mark Matthews would make a good choice."

"When you think he's ready to fill your shoes, you could step down," I suggested. "Maybe you could work part-time."

"That's what I figured," Alan nodded. "You and I could travel or just enjoy the mountain views together. I'd like that."

"Me, too," I agreed.

I thought it the perfect opportunity for me to introduce my decision to start a business using Abe's cabin as a garden shop. I didn't know if Alan would consider me crazy for wanting to take on such a responsibility, but I explained that I felt compelled to carry on Clara Whitman's legacy.

Alan reminded me that it took a lot of time and resources to open a storefront yet, in the same breath, assured me of his support. He agreed that we could showcase the town's history, and I could set my own hours of operation.

"My sentiments exactly," I replied. "I told Evelyn, and she thought I had a great idea. In fact, I think she wants to help."

"You have a good friend," Alan smiled, "and you can't do better than that. I guess we'll need to winterize the cabin."

"Deke and John said they can help with the upgrades," I said with a sly grin, "and they're almost finished with the work in the house."

"You've been scheming," Alan teased.

Laughing, I reached for our glasses of wine on the coffee table and handed Alan his. We took our final sips, and toasted to success for our endeavors, then we kissed.

"I guess we'd better call it a night," I said. "Morning will arrive before we know it."

"Lou told me to take the day off," Alan noted. "Sergeant Matthews will hold down the fort."

"That's even better," I mumbled, settling back into Alan's embrace. "Have I told you lately how much I love you?"

CHAPTER 56

The next morning, I felt rather pampered when Alan suggested that he make bacon and eggs for the two of us after he took Sophie out. I filled her bowl with kibbles and made the coffee, then we enjoyed a leisurely breakfast, despite John and Deke's early arrival.

Deke reminded us that the electrician would arrive for his jobs in the bathroom, walk-in closet, and cabin. John planned to paint the drywall in the *en-suite* and closet, so they'd contain all work to the master bedroom, except for their comings and goings.

"You don't need us to get out of the way?" Alan asked.

"As long as you don't mind the chaos," John replied as he accepted a slice of bacon I offered. "And, by the way, sir, you did our town proud. A lot of folks have said good things about you."

Alan accepted the compliment graciously and I beamed my pride. Despite my residual aches and pains and a few scary days, I knew that we'd made the right decision to move to Aspen Notch. Alan glanced my way and winked.

"Since Alan has the day off," I said, "we'll plan something to occupy ourselves while you finish what you need to do. I'll give a call to Maggie White at Hickory Glen to see if we can drop Sophie off for the day. She'll enjoy romping with other pups while Alan and I explore the area."

"That sounds like a good plan," Alan chuckled, with John echoing something similar. "I heard about a quaint town not too far from here that has all kinds of little stores and bistros. They might also have a garden shop."

"Are you talking about Oakville?" John asked. "It's a great place to visit."

"Yes, that's it," Alan nodded. "How long's a trip there?"

"I'd say about 40 minutes," John said, "if there's not much traffic. My mother used to love it when I took her there, and her favorite place to have lunch was Millie's."

"We'll definitely check it out," I smiled, taking our plates to the sink. "It sounds like fun."

"You deserve some of that," John replied, giving me a pat on the back.

I didn't disagree.

∾

ALAN TOOK the scenic route to Oakville and, though it extended our travel time, I didn't mind. The mountain backdrop looked beautiful in every direction, with low clouds that hovered over their peaks, as if to blanket them in wispy comfort.

Each of the small towns we passed through were carbon copies of Aspen Notch, as if families settling a new location used a master plan, and modeled one Main Street after the other. Each had a couple of storefronts, an eatery, and a church, with the only distinction an unobtrusive sign on the road giving the town an identity.

Oakville seemed different, I noted as Alan slowly cruised the main drag. The place bustled with visitors who enjoyed the eclectic shops or strolled to the gazebo near town center, and I thought it looked quaint, yet current in appeal to all ages.

Centralized parking, not curbside, afforded a good view of the stores with their beautifully decorated front windows, as well as safety for the people milling about. Alan found a parking spot near Millie's, yet directly across the street from *Fireflies and Flowers*, a garden shop of the same character that I imagined.

"What do you think?" Alan asked as he turned off the engine.

"Perfect," I sighed.

"Let's go see how you can transform Abe's cabin into the garden spot of Aspen Notch," Alan smiled.

ALAN and I sat at a booth in Millie's Eatery which reminded us of an old coal-town general store. One section of Millie's had a candy counter, cracker barrels with a variety of crackers and cookies, and racks of gift items. The other offered seating at a counter or booths, with a number of tables interspersed.

We had planned to take a look around the place, but they called our number rather quickly, making it obvious that the staff knew how to move guests in and out with efficiency. As we slid into our seats, my eye caught sight of a striking display of home-made jams and jellies.

"Check out the side wall," I whispered to Alan. "Wouldn't that look cool in our garden shop?"

Alan followed my gaze. "You're also going to make things like jelly? Are you kidding me?"

"Maybe," I chuckled. "I'm just gathering ideas."

"What about the wreaths and floral displays like we saw at *Fireflies and Flowers*?" Alan queried. "I thought you planned to have some of those."

"Definitely," I nodded, "and I also want bird feeders."

Alan encouraged me with more ideas and we both had a good laugh with the bantering, even as the waitress arrived to take our orders. I enjoyed seeing him relax for a change, and I could sense a weight lifting from both of our shoulders. In fact, I pictured our lives together this way: enjoying a meal, visiting new places, and reveling in each other's company.

In no time at all, our food arrived. We had both ordered the deep-dish chicken pot pies, each one enough to feed two people, with an impressive amount of chicken and vegetables, a nicely browned homemade crust, and a cream sauce that looked and smelled delectable.

"For some odd reason, this reminds me of Thanksgiving," I said, blowing the steam from my first spoonful of sauce. "Shall we invite your kids to our house?"

Alan looked pleased with my suggestion. "I think George and his family might want to come, since George suggested our move to Aspen Notch, and he hasn't yet seen our home. I'll give him a call later."

"Tell them to make a weekend of it," I added. "We'll have a good time."

"Do we have enough room?" Alan questioned.

"Sure," I nodded. "We'll take the master bedroom, George and Marianne can have the guest room, and the two boys can have the den to themselves."

"Two teens with full access to a TV and computer," Alan chuckled. "They'll love it."

We decided to hold off inviting my Michael and Alexa until Christmas, and Alan didn't think his daughter and other son could make it because of distance, but he'd check on it. Of course, the weather would play into our final plans, but at least we'd get the ball rolling now.

By the time we'd finished our lunch, the waitress arrived with our check while someone else cleared the table. It made me think about Dottie and how she could use another pair of hands. With additional help, she could handle a faster turn-over in her café, and my musings made me realize that already I strategized as a businesswoman.

Alan and I browsed the other side of Millie's. I purchased a jar of cherry jam for ourselves, and two jars of grape jelly for John and Deke before Alan could pull me away. He knew that I eyed the chocolates and I'd regret it, especially since we still had a bag of Snickers at home.

Similar to the other Oakville visitors, Alan and I strolled to the gazebo and admired the town from its vantage point. Alan took my hand in his as we gazed at the scenery, and a few snow flurries brushed my nose before I leaned into Alan's embrace.

"Do you have enough ideas for your shop?" Alan asked.

"I have plenty for now," I nodded. "Let's check out the bakery and gift shop, then head home. We've had a wonderful excursion."

Alan smiled, giving my shoulders a squeeze. "It couldn't have been more perfect."

CHAPTER 57

*E*velyn called while I cleared the table from our easy supper. After our hefty lunch, I just opened a can of soup and cut into the crusty loaf of bread we'd bought at the Oakville bakery. Sophie, as tired as Alan and I, rested at Alan's feet while he channel-surfed the TV.

"I planned to call you later," I said, rinsing our bowls to put into the dishwasher. "We've had a busy day."

"It's OK," Evelyn said. "I got all the gory details I wanted on the news. I guess you know that Alan's a hero."

"He's a keeper," I replied with a smile. "Anyway, we went to Oakville today. What a great place to visit."

"Gosh," Evelyn sighed. "I never thought to tell you about all of the quaint little shops there. I usually drag Marty during the Christmas season, and you'd love the decorations."

"You and I will have to go back," I suggested. "They have a wonderful garden shop called *Fireflies and Flowers*. It's exactly what I imagined doing with Abe's cabin."

"You're right," Evelyn agreed, "I love the name. In fact, it's what I meant about coming up with a catchy title for your place."

"I know," I chuckled. "Put your thinking cap on."

"I will. The reason I called is to invite you and Alan to our house for dinner on Saturday evening. You can't say no because it's in Alan's honor. Lou and Mildred Greene, as well as Bernie and Gladys Calamito, have already confirmed."

"I'll check with Alan to make sure that the date works for him," I said. "Otherwise, we'll be happy to come."

"Great," Evelyn stated, "but don't get dressed up. Marty and I prefer a casual get-together."

Disconnecting the call, I realized that I'd formed negative opinions about a few people too soon. To my regret, I misjudged Bernie and Gladys, and I had acted rather snobbish with Lou and Mildred, so I considered it time to make an attitude adjustment.

"Who was that?" Alan asked when I settled myself on the sofa. Sophie jumped up to lay beside me.

"Evelyn called," I replied. "She's throwing a dinner party in your honor. Are you free on Saturday night?"

"Only if you'll be my date," Alan teased. "Who's invited?"

"Your favorite people," I said. "Besides celebrating your success, she wants me to get to know Mildred and Gladys since she thinks I'll like them."

"That sounds like a good idea," Alan remarked, glancing at the TV.

"I only hope that Bernie and Gladys can forgive me for all the trouble I caused them," I sighed.

Alan turned his attention back to me. "You don't have to worry about that. I showed Bernie the paper from Sal's trash, and he told me that he'd have come to the same conclusion. He's sorry that he overreacted."

"I'm glad no one harbors hard feelings," I nodded. "By the way, I spoke to Deke when you played in the yard with Sophie."

"What about?" Alan questioned.

"I asked if he knew where Clara had kept the key to the front entrance of her shop."

Alan raised an eyebrow, then said, "I thought you had the locks changed."

"I did," I agreed, "but do you remember about my hearing noises outside when we first moved here?"

"Yep," Alan said, giving me his full attention, "though we never found anything or anyone there. You just felt nervous in a new environment."

"Not so," I countered. "I knew someone was out there."

"Clara's ghost?" Alan teased.

"That would have been interesting," I smiled. "If it was, she's resting in peace now."

"What's your point?" Alan sighed.

"Deke admitted he had the key to the old padlock. He'd heard that Clara's place had sold, and wanted a chance to search the cabin before we took ownership, only he didn't know our settlement date."

"He wanted to find his grandmother's ring?" Alan asked.

Yes," I nodded, "but he had no luck in the cabin, so Deke returned several nights later with a metal detector to explore the yard. He thought it fortunate when he got John's call about the project management job because he no longer needed to risk trespassing."

"Deke *did* trespass," Alan said with a frown. "Do you want to press charges?"

"Of course not," I replied. "He's my friend. Anyway, I just wanted you to know that I wasn't crazy."

Alan laughed, turning off the TV. He stood and stretched, then pushed Sophie off the sofa so he could sit next to me. After putting an arm around my shoulder and pulling me closer, he whispered into my ear, "Honey, the thought never crossed my mind. If anything, I've learned to trust your instincts."

"It took you long enough," I sighed, before locking my lips with his.

CLARA'S RIDDLES

Red and blue, flickering flame,
Eats the wood, knows no shame.
Winter is coming, time to chop,
Fill the bin to the very top.

Time stood still for one so young,
Dark and bitter, melodies never sung.
Ashes to dust, deep in the ground,
Happiness again never to be found.

Blade upon blade, pewter and green,
One will meet its match, as we have seen.
It won't last long, this ongoing fight.
The stronger will fail, the weaker has might.

With bright moonlight they appear,
Looming dark, causing fear.
Always silent, calm as a lamb.
Unless some movement makes them scram.
The wind is the culprit, I so often say,
Though I'm happy they're gone with the light of the day.

Made of tin, wearing a hat,
We fill it up with this and that.
Full to the brim or begging for more,
It must be gone from the store.
Don't worry, I tell it, you'll be back soon.
But it must wait until the afternoon.

A broken heart finds no relief,
Absconding joy, like a thief.
The wound a chasm, black as a crow,
Holding sadness, angst, and woe.

No one can know the secret I bear,
Sins of the past, never to share.
Hidden beneath the soil of the earth,
No bed for her head, no crib for her berth.

Paper and silver in a shallow grave,
No one must know how much I save.
Tins or jars, either are fine,
Safe from those who believe they aren't mine.

Who goes there? Who traipses at night?
Who crosses the lawn, causing my fright?
What search they, those bold,
Is it bones or is it gold?

Too many secrets for a woman, now old.
They must go to my grave, never to be told.
Falling prey to desires with only a boy,
It wasn't a ploy, nor did it bring joy.
Sorrow and regret are all I have left,
My heart is heavy, my soul bereft.

ABOUT THE AUTHOR

Kathleen McKee is a retired educator and registered dietitian who enjoys crafting stories that are uplifting and moving. Regardless of genre, she likes to include a touch of romance and mystery, with narratives that bring the characters to life.

Kathleen's heart-warming stories and their settings are often inspired by experiences of people she has met or places she has lived. Kathleen has fond memories of her years in northeast Pennsylvania when she taught at a school in Scranton. Although Aspen Notch is a fictional town, it provides a fitting setting for Alan and Sue to make their home after their wedding, since they both love the mountain vistas of the Poconos.

Kathleen currently lives in southeast Pennsylvania with her springer spaniel, Maggie. You'll find her there, working on her next novel. Visit her website at: https://kathleen-mckee.com/ and sign up for her newsletter at: http://eepurl.com/crzIUv

Honest reviews of my books help bring them to the attention of other readers. If you enjoyed *Murder in Aspen Notch*, please post a brief review on Amazon.com and/or Goodreads.com. It's unbelievably important and I'd appreciate it so much.

ALSO BY KATHLEEN MCKEE

No Gifts to Bring

(Prequel to the *Aspen Notch Mystery Series*)

The Aspen Notch Mystery Series:

Murder in Aspen Notch

The Garden Shop Mystery

A Cameo Appearance

Below the Landscape

Bedlam in the Blizzard

The Poustinia Series:

Poustinia: A Novel

Joyful Encounters

Bountiful Legacies

A Specter of Truth

Living with a Springer Spaniel:

Pete and Me

THE ASPEN NOTCH MYSTERY SERIES

No Gifts to Bring (Prequel to the Series)

A young child with disabilities, a flamboyant singer, a handsome traveler, and an irritating private detective bring back Sue's spirit in an endearing story of love and hope, including an engaging mystery.

Murder in Aspen Notch (Book 1)

Sue and Alan fell in love while solving a murder mystery in *No Gifts to Bring*. Now married, they've moved to a small town in the Poconos. Alan becomes the police chief in Aspen Notch, while Sue finds a dead body, inherits an unruly puppy, and receives a death threat.

The Garden Shop Mystery (Book 2)

Sue plans to use the historic log cabin on her property as a garden shop, but mischief and vandalism escalate in her first week of business. Alan believes the incidents are pranks until he finds her unconscious in the shop. Sue thinks that someone is trying to force her to close *Butterflies and Blooms*. But why?

A Cameo Appearance (Book 3)

Sue's daughter and granddaughter come to Aspen Notch for a long-overdue visit. The cameo necklace they buy at *Trinkets and Treasures* becomes the key for solving the cold case mystery.

Below the Landscape (Book 4)

Sue purchases oil paintings at *Trinkets and Treasures*, only to learn that her friend's fiancé, missing for 40 years, is the artist. When Sue discovers that the actual location of the landscapes lies above an abandoned coal mine, she finds the missing piece of the puzzle.

Bedlam in the Blizzard (Book 5)

Sue and Alan return to the Alpine Holiday Lodge where they meet up with Alan's estranged daughter, Judy. During a power outage caused by the blizzard, Judy is found in shock, covered in blood, then guests report items missing from their rooms. Is the thievery connected with the murder?

Made in the USA
Columbia, SC
30 April 2022

59745392R00139